The Book of Lazarus

Fiction Collective Two  Normal

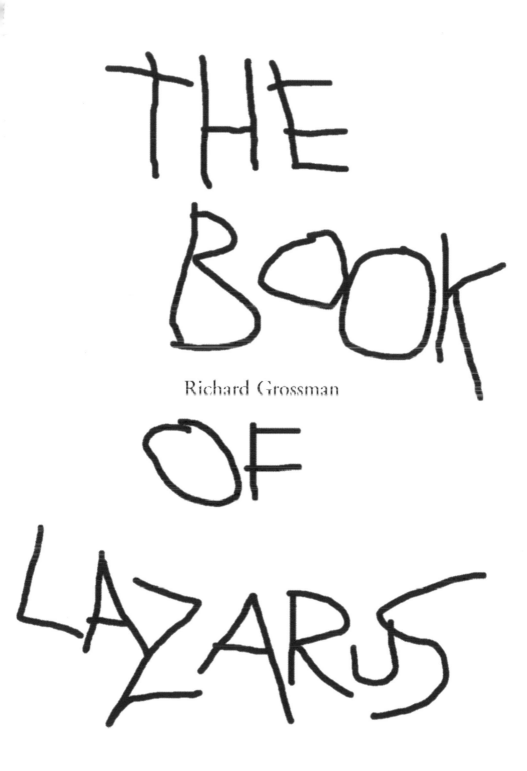

THE BOOK OF LAZARUS

Richard Grossman

Published by FC2 with support given by the English Department
Unit for Contemporary Literature of Illinois State University
and the Illinois Arts Council.

Address all inquiries to:
Fiction Collective Two
Unit for Contemporary Literature
Campus Box 4241
Illinois State University
Normal IL 61789-4241

ISBN: cloth 1-57366-029-9

Produced and printed in the United States of America
Distributed by the Northwestern University Press

Designed by Richard Grossman
and Jensen & Wilcoxon, Inc., Minneapolis

For Sandy

Only a tramp was Lazarus' sad fate,
He who lay down at the rich man's gate.
He begged for the crumbs from the rich man to eat.
He was only a tramp found dead on the street.

He was some mother's darling; he was some mother's son.
Once he was fair and once he was young.
And some mother rocked him, her darling to sleep,
But they left him to die like a tramp on the street.

Hank Williams

•

Oh that my words were now written! oh that they were
printed in a book! That they were graven with an iron
pen and lead in the rock for ever!

For I know that my redeemer liveth, and that he shall
stand at the latter day upon the earth: And though after
my skin worms destroy this body, yet in my flesh I shall
see God.

Job 19: 23-26

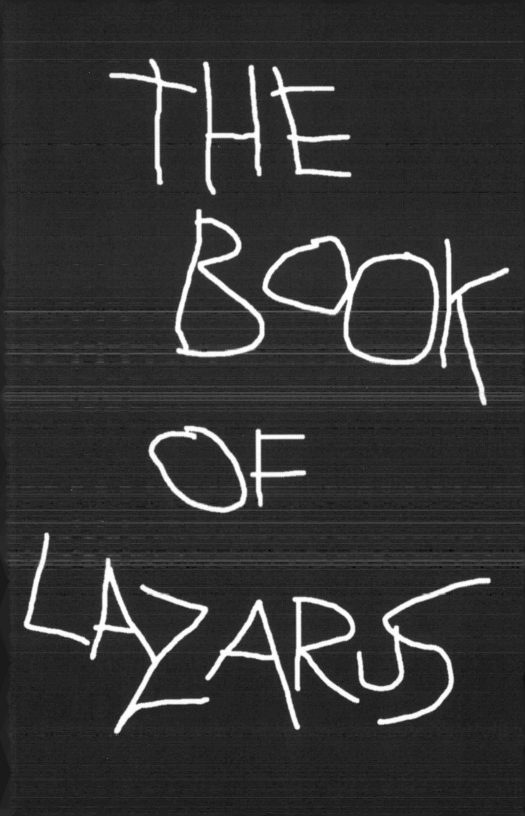

In Memoriam

The People's Liberation Brigade

Gretchen Halder (June 15, 1949–January 2, 1971)

Gerald Oren Holt (March 22, 1936–January 2, 1971)

Tubby Hyams (May 25, 1922–January 2, 1971)

Thomas Kearns (April 8, 1946–March 27, 1993)

Martin Kulander (March 4, 1940–June 20, 1976)

Cynda Lazarus (July 6, 1945–January 2, 1971)

Robert Simon Lazarus (August 15, 1944–September 5, 1993)

Mitchell Emerson O'Banion (October 2, 1927–October 24, 1991)

Helen Kearns Scott (May 5, 1943–October 28, 1991)

and

Jaynie Cannavota (December 1, 1960–January 2, 1971)

Emma Stronghorse O'Banion (March 15, 1961–April 8, 1996)

Gina Gozzi O'Banion (November 8, 1937–April 14, 1974)

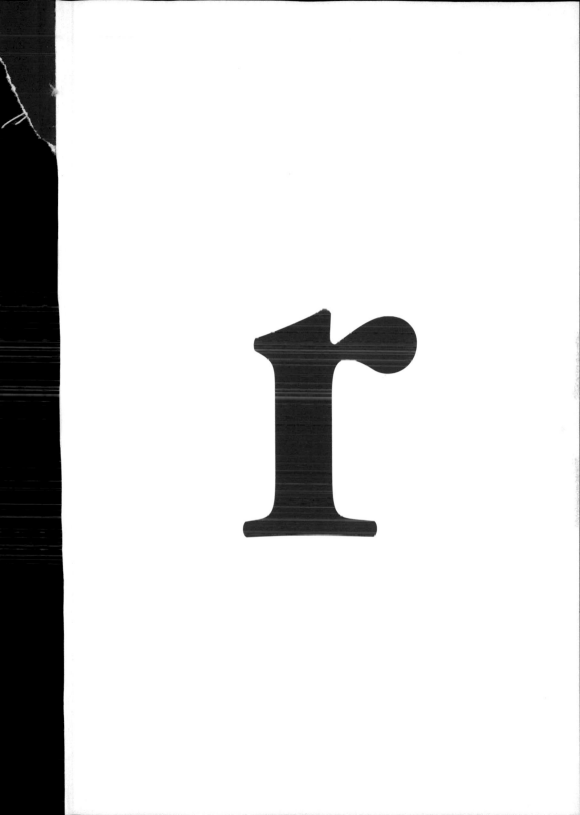

Gretchen

♡ New Year's Resolutions ♡

I promise to stop doing a lot of drugs especially when I'm with Gerald and Marty together because they take advantage of me.

I promise to stop eating animals.

I promise to try to understand about what's wrong in our country and to do my best to promote kindness among all peoples.

I promise to say a prayer at least once every day.

I promise to stop thinking I'm so beautiful when I know I'm not.

I promise to try to not lose my temper so much.

I promise to work harder so that I can stand on my own two feet.

I promise to think of what I can do for another person and to try to make people happy before I think about myself.

I promise not to eat so much candy especially when I smoke grass.

I promise to take better care of my nails
and to present a cleanly appearance.

I promise to try to be nicer to Bobby
and Cyndas because I know I have
acted small with them because I am
jealous of their brains.

I promise to forgive my dad and
to call my mom at least every month.

I promise to make something of myself
and not to hate another human being
because we are all children of love. ♡

I promise to be more quiet about my
feelings and not to think that my
friends want to know everything
about me.

I promise to try to change
to become a better person every day
and to make this a good year
for me and my friends.

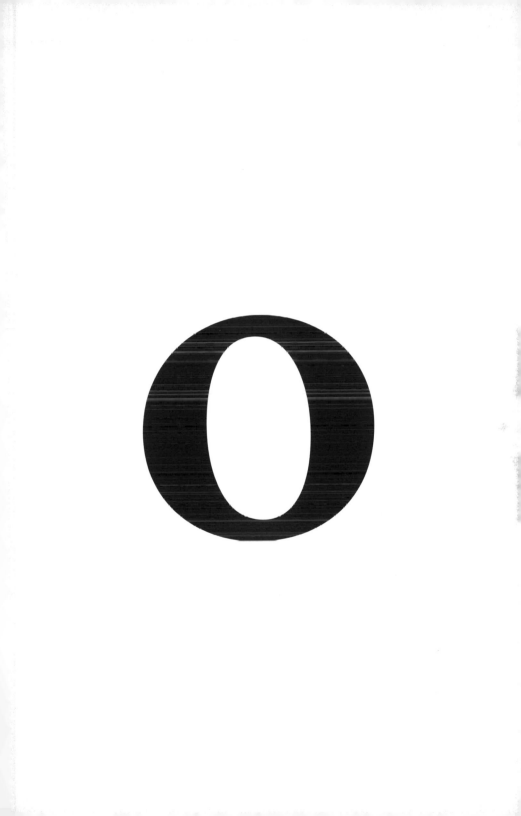

Jennifer Katz-
Gach died
trying to save
the life of
Joshua Katz-
Gach who was
eloping married.
Death by burning

Better government rarely makes for better citizens.

Men dream of flying because they thirst for a state of mind where they need not worry about the placement of their feet.

No man with a belly full of Wheaties and a mind filled with Mickey Mouse can be an effective lever of democracy.

The pursuit of wealth is a cowardly action.

America is the first civilized society in recorded history that has refused to venerate eloquence.

When a dictatorship collapses, everybody feels naked.

The faceless unit of the masses is an insect at heart: a plodding creator of historic systems. The ant has his hill; the spider has his web; the bee has his hive; and man has his own technology of bloodless structure.

A salamander raised in a cave turns blind and white. So do men in corporations.

Fichte believed that higher culture would only commence when culture was spread uniformly over the surface of the earth. Instead we shall soon be treated to the opposite: a uniform culture, devoid of culture, spread over the surface of the earth.

The purpose of life is to die with a purpose.

The moral bedrock of political and economic power is a tawdry heap of insignificant criminal acts.

Allen Bell
died trying to
save the life of
Carolyn Bell
who was trying
to shoot herself.
Death by bullets.

Marty

July 13, 1970

Mitch—

The fucking twat I'm living with is a real piece of
shit and doesn't see the significance of the bourgeois
revolution. I mean the bourgeois revolution in the
sense that the revolting assholes are revolting because
they don't have enough fucking money in their pockets
and they don't like to have to look at poor people. The
goddamn planet is coming unglued. It's not really a
planetary thing but more of a mind thing. It's a
control issue where the minds of all these stupid
fucking dingbats have given up on living and want to
live through things. McLuhan was right, and what's more
they have given up on expressing themselves because
self-expression requires work and thinking about what
they're saying is hard. I predict that within forty
years everybody is going to be listening to and talking
through machines and the machines will turn everything
these fucking morons say into Cream of Wheat. Our
children's children will think these goddamn machines
are terrific and that they are really complex, but
everyone with any fucking brains knows that machines all
have limits. I read in the papers that they are working
on a concept called artificial intelligence, because
they think there are no limits to what machines can
do, but the only thing these fucking monster computers
can do is to turn the wimps on this planet into
horseshit. All these nerdy numbers-crunchers should be
forced to read a page a day of Plato, and in no goddamn
time at all they won't be needing their stupid

calculators and slide rules and all the shit they use
to justify their miserably small existences as fucking
goddamn gnats.

Right now it's cool to be hip, but that won't last for
long. I predict it. The only strength in this fucking
pigsty of a country is in numbers. That's what's wrong
around here. Numbers always win. The largest number of
votes, the largest number of fucking dollars, it's all
that matters. Everybody worships the biggest thing in
the neighborhood. It's big that counts. Not smart. Not
kind. But huge. But it's not only this obsession with
more and more, it's also the fact that this fucking
bigness worship causes blindness. I see it all the
time. Take a look at people's language. The whole
fucking notion is that slang is good, which it is.
Ghetto shit is great. Any street language shit is cool.
But there's a language control bureau in Washington DC
where they work on removing any form of indecency from
what we say and they have all these bureaucratic
expressions that are slowly creeping into the everyday
thought of the average Joe Prick. Even the goddamn
plumber is becoming a fucking go-getter. Look at this
new thing with business cards and print shops. Everyone
has to have a title, like, for instance, I'm John Q.
Diarrhea, and I have an advanced degree in rectology
from Blow Me University. I mean who the fuck cares?

Take a look at it this way. What's the real enemy of
all Americans? What do all those guys in front of the
tube really hate? The guys watching sports. They never
hate the opposing team. They don't hate the announcer,
unless he talks too fucking much. They don't hate the
factories that pour out useless products that buy
advertising that support these idiots who are running
around bases and dumping balls in baskets. They don't
hate the networks. They don't hate the government that
subsidizes the networks so that they say nothing that

isn't fucking red white and blue. They don't hate their
neighbor unless he's a nigger. They don't even hate the
blacks who play sports. They only hate the non-sport-
playing fucking niggers. They don't hate the shitheads
who act in movies. They love to go to the movies and
slobber on their goddamn popcorn. They don't hate
themselves. That's all psychological shrink bullshit,
that people underneath it hate themselves. They don't
hate themselves. They fucking love themselves. Even if
they hate themselves, underneath it all they love
themselves all the more because of something that
someone else did to fuck them. All right, I admit that
most of them hate their boss and spouse. That's true.
Also, a lot of people really hate their kids, because
the fucking rug rats hate them just as much. The
trouble with kids is that they see what assholes their
parents are, and their parents hate them for it.

People always hate the circumstances of their
miserable pathetic fucking lives. The job. The rashes.
The headaches. The boredom. The same fucking faces
surrounding them day after day. Like my girlfriend.
She's beautiful but she's a stone-cold bitch. It's only
temporary, I know. But I can't help hating her, even
though I'll dump her fucking cunt after I get sick of
her body.

But the thing that everyone who is a true-blue, died-
in-the-wool, fucking red-blooded American dumbbell
hates is imagination. That's the great enemy of
America. That's what they always hated about communism.
Sure, it was a question of somebody who wanted to get
the money away from the WASP morons in their golfing
clothes who smoke cigars in their country clubs and
worry about the stock market. Those guys go apeshit
when they think of some smelly Slavic commie fruitcake
coming over and taking the cash out of their miserable
paws. But it's more than that, which is what I tried to

tell that fuckhead girlfriend of mine. It's about free thinking. That's why they equate communism and free love. Because thinking is equal to fucking. Free thinkers are free fuckers.

They can't stand it. Take artists for instance. Everybody hates artists. But the hatred isn't like the hatred associated with hating the brothers. It's kind of like hating Jews. It's kind of mild hate is my point. It's strong but mild. It's the kind of hate that all these pathetic powerless pieces of shit need in their lives. Mild hate is like a background kind of hate. It's like real faint background noise. If you lived with it all your life, and as a result of some fuck-up it was taken away, the silence would drive you crazy. You'd need to hear it again. Nobody has to say they hate the Jews, but most people do, because the Jews are smart, and most of them have more money than most of the dimwitted fucking working class stiffs that hate them. It's just not cool to admit it. There are a few places it's OK, but not many. Now hating artists is even a milder form of hate but the milder the hate the more pervasive it is. When I mentioned it to Gretchen, she claimed that nobody hates artists, which just goes to show how fucking dumb that cunt can be. Her sensors are totally out of order. The goddamn bitch doesn't see anything.

I mean most guys would rather be fucked in the ass with a harpoon than have to think of something that requires imagination. That's a straight-on fucking comment. I predict that within the next fifty years they'll have concentration camps in this country for artists. That's not an exaggeration. They'll lock them up and then they'll have a contest to find out the most unimaginative ways of taking it to them. Gassing or shooting will be too fucking imaginative. Maybe they'll just spit on them. The whole goddamn empty-headed population with their whining fucking voices will line up on the other side of the barbed wire and gob on them. They'll drown them in spit.

It's imagination that threatens the power structure. It scares the shit out of them. They spend all their time teaching kids how to avoid being imaginative. Take that new program Sesame Street. Who wants to fucking think like that? It's a moron's wet dream of what a kid will want and so they teach their kids how to play and count while looking into a goddamn box. I hate that shit. Cookie Monster. Goddamn fucking baby talk that leads to nothing. That's why Jesus said that kids were boss. I mean kids were everything to that cat, which is why they crucified his fucking ass. It wasn't that he was a heretic. It was that he treated children right, and since everyone is afraid of the honesty of their children, they terminated him. The whole cultural machinery is based on turning kids into liars, because you don't have to listen to a liar when he's calling you a liar. It's elementary.

One day everything will be ordinary. The whole planet will be one ordinary trip down memory lane. It's just going to be hamburger stands and movies and junk food and that's going to be the whole thing. There will be machines to beat you off and machines to tell you what a great guy you are. One day, mark my fucking words, they'll take newborn babies and dump them into slots in machines and the babies will spend their whole fucking lives in an artificial machine world being happy. The machine will be their womb, their lover and their coffin. They'll never leave the fucking thing. And when they finally die, the machine will grind them up. It'll grind up the bones of the person and lay them out on a fucking tray. Then the machine will entertain the next life cycle. The people will be disposable, not the machine.

Sometimes I think about these issues while I'm screwing Gretchen. I mean the last thing I want to do when I'm fucking her is think about her. Last night I was thinking about armies. It's really a sadistic thing, a goddamn human fighting machine. It's the machine part of the equation that the idiots respond to. They love the notion of a machine kill. Yeah, the machine mows the fucking Commie assholes down. Fucking fodder. Good riddance. You don't see the enemy suffering on the battlefield when you're winning. You move on by. Get to the goal. Salute. Grab a brewski. One day there's going to be a new kind of army. Ray-gun shit. You'll join the army to become a target, because there will be nothing else to do. People will line up on either side of the border and then the machines will go to work. The people will just fucking stand there. And then the beams will cut them in two or make them explode and thousands of miles away, some suit will be keeping score. Then he'll take the results upstairs to his boss who will be fucking some babe just like I was fucking Gretchen. It's a vicious fucking circle.

People are becoming zombies. They're turning into polite people with no manners. I hate the fucking younger generation. There's no emotion in their voices. It's fucking freaky. When they try to feel something, it's like they're taking a shit. They're totally desen-sitized. I think it has something to do with the drinking water. Fluoride. It always was a bad idea. It puts some kind of weird coating in the brain that doesn't affect people that have already developed. It only attacks the kids. It makes it impossible for them to feel emotion. Maybe that's why they don't think. They don't think because they have no way of feeling. The fucking lack of feelings makes it impossible for them to keep anything important in their heads.

But it's also the hatred. When the entire country is filled with pathetic cripples, there can be no brotherly love. That's the myth of America. It's the love thy neighbor myth. It's just a pack of animals. I mean what kind of sane human being could ever vote for Nixon? But he blew Humphrey away. Not that Humphrey was any great catch himself, but Nixon?

I don't mind what we're doing, and I don't mind killing people. It's not that the ends justify the means. They don't. It's just that people nowadays are unimportant. They aren't human. They're nothing. They're stupid and selfish and worthless. I've been on this planet thirty years and I haven't met thirty decent human beings. I'd be pressed to name ten. Everybody's a slimeball. Then there is the argument that given the way things work, if we go around killing people to change the nature of society, we're bound to kill some good people. And the bad will survive to coopt us.

But I don't agree. This society has to be destroyed. And if the people have to be destroyed so that the society can be destroyed, then that's the way it'll have to be. Everybody's going down way one or another. Besides, if we don't change things, then things will change themselves. And in either case it's going to be bloody. Look at what's happened over the last hundred years. After the aristocracies fell apart, and the street people took over, led by the merchants, an immediate global plan was put into action to kill the intellectuals. And that's what they did. In every country, wars were conducted, and anybody with a triple digit IQ got axed. Every decade, they get more sophisticated at this. Pretty soon they'll start moving the IQ down. There'll be a point in time where an intellectual will be a person who can spell his fucking name. No fucking shit. That'll be the deal. There'll be limousine liberals parading down the streets with signs

saying power to the illiterates. But nobody who
sympathizes will be able to read the signs. That's the
way it always is with those stupid fucking New York
intellectuals. They truly are morons. Pompous pieces
of crap with their stupid soirees and dry as dust
opinions. Old farts.

Nobody asked me, but I'll tell you. I'll rap down what
will happen. Not in this cycle but later. First there
will be the general destruction. We'll put our
shoulders to the wheel on that one. I know that's not
the way most revolutionaries think, but fuck them
anyway. It's the way I think. I can smell blood and I
like what I smell. Anyway, first there'll be the general
destruction. Chaos. About two hundred years or so from
now. My prediction is that it will start with sickness.
The planners will make a fatal error in the planning of
their robotic mass jerk-off population. They'll leave
out an element and people will just stop moving and
start dying. The virus will attack their soft spots.
They'll whimper themselves to death. All over the
planet people will just fucking give up. It's not that
they'll want to die, but they'll no longer be able to
understand the issues. They won't have the brains to
want to survive. You know, that's the basic thing
that's supposed to be in us. The will to fucking
survive. But that's what the global planners will have
left out. Nobody will know how to want to live. And
they'll just fucking die. My guess is that about half
the planet will die that way. And it will be the first
time in hundreds of years that natural selection will
work in favor of humanity. It'll be the worse half that
will kick and that will provide the impulse. The
survivors will get angry and murder the planners.

And that's why I'm fighting. Because I hate the geeks. I
hate the fucking idiots who wear their pants up around
their armpits. I hate soft feelings. I hate soft heads.

I'm a compassionate man. I live my life to help to save
humanity. I'm a dope-addicted criminally-constituted
socially-subversive writer. But I'm also a long-term
fucking thinker. I'm hard enough and strong enough and
smart enough to look ahead. I see what's coming and I
don't like it, and I'll do whatever I fucking have to
do to change it. So don't turn your back on me. Not
that I would hurt you, I'd never threaten that. You're
too fucking rough yourself. We need to be on the same
side. I'm coming down there, once I dump this stupid
fucking bitch. I know we have to talk but I'm still
getting used to fresh air and pussy. I still have San
Quentin bouncing around in my fucking head. I'll bust
loose and join you. I know how to find you. I remember
the good times. So see you soon.

Marty

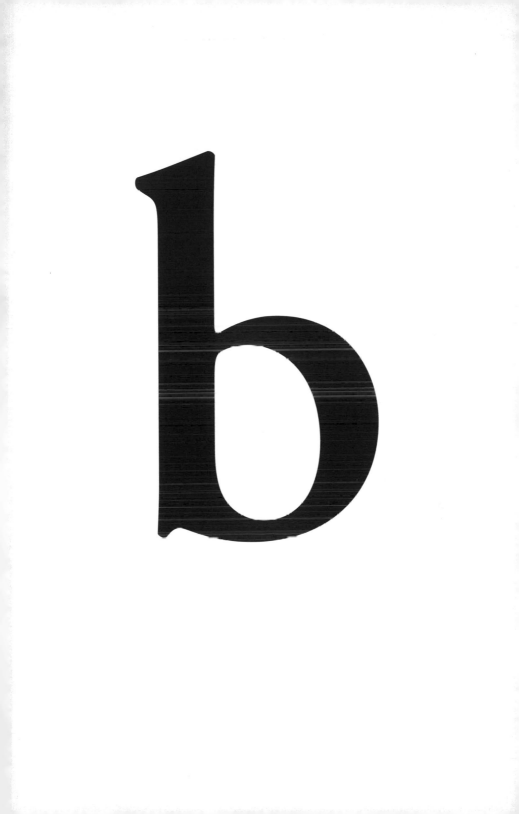

Tasker Brown
died trying to
save the life
of Patricia Jo
Hoyt who jumped
off a bridge.
Death by drown-
ing.

Entertainment has already replaced art under the name of art; and soon information will replace entertainment under the name of entertainment.

Political organizations are established in order to eliminate the common and reasonable fears that human beings have of each other.

Within the next century, people will walk down the streets swinging their arms from side to side like apes.

Hegel pointed out that there is no way for just men to compete in the world, because they are limited by the effects of their own morality. Given time, they are always overwhelmed by the corrosive forces of the masses. The best that a society can offer a virtuous man is temporary breathing room.

The individualist, the artist, the exception, cannot afford to be isolated and trampled. He or she must be public, must be armed, must be brave.

I have heard that Mao Tse Tung lives his life beside a swimming pool. So much for running dogs.

Technology demands the abandonment of dignity.

How much better to say that all men are to be treated equally before the law than to say that all men are equally capable of creating or respecting law.

The ideal form of government is probably an agrarian meritocracy, but even if a simple history test were required to be passed in order to register for an election, how the urban ignoramuses would howl!

Clarissa Flam
messmith died
trying to save
the life of Joanna
Drew who was
stuk on a trak.
Deth by crush
ing

Jaynie

January 1

Dear Mommy and Daddy. I am ok
but I am scared I want
to come home now and
miss you. They come with masks
and took me when I was
going to the store. They say
they will not hurt me. They
want you to give them
2 million dollers. Please give
them what they want so
I can go home.
I miss you so much,
but I am ok. I love you

Jaynie

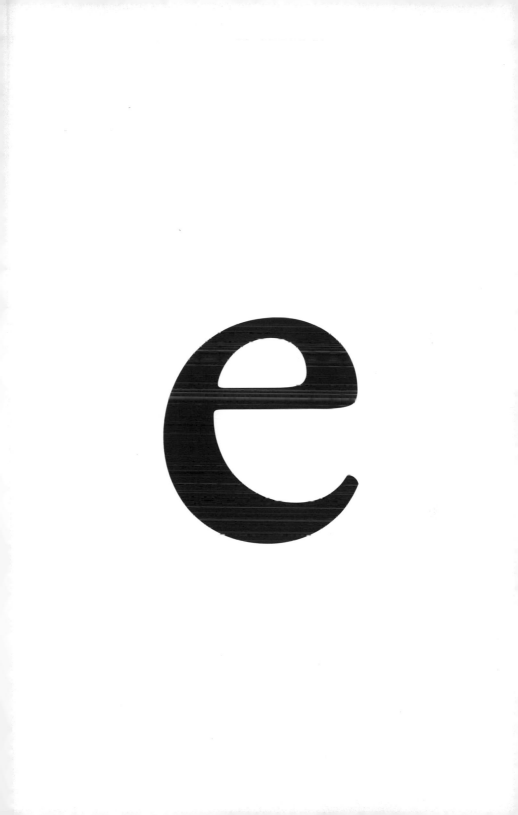

Heinz Locken died trying to save the life of Dor other Locken who was traped in her house.

Death by burning

In a capitalist democracy, the poor buy groceries and the rich buy the poor.

There are diseases of the spirit that are passed from person to person. These illnesses have their own structures and mechanisms of transmission. They are most visibly present in the form of mob psychoses, but they operate just as maliciously and effectively when transmitted between lovers in the form of an intimate kiss.

The revolutionary ideal of an afterlife, assuming there is one, wouldn't be beautiful or pleasing: it would simply be just.

Power can never mold the passions of the heart.

If the world were fashioned solely out of doctors, there would be no possibility of alternative medicine.

Character is rapidly disappearing from the facial features of the masses.

Neitzsche wrote that the man of the future would be defined by one word: mediocre. One hundred years later, half the population of America doesn't know what the word "mediocre" means.

The most admirable achievement in life is to change one's destiny.

Terrified men, who have nothing to hold on to and no protection and nothing to lose, gladly embrace the new.

If there were guns at the time of Tiberius, there would be no Christianity. One can build a religion around the Cross, but not around a bullet. That is why the revolutionary is in constant search of a new iconography, a symbol of reform that will last for thousands and thousands of years.

Jimmy Chong
died trying to
save the life of
Lahoya Cont is
who fell off a
Boat. Death

by drowning.

Emma

Mother had seen bodies rising out of the ground, and for the rest of her life she washed her hands.

She had witnessed the Apocalypse, and it made her feel dirty.

When the Spirit of the Lord first descended upon her, the trees in the park erupted in flames and the dead began to choke. It was so intense—this collective desire of the dead to breathe—that a tortured strangulation haunted the living as well; and as the corpses rose through the smoke, their mouths filled with worms and mud, those that were alive were forced to fall, so that the living and dead were entangled on the surface of the earth, a sphere of useless stuffed-up flesh begging for release. In the most violent pain imaginable, my mother lost both hearing and sight, as the suffocating bodies, like crated carcasses heading for the butcher, slithered against her skin.

I shall spare you, for the time being, her ultimate conversation with Jesus.

Mother had dropped a lot of acid that summer. Under different circumstances, she might have recovered her sanity, but the events that preceded her nervous breakdown were so emotionally crippling that even her sense of being strangled, which continued on for years, seemed preferable to the feeling of terror she had experienced in her former existence, when her marriage, her hopes and her defenses against fear had collapsed in the course of a few bloody hours.

It's hard to describe the effect this insanity had on me, an only child, abandoned by my father several months before. One day I had a mother, and the next day she was a zombie. It would have been far better if she had been institutionalized and I were taken away from her, but at the time, in 1971, there were so many freaks and burnouts in West Berkeley where we lived that no one cared much about Gina's disappearance into the killing-fields of Armageddon. Besides, in those early years of heavy psychedelic overdoses, everybody seemed crazy about something, whether it was Yogananda, Meher Baba, Sri Aurobindo or the Holy Ghost. I had a wealthy uncle in Chicago, a stable, settled man, and my mother's father, the *pater familias*, was living in the same city, but they didn't discover the horror of my situation until after she died. By the time Uncle Jack flew out to dispose of her mangled body, I was like a monkey being separated from an organ grinder.

I don't remember the events of those last three years with Mother as well as I remember the feeling of panic that constantly surrounded them. Gina's hands were the only parts of her body that were clean, and it seemed that she spent much of her time thinking about where she was going to find the next faucet, where she could mumble her Hail Mary's and wash. When she addressed other people, there was barely any sense of presence about her, all of her thought and energy being concentrated in a different place, in that desperate world of suffocating, resurrected bodies. Ours was a lurid existence of bhangs, scratchy music, foot odor, drug sickness, multilayered sex and narcissistic doodlings; and our possessions—a Bible, a few changes of filthy clothes, a meerschaum hash pipe with crinkled bits of foil, some tattered bedding and astrological ephemerides—were carried over her shoulder in a knitted sack.

Then one morning Mother walked out of somebody's apartment and never came back. Later that day, she fell from the seventh-floor window of a fleabag hotel.

When her corpse was finally identified, nobody knew how to locate her husband, Mitchell O'Banion. By anyone's standards my father was wild—an antisocial immigrant who worked tirelessly to save society. He was a union organizer, freedom marcher, an anarchist college-educated free-thinker, a Weatherman, and then something else, and then something else, belonging to this or that foco or brigade, eventually getting into so much trouble that he had to go underground. He was older than most of the revolutionaries of his time, in his mid-forties when I last saw him, and he was one of the few genuine bomb-throwers to have emerged from the labor movement. For many years he worked with the longshoremen, but by the early sixties he had shifted from the class to the racial struggle and begun his career of jail-hopping in the South. My mother, who maintained her job as a sales clerk in downtown San Francisco, had stayed at home and raised me. We lived in the Potrero district, and I remember my early upbringing as poor and outwardly conventional, with many residual friendships from Dad's old days at the docks. Friends of Dad who became lovers of my mom. My father, whose mind was evidently elsewhere, I saw maybe three or four times a year.

Then he left us for good, and shortly thereafter Mother had her apocalyptic vision in Tilden Park, as a result of which our circumstances changed radically. In the spring she wore an apron, and by the following winter we were homeless.

Mother was an Italian, although one of her grandmothers had been Chippewa. Her father sold auto parts, and my uncle, Jack Gozzi, inherited the family business, which was national in scope. When I was flown back to Illinois after her funeral, it was to a barn of a house in Winnetka containing two pampered cousins and a neurotic schnauzer named Lulu. Jack and Donata tried to raise me in their own clumsy ways, but I was a hardened creature with my own nasty habits, and I kept pretty much to myself. I became obsessed with education as a means of reconnecting with the world after so many years on the streets, and every afternoon after school I would shut myself in my room, where I read history and philosophy and practiced Parker, Dolphy and Coltrane riffs on the saxophone.

Shortly after I moved in with them, my aunt and uncle changed my last name to theirs because they thought I would be happier that way, but when I was twenty-four, I changed it back to O'Banion and added a traditional Indian name as well. I became Emma Stronghorse O'Banion. Quite consciously, I wanted to preserve within my name the presence of my departed parents.

Unfortunately, I was never able to accept any kindness from my adoptive family. Their plastic and shag existence, of pinks and blues and lime-green furnishings, emitted an antiseptic odor of betrayal, the stagnant smell of suburban emptiness. They put me through the University of Illinois, and then through graduate school at Duke, but by the time I was preparing for my orals in sociology I no longer wanted to maintain a relationship with them. After all I'd experienced in California, I couldn't brook their pusillanimous cowering in the face of any thought or emotion that challenged the normal ordering of their lives.

They did, however, continue to support me, and I am still being supported, although both Jack and my grandfather are long dead. I have a trust that pays me sixty-thousand dollars a year. Every three months, like clockwork, I receive a letter from Aunt

Donata, which I rarely answer. Recently, she started going to Al-Anon meetings, because my cousin Paulie, a simpering little swine with a gigantic superiority complex, can't stop drinking. She writes that she is applying what she learns there to her situation with me, even though I'm certainly not an alcoholic and haven't done drugs since my mother died. She believes that I was permanently damaged by the massive amounts of LSD I took as a child and by the emotional coldness I experienced before I came to live with them. She thinks, mistakenly, that I live in a marginalized world of sexual perversion and bitterness. My aunt is a bit loose-brained. I understand that our rupture is my problem and that she is basically a fine person, but some things can't be altered, no matter how much one may wish to change them.

Over the intervening years, I've grown into a large, muscular and fairly intimidating woman. I have cropped red hair and green eyes that my lovers claim can smolder, and I've adopted unconventional tastes in the way that I dress—even at an early age I was mostly into chains and leather—and in what I pursue. I'm considered something of a renegade, an abrupt and mannerless person who throws her weight around: I'm rough and tough, and I'll walk through fire to get what I want. I'm also deeply conservative in my views, in the main as a result of the insincerity and radical softheadedness I encountered in hippie pads and on the streets as a child. In my creative life, I am wedded to an unbending formalism; in my political life, I am libertarian; in my spiritual life, I have surrendered to the infinite mercies of Jesus Christ; but in my social and private life, I've come to relish the ruffian energies of precipitate action and harnessed sex. All in all, I'm a fairly complex animal: a lesbian rough-trade Catholic intellectual.

Back when my mother and I were wandering from place to

place, through the tenements of Berkeley and Sacramento, Gina had made a habit of filching coffee-table books from libraries, and I remember in particular two of them, on Bosch and Escher, which I examined hour after hour, stoned. I would sit cross-legged at the edge of stained mattresses and fashion iridescent landscapes, epic battles, orchards of anthropomorphic trees, a psychedelic kiddie-art that everyone seemed to admire. After I dropped out of the graduate program at Duke, I returned to my original interests. I moved to Brooklyn and took up life as a figurative painter. As I struggled to refine my abilities, I came to realize that it doesn't matter to the modern world, which feeds its appetite for aesthetic stimulation on the fourth-rate production of nincompoops, whether masterpieces are produced or not. I always understood, on some instinctive level, that my efforts would necessarily go by the boards. Yet in spite of all this, I did try to establish a source to sell my paintings, and a gallery on West Broadway offered to represent me—not a Mary Boone, Leo Castelli or Sonnabend-type gallery, but a second-floor walkup run by a pair of fashion-forward femmes with crimson lipstick, powdered skin and hennaed hair, who thought they could promote their artists by consuming lots of Ecstasy and haunting the clubs. They were pathetic and had little success with my work. Finally, I decided to leave the country.

I am writing this commentary in Rome, where I've been painting for the past seven years. I felt when I left the States—and it turned out I was right—that it would be possible to live here in a way that was impossible to live elsewhere; that I could experience the full range of art history and survive outside the confines of my age; that I could locate myself in the midst of a bustling city and yet find refuge in prayer, in beautiful women, and in my painting. I occupy an apartment on the Via di Monserrato, a medieval street speckled with small antique stores and sundry shops that runs into the Piazza Farnese. My building adjoins the Church of St. Thomas of Canterbury, a ludicrous piece of architecture constructed by Offa, King of the East Saxons and gradually downgraded, over more than a millennium, to twentieth-century standards. The apartment, which is quite spacious, is effectively shielded from the noise of the street, from the maddening blasts of the *motorini* and the incessant babble and hoopla of Italian life, and I have a separate area with access to a terrace, a narrow studio with high windows and northern light for my easel and paints.

When I came to Italy in 1989, I was sharing my life with a novelist, Katrina Heutz, a talented woman who has become wildly successful in the past few years and is something of a household word in literary circles. Katrina isn't the most orderly of people, and our working conditions were chaotic at best; but she left me suddenly in the fall of 1990, shortly before the events I'm about to relate. During the course of our love affair, we had become more and more interested in threesomes, and one evening she met two Swiss women in a trattoria, fell madly in love, and within a week had packed her bags and was gone. When she deserted me, I was distraught, but I refused to wallow in the shambles of my emotional life, knowing that to do so would detract from, if not destroy, my ability to continue painting. In the wake of her departure, I turned my back on my few Italian friends. I studied Latin literature with a Franciscan tutor and took a vacation, by myself, in late spring, in the Dolomites.

If I had been more successful in dealing with the upset of being abandoned by my lover, I might have handled the murder of my father, which occurred the following year, and with which my story begins, in much better fashion. Yet I now believe that the bizarre sequence of events that followed his passing have constituted a trial by ordeal, and that my survival—insofar as anyone can survive something as brutal as what I'm about to relate—has made me a stronger person and has ultimately brought me closer to Christ. Although I am now in grave danger of being murdered myself, I have developed a deeper courage and a stronger faith, which have continued to sustain me.

Late one night, shortly before my mother died, she related in a frantic whisper, while staring into the guttering light of a candle, how she had conversed directly with God.

The corpses that rose from the ground had begun to melt, she told me. The entire population of the planet was dissolving in a soup of fuming, incandescent bodies. Jesus summoned her to her judgment, and she rose above the chaos and screams into a refrigerium of turquoise that was embossed with spinning planet-wheels and stars. There she finally heard His words, that the damned and blessed are both, in their own separate ways, quickly driven to their destinies, but that the worthless multitudes, the nine-hundred-ninety-nine middlings out of every thousand, the semiconscious crap of the human race, are forced to suffer and wait; that each mediocre spirit must wander through a closeted, silent universe, helpless and alone.

Therefore, she had known since that time what her own destiny would be and how, awash in a god-inflicted madness, she would be set endlessly adrift.

Soon afterwards, she fell asleep in the corner of the room. Others around us had remained awake. A few were tying off and shooting. A couple high on peyote were making love—banging together and emitting strange grunting noises—in a curtained alcove next to a kitchen. I walked out into the hallway and through a metal door onto a garbage-strewn balcony that ran along the rear of the building. Directly below me was a maintenance yard filled with laundry-service vehicles. I sat on the wooden floor, with my back to the wall, and gazed through the railing at the throbbing constellations. I was high on peyote, too. The stars took on symbolic shapes, dimly understandable, and I realized that the astrologers were right and that every creature lives his life beneath a book—a luminous volume that rewrites itself with every twitch and impulse in the cloud of life.

I was thirteen years old at the time and had been raped twice.

And my mother, who woke in the middle of the night gasping frantically for air, could hardly remember my name.

• • •

It was one of those oppressive, breezeless August afternoons in Rome when the temperature mounts towards a hundred degrees and nobody moves except out of habit. This was the third week of terrible weather, and except for an early-morning trip to the stores for food and cigarettes, and my occasional hike across the river to a monastery in Trastevere where I met with my tutor, I remained shored up in my apartment and out of the sun. My choices at home lay between mindless labor and passive oblivion, and on this particular afternoon I had chosen to labor. I owned a large table fan, a battered piece of Neapolitan goods with three speeds, slow slower and slowest, and I'd placed a bowl of ice in front of it in order to gain some marginal relief. Stripped to a bra and shorts, I concentrated on building stretcher bars. Normally I let my machine take my calls while I'm working, but I felt distracted and restless, and reached for the telephone when it rang.

"*Pronto.*"

"Do you speak English?"

"Yes, I do."

"May I speak to Emma . . . Goldman . . . O'Banion?" an older man asked.

"This is Emma Stronghorse O'Banion."

"No, I don't want you. I want to speak with Emma . . . Goldman . . . O'Banion."

"I already told you that I'm Emma O'Banion. I changed my name a long time ago. Who is this anyway?"

"You used to be Emma Goldman O'Banion, is that it?"

"Yes, yes," I replied irritably. "I already told you that."

There was a pause, as if he were trying to decide whether I was the Emma O'Banion he wanted or not.

"Emma, this is your father calling," he finally said. "I'm dying!"

I was speechless.

"I'm sorry I haven't been in touch," he continued after another short pause. "I'm going to have a funeral with lots of flowers!"

I still said nothing.

"Why aren't you talking to me? What's wrong with you?" he demanded. "Has the cat got your tongue?"

"It's been over twenty years . . . "

"I told you I'm dying! Talk to me, Emma. Say something!"

"I don't understand . . . " I was stunned.

"What don't you understand?"

"Are you calling to say good-bye?"

74

"Why would I want to say good-bye?"

"Where are you?"

"I'm in Tacoma. I need you to come here. I have some important things to tell you. I'm going to have a funeral with lots of pretty flowers."

"You're thousands of miles away."

"So what? Fuck it! I'll pay. You can fly first class! Come immediately."

"I still don't understand. . . . How did you find me?"

"I've always known."

"You've always known what? Where I was? I find that extremely difficult to believe."

"It's raining, it's pouring, the old man is snoring," he suddenly sang.

"Why are you singing nursery rhymes?"

"Come right away. Drop everything."

"Why were you singing that ludicrous nursery rhyme just now? Are you OK?"

"It's raining, it's pouring, the old man is snoring!"

"Stop singing that! What's wrong with you?"

"I'm nervous. It's raining, it's pouring, the old man is snoring. It's raining, it's pouring, the old man is snoring. It's . . . "

"What did you mean when you said you've always known where I was?" I interrupted him. "If you've known where I was, why didn't you ever contact me? It sounds like you've gone crazy!"

He stopped singing. There was a long silence.

"I'm not crazy," he finally said. "I'm physically maladjusted."

"Why did you wait until now?" I continued. "Did it ever occur to you that I might have needed a father? I was a little girl with a drug-addled mother and no one to protect me! I was abused by strange men. Mother went insane, and now you're insane. This is insufferable!"

"I'm maladjusted," he protested again. "I did the very best I could."

"It's been twenty years, goddamn it! Why didn't you find me before? Didn't you care? What the hell's wrong with you? What kind of person are you anyway?"

"I couldn't get in touch with you. . . . I would have had to tell you. I couldn't live with myself and they would have cut your throat, Emma! Honest!"

"What in God's name are you talking about?"

"They wanted to kill me, but as long as they didn't find you, they couldn't kill us both together," he explained in a frustrated tone. "They couldn't get even for what I did."

"I don't understand what you're saying. Whom are you talking about? You're not making any sense at all."

"Those oily dagos!"

"I can't believe you're using a word like that!" I exclaimed in shock. "In case you've forgotten, you were married to an Italian. I have Italian blood!"

"I didn't want to kill that child, I just wanted them to feel what it was like to have someone like that. . . . what they had done to so many other people but I had to hide because I loved you so much and didn't want them to do the same to you . . . what we did to her. I had people until I . . . but never spoke until I . . ."

"What are you saying? What child? I can't believe this!"

"It's raining, it's pouring . . . "

"Stop that!"

"It's raining, it's pouring, the old man is snoring, it's raining, it's pour . . ."

"Stop it!"

There was another long pause. I reached over to my worktable and grabbed a pack of cigarettes and quickly lit one.

"I always loved you, Emma . . . so much." He suddenly began crying. "You're my little girl."

"I don't know if I can stand seeing you," I said. "I have a different memory that I want to preserve."

"But you can come to my funeral," he suggested hopefully through his tears. "It's going to be beautiful. They're going to be lots of plants and . . ."

"I know about the flowers already," I cut him off. And then I had a perverse thought.

"Are you certain you're dying?" I asked. "Maybe you just think you're dying."

"I have AIDS," he said. "I was a naughty boy."

"That's disgusting! A naughty boy? You're dying because you think you've been naughty? That's disgusting!"

"No one can help me except you. You're still in one piece."

"Don't guilt me!" I snapped.

"I know you're good. The truth has to get out. I'm going to fuck the bastards who are trying to kill me," he said, getting excited again. "They won't have the last laugh on this one. I'm going to smash their balls!"

"You just said you had AIDS."

"Yes," he said, "I'm dying. They're going to . . . "

"Why would someone want to kill you if you're already dying?"

"I won't give them any money. I won't do it, I told them they can do whatever they want. They've always treated me like a cripple and they can cram it. . . . The fucking assholes! Please, if you don't come, nothing will work out. Nothing at all. It's planned.

For months I planned this out . . . since I heard . . . I have to tell you about this man. He's brilliant!"

"Are you gay? Is that why you left Mother?"

"She stabbed me in the back!"

"What are you saying?"

"I was wrong, what I did, but your mother stabbed me in the back. She ruined my life! I did the best I could for her, but it was too late."

"What do you mean, 'you did the best you could'? You didn't do shit! She supported you," I said. "She stayed at home and raised me while you were wandering around, being heroic. It broke her spirit."

"That's not important . . . you have to come. . . ."

"It's not important?"

"No."

"I refuse to be part of your stupid, pathetic plans! You stood for something. Even if it was the wrong thing, I thought you stood for something!"

"But I want to apologize. To you, Emma. You're the last one, I have to apologize before . . . I want to say I'm sorry I . . ."

And automatically, without another thought, I slammed down the receiver.

I was dizzy, and my hands were shaking. I went into the kitchen and poured myself a glass of wine. I tried to drink it, but I had trouble swallowing. In the worst moments of my life I had been sustained by a belief that some day my father would come and rescue me: from the spiraling madness of my mother, and later from the misery of my teenage years in Winnetka. Even in adulthood I dreamt that he would come, with an embrace and an explanation, to save me. I crossed the studio and sat in a chair and smoked cigarettes and stared out the window until the sun went down. I lacked the willpower to move and remained seated with sweat pouring off me. I was pleased I'd hung up on him. He was filled with disease. He was a crippled and depraved bastard! I confessed it to myself: I wanted to hurt him because he deserved it for everything he'd done to me. For all the neglect, for all those years, and for not being what I thought he was.

Finally I tried to stand, but there was no strength left in my legs. I stumbled into the kitchen and retrieved my glass, which was still on the counter, and drained it. Then I went into the bathroom, turned on the cold water, removed my clothing and climbed into the tub. I switched on the hand shower. The water felt hot. I got out and dried myself off and lay down naked on my bed.

During the following weeks I was so depressed that I was unable to accomplish any work. Moreover, I began to have serious doubts about what I'd done. I called Tacoma information, only to discover that there wasn't any Mitchell O'Banion listed in the state of Washington. I tried to put him out of my mind, but I continued to be haunted by morbid thoughts. I became panicked by the notion that I would never hear from my father again, that I would never get any more information, and that I would be left with only the ravings of a madman as the final testament to my origins. I had no idea how he had contracted AIDS, to whom he owed money, who his mysterious "brilliant" friend was, and most importantly, if there were actually a legitimate reason why he never had gotten in touch with me. I had no idea what he had done for the past twenty years, except for chasing after some cockamamie political dreams. I realized that I hadn't given him a chance to explain and that there was really no reason, financial or otherwise, why I couldn't have gone to visit him in order to learn the truth. Yet there was nothing I could do, because in a sudden access of rage I'd foolishly cut him off.

In thinking about what had transpired, I was forced to acknowledge that unless I received more information I would remain perennially in the dark, since my early impressions of my father were little more than vague snapshots. Mitchell O'Banion had lived in my head as a concept. He was a hard-nosed, burly Irishman, a radical republican and devout Catholic, who had come to America as a teenager, fleeing a shattered home. He was extremely intelligent, charismatically handsome, physically domi-nating and miserably drug-sodden, but there was little else that I could remember about him. I understood for the first time that all the stories I'd heard about his humanitarian exploits had come from my deranged mother. Later in life, when I'd mentioned his essential goodness to my aunt and uncle in Winnetka, they were embarrassed and said little. To cloud matters still further, I'd never bothered to look up any of the people who had known him as an organizer, freedom-marcher or urban guerrilla. I'd taken every-thing my mother had told me at face value, without reflection, and not once, even for a moment, had I allowed myself to think the obvious: that she had fantasized an epic role for my father in order to rationalize her own abandonment.

I can barely remember what I did during those final weeks of summer, except to brood and suffer. My feelings of anger and loss were overwhelming. I went to church and prayed that he would contact me again, but my prayers weren't answered, since he never did.

Late one night, in October, I received another call from Washington.

"Is this Emma O'Banion?"

"Speaking."

"Miss O'Banion, my name is Joseph Blumenson, and I'm a senior partner in the law firm of Branner, Blumenson and Davies, here in Seattle. I'm afraid I have some rather sad news, if you haven't heard already."

"You're calling to tell me that my father is no longer alive, is that it?"

"You know already?"

"No, I didn't know."

"Yes, he passed away yesterday in his home. He was sitting in his living room, reading a newspaper, and his heart stopped. It was apparently a peaceful death. We were just informed."

"But he had AIDS?"

"Yes, of course."

"Did he ask you to notify me when he died?" I asked.

"Not exactly. His funeral is tomorrow at two o'clock. There is an Alitalia connection through Kennedy that would get you here on time, if you wish to attend, but you'd have to go to the airport first thing in the morning."

"I'm not certain that I want to come, Mr. Blumenson," I replied with some bitterness. "I'll have to think about it."

"If you miss the flight, you'll miss the funeral."

"Can't the starting time be changed?"

"I'm sorry, but your father was specific about his arrangements. He asked for a prompt burial."

"Well," I said, wondering to myself why there was such a rush, "I'll either be there or I won't."

"Our number here is 206-734-5500." And he waited for a moment while I wrote it down. "If you decide to attend, please call us and ask for Miss Harmon. She'll give you flight information and directions to the chapel."

"Thanks."

"There is, however, another reason for my call."

"Oh, yes? What's that?"

"Your father left a sizable estate, and you stand to benefit. The day after the funeral there will be a formal reading of his will in our offices. I recommend that you attend, and I strongly suggest that you bring along your own legal counsel."

"You expect me to mourn my father, fly to the funeral, and somewhere along the line pick up an attorney? What's wrong with you?"

"I'm required to give you this advice. I'm sorry if this sounds insensitive, because I certainly don't mean it that way."

"Don't you think this is a bit heavy-handed?"

"Perhaps. But I'm just following your father's instructions."

"And what if I don't show up?"

"I'll be happy to contact you next week and discuss the terms of his will, but I encourage you to be at the meeting and bring a lawyer. It would be to your advantage."

"I don't really want to discuss this kind of thing right now."

"As you wish. Again, Miss O'Banion, I want to express my sincere condolences."

"What are 'sincere condolences'?"

"I understand that you're upset, but there is no reason for you to doubt that I harbor genuine feelings."

"Thanks for the boilerplate sympathy and concern," I said sarcastically.

I wasn't particularly interested in the phony sentiments of a mouthpiece.

• • •

One of the few clear memories I had of my father was of our attendance together at Sunday mass. My mother never seemed attached to churches the way that he was—even in her days of ceaseless praying, she simply wandered through them, distracted—so that as a small girl I truly believed that my devotion to the Virgin Mary was something I shared with him alone. In spite of his revolutionary activity, Mitch was a deeply religious person, and I always believed, rightly or wrongly, that at least in this one respect we shared the same mentality. Both of us were "fearless beasts" with obsessive missions, and yet in order to compensate for the chaos of our lives, we needed a spiritual anchor for our craziness and a loving, benevolent power to mitigate our tendency to bust into things abruptly and shake them up. This lifelong identification with my father will explain, in part, why my reaction at his funeral was so violent. To attack his religious convictions was to attack my own.

Even though I followed the lawyer's instructions to the letter, there was no way I could have arrived in time for the beginning of the service. I had taken a cab from the airport through downtown Tacoma and then out through a large urban park into a neighborhood of working-class homes. The chapel, on a commercial street across from a cineplex, was a gabled mansion with redwood shingles, shabby turrets and a porte-cochère for a hearse. At the head of a stone staircase leading up to the entrance of the building a sign hanging from chains identified the hulk as the Edelman

Memorial Sanctuary. It was a stormy day, and I found myself in a stuffy room containing a fireplace, surrounded by a pink-marble mantelpiece, in which a Dura-Log was burning. A wizened man in a shiny suit shuffled up, eyeing my leather jacket and duffel, and offered me a plastic coat-check as I shook off my umbrella. I handed him the bag and umbrella but decided to leave my jacket on.

It took only a few moments to realize that something was terribly wrong. There was no crucifix in the room nor was there any representation of the Blessed Mother. There were only a small divan covered with atrocious beige flocking and a waist-high mahogany stand with a guestbook resting on blue-lace cloth. I went up to sign my name in the register. Surprisingly, there was only one other signature in the book, which I made out to be "Adele Marie Layosa." When I turned around, I noticed that the elderly man who had relieved me of my coat was wearing a black skullcap. With trembling hands, he blew his nose into a handkerchief.

Ahead of me was a set of swinging doors, through which I heard the booming voice of a woman:

"Deeep in my heart, I doooo believe
We shall overcome somedaaaaay."

I hurried into the chapel.

The space for worship reminded me of the backroom of a florist shop. The walls were lined with jumbled bouquets, gaudy wreaths, and orchids in colored pots. A trellis resembling a tasteless garden ornament from the fifties, strung with a drooping patchwork of mums, pink roses and vines, arched across the dais. The seating area, approximately fifteen rows of battered, freestanding benches, was divided by aisles into thirds. On a catafalque in front of the pulpit, a cherry-wood coffin in open position contained the remains of my father. The lady who was singing was standing by the bier. She was a brickbat of a woman, an absurd creature as wide as she was tall, and her upstretched arms were waving rhythmically in the air. As she repeated the final verse, her eyelids nictated with fervor and her fat face reddened with exertion. She was draped in white silk and wore a prayer shawl.

Directly behind the coffin, a man waited patiently with his hands on a lectern, head bowed. When the woman had finished emoting her way through the protest song, he straightened up and scanned the audience, which consisted of two other people, one in the central section and the second off to the side near an exit door, as if strategically positioned for escape. The rabbi was a trim, unctuous specimen in a pinstripe suit and conservative tie. He muttered a few incomprehensible phrases in what I presumed was Hebrew. Then he led the audience through the psalm which began, "I will lift up mine eyes unto the mountains: from whence shall my help come?" This was supposed to be read responsively, but he wound up doing both of the parts himself.

I had remained at the back of the room. For the first minute or two I had assumed that I was at the wrong service—until I noticed a gigantic horseshoe wreath of crimson blossoms, tied with a banner lettered in green, positioned below the bier. It read "We'll miss ya, Mitch!" At the end of the recitation, I walked up to the front and seated myself in the middle section. I was able to catch a glimpse of my father's forehead and nose but nothing else. The smell of the flowers was unbearable.

The rabbi launched into his eulogy.

I turned around to examine the other people in the room. A

tall, handsome man, a Nordic type with bleached features and tow hair pulled into a ponytail, returned my glance and smiled. The other mourner, farther back and to the side, was dressed in a dark-blue suit. His skullcap was perched uncomfortably on top of his haircut. He sat with eyes closed and mouth slightly open, seemingly asleep. I again faced forward. I was disgusted to the point of nausea.

" . . . are quiet men, for the best that life affords us comes not through words alone but through noble action as well. Jacob tended the scattered flocks of Laban out of love and accepted the petty deceits of this world with a patient, gracious heart. Moses, Saul and Mordechai—all were constant men of our people, men of great wisdom and compassion and of very few words. And so was Mitchell, beloved friend and father, who led a modest life, first in Port Hamilton, and then, for the past few years, here in this marvelous city of Tacoma.

"I had the opportunity of meeting Mitchell for the first time a couple months ago. Although he was a man of substantial means, the charity he extended to his fellow Jew and to the State of Israel went well beyond the common bounds of generosity. He walked in paths of righteousness for His namesake, while tending to those around him, for the needy and forsaken, for the bereft and bewildered, for the forlorn and forgotten, for all those unfortunates among us who require a helping hand. Mitchell had contacted the offices of the Federation of New York, wishing to make another large contribution to the United Jewish Appeal, and as a result I had the privilege of traveling from Manhattan to meet with him. During the brief afternoon I spent in his beautiful home, I came to know him intimately—as intimately as one can get to know a stranger when time and the means of communication are so severely limited by circumstance and disease.

"The man I came to commune with had had many problems in his life, it's true, and many burdensome sorrows, which he handled with *menschlichkeit* and dignity. Never one to assert himself or cause difficulties for others, Mitchell was among the meek who labor quietly behind the scenes in order to make the world a better place through the exercise of kindness and justice. I discovered, from my conversation with him, that he had been a wonderful father, an attentive man who cared deeply for his child—that he was all that one could possibly have wished for in a parent, someone who could be counted on to put aside his own interests at any time in order to show loving tenderness to his own offspring. Throughout life Mitch had been there, he told me, whenever his child needed him, to provide a loving embrace and brush away the tears. The name of Mitchell Emerson Finkelstein won't go down in history, but it will be written on the hearts of . . ."

I bolted to my feet.

"His name was O'Banion, you fucking asshole!"

The fat cantor, who had been resting on a folding chair against the back wall in a crowded space between the bouquets, leaned forward from the blossoms, as if she hadn't heard me correctly. The rabbi stopped his speech.

"This is hardly the time or place," he said sharply, "to begin an argument."

"His name was O'Banion, you fucking hypocrite," I screamed. "Mitchell Emerson *O'Banion*, and he was a horseshit father! He was never there for me!"

"My dear," the lady cantor said, "please . . ."

"And he wasn't any Jew either!" I yelled at him. "He was a good Catholic!"

I pounded my fist against the side of the coffin.

"He was a good Catholic, do you hear me? You can't steal away his identity like this. It's bad enough . . . this insanity and your stupid saccharine speeches about money!"

"Please," the cantor said, "let him rest in peace. Sit down and try to calm yourself."

I slammed my fist into the coffin again.

"You animal!" I screamed at the corpse. "You left me to rot!!"

The cantor waddled down the steps and walked over to my side. Her sugared look of pity had changed into something snarling and vicious. I clutched the edge of the coffin, as if to defend it, and then for the first time I looked at the body it contained.

The man inside was distinctly Jewish.

I fell back onto the bench. I began rocking back and forth.

"Pull yourself together," the cantor snapped at me, as she grabbed ahold of my shoulder and pressed her fingers into my leather jacket.

"Young lady . . . " the rabbi began again.

"Don't 'young lady' me! I don't need any patronizing from the likes of you," I replied, without looking up. "That isn't my father!"

"What are you saying?" the rabbi asked me.

"This isn't my father! Where is my father? What have you people done with him?"

"Perhaps you're attending the wrong funeral," he suggested.

"I was told to come here. This is supposed to be him, god-damn it, so where is he? Why did you call him Finkelstein?"

"Please watch your language," the rabbi admonished me. "There is a saying in the Talmud that if . . ."

"Keep it to yourself! I don't want to hear it!"

I stared at the carpet. Perhaps it was my father. Perhaps I was actually part-Jewish. My middle name had been Goldman. Perhaps I never knew who my father was. I didn't know what to think. I stood up and looked closely at the corpse. He had purple lips. He was wearing a cap and prayer shawl. He seemed old and frail. His face was covered with yellow makeup.

The cantor took hold of my wrist and pulled me toward her. I was certain she was trying to inhibit my movements, and I yanked myself away. Then, without another look at the body or at anybody else, I hurried out of the room. I reclaimed my gear from the old man in the vestibule and stumbled into the rain.

The water was coming down in sheets, and as I waited, trembling, at the curb in front of the funeral home, I realized that I had no transportation. Luckily, a few doors down the street there was a Greek restaurant, its sign-bulbs twinkling through the downpour, and turning my umbrella into the wind, I headed for the place, where I assumed I could order something hot to drink, dry myself off and telephone for a cab. As it turned out, the front of the restaurant was a bar, with leatherette booths, an array of raffia baskets, plastic grapes and stringless bazookis dangling from the ceiling, and the usual travel posters of white-washed buildings and rugged shores lining the walls. I seated myself and stowed my gear underneath the table, and when a waitress approached, I ordered a cup of coffee and asked her to call me a taxi. Then I went into the bathroom and threw up. I wiped my mouth and looked in the mirror.

My face, which was haggard to begin with, was covered with splotches. I used the paper towels to absorb some of the water, and then I promptly threw up again. I washed out my mouth and stood for a moment staring into the basin. I tried to empty my mind of the image of my father, or of his impostor, lying in the coffin, and started—God knows why—to count in Italian: *uno, due, tre, quattro, cinque, sei, sette. . . .* up to one hundred, in order to steady myself. Then I inhaled deeply and headed back to the bar.

A heavyset man in his thirties was sitting in my booth, his raincoat slung over the banquette behind him. He was dressed in urban western wear: a cowboy jacket, flannel shirt, and a bolo tie with a gold-plated clasp of a bucking bronco. As I approached, he mustered a raw, superficial grin, and I realized that this was the mourner with the ponytail who was seated in back of me at the funeral. On the table were two cups of coffee.

"Are you feeling any better?" he asked, as I sat down.

"How did you know where I was?" I replied with suspicion. "Were you following me?"

"That's right, I was following you," he said. "I'd paid my respects, and I really had no desire to accompany Mitch to the gravesite. The dead don't catch cold."

"That's not a particularly sensitive comment, considering I'm his daughter."

"Apparently, you're not so sure."

"Sure about what?"

"You're not so sure you're his daughter," he said in a tone of voice that was faintly feminine and aggressive.

"Who are you anyway, and what the fuck do you want?"

"There's no reason to be rude. I haven't done anything to hurt you."

"You couldn't hurt me if you wanted to, pal. Just answer my question."

"My name is Carlos Byrd, and I came in here because I wanted to make certain you were OK."

"You felt sorry for me, screaming and swearing at everybody, is that it?"

"You were under a lot of pressure," he said. His manner seemed far more patronizing than sympathetic.

"It had nothing to do with pressure," I objected. "He didn't look like my father. There are certain characteristics one remembers as a child, and I couldn't find them on his face."

"Well, he told me he had a daughter named Emma O'Banion, and you said that you're an O'Banion, so there you have it."

"You're absolutely certain he said that, are you?"

"Yes, he said you were some sort of painter in Italy."

"He knew that I painted?"

"That's what he told me."

"Did you take a look in the coffin?" I asked.

"Of course. It was Mitch Finkelstein."

"His name wasn't Finkelstein. That's an absurdity and an outrage."

"Maybe in your opinion it's an outrage," he said, seemingly taken aback by my comment, "but that's the name he chose to go by."

"So how did you know him?" I asked.

"How did I know Mitch? We shared the same problem."

"What does that mean? Are you also a Catholic who feels the need to parade around as a Hebrew?"

"What do you have against Jews, anyway?"

"Why don't you get lost?" I replied, not deigning to answer his question.

"Perhaps you also have something against gays?" he said, as he took a sip of coffee. He apparently had no intention of leaving.

"Why would I have anything against gays? Is there something wrong with your eyesight?"

"What do you mean by that?"

"Well, who do you think I look like? Julia fucking Roberts?"

"I get your point."

"In any case, I have absolutely nothing against Jews," I replied wearily. "I have nothing against gay Jews, black lesbians, or transsexual Armenians. I have nothing against anybody. I don't give a shit about anybody, if you want to know the truth. I just don't understand what's going on."

"When I said that your father and I shared the same problem, I meant that I'm also HIV positive," the man explained, "so you'll pardon me if I'm not particularly adept at turning the other cheek. I'm Executive Director of Project Love Tacoma, which is a meals program for people living with AIDS. We deliver lunches to over seventy people here in town. A couple months ago we received a call from Mitch, who said he wanted to make a significant contribution to our organization and become a client."

"Apparently my father loved to call people on the telephone and offer them money," I said. "He did the same thing with that rabbi."

"Your father was a charitable man. He asked if I would come over to his house to meet with him. It was a creepy place."

"I don't understand what you're talking about," I said peevishly. I looked around for the waitress, wanting to get more coffee. There was no one in sight.

"In many cases," he explained, "as the disease progresses, AIDS victims seem to shrink inside their houses. Their homes become hostile environments, as if they were camping out on somebody else's property. The people seem small and displaced. In the case of Mitch and Bobby, when I visited them . . ."

"Who's Bobby?" I asked, interrupting his silly AIDS lecture.

"You don't know?" He seemed genuinely surprised.

"No, I don't have any idea what you're talking about, Mr. Beagle, or whatever you said your name is."

"I already told you that my name is Carlos Byrd. I assume that Bobby is your brother."

"That's utter nonsense. I don't have a brother," I answered flatly. "I'm an only child."

"Well, then maybe he's a half-brother."

"So that's what that slick rabbi meant!" I suddenly understood. "He wasn't referring to me at all when he mentioned all that 'brush away the tears' crap!"

"No, he was obviously referring to Bobby."

"And my father had no girlfriend or wife around?"

"You're talking about someone who could be Bobby's mother? That person would have to be well along in years."

"I don't get it," I said, bewildered.

"Bobby's not younger than you," Carlos said. "In point of fact, he's much older. I would guess he's in his late forties."

"Sorry, but I highly doubt it. No way. Not possible."

"You must be around thirty?" Carlos asked.

"Exactly."

"And how old was your father?"

"He was born in 1927, so he'd be sixty-four."

"Well, how would you have any way of knowing what your father was up to fifteen years before you were born? Bobby could be the result of an early relationship that Mitch decided to keep secret."

He leaned back against his seat.

"I suppose you're right," I admitted, feeling somehow defeated. "That other mourner, sitting near the back at the funeral, was that Bobby?"

"No, it wasn't. I don't have any idea who that other guy was."

"Then why wasn't Bobby at the funeral?" I asked.

"He might not have been capable of making it to the funeral."

"What do you mean?"

"Bobby is disadvantaged," Carlos said. "He's got scars on the back of his head. Out of delicacy I never asked where they came from, but in any case he can't think clearly."

"He's retarded?"

"He talks like he's from another planet."

"So where is he then?"

"I have no idea. I only saw him once—that time I went over to the house to discuss the contribution. Mitch came to the door. He had Kaposi's on his face, and a slight limp, and it was obvious he was demented. He would be lucid for a couple minutes, and then he'd go off into hyperspace, into a kind of dream state. He invited me in, and I saw through an archway leading into the dining room an Oriental woman, maybe a maid or a nurse, fidgeting with something, like a clock or something. The place gave off a strong smell of grass, and there was a stop sign."

"A stop sign?"

"A sign that you hold in your hand. I guess they're called 'lollipops'. This strange head peered around the side of the arch. He jumped into the center of the door—he was wearing one of those orange shine-in-the-dark jackets and an orange cap—and he raised his hand in the air and blew a whistle. With his other hand, he held up his stop sign. Then he mumbled something and disappeared behind the jamb on the opposite side. Mitch started laughing and commented that there was too much traffic in the house, and then he told me, in a mocking tone, that Bobby was practicing his moves. Suddenly, it was as if somebody had flicked a switch in Mitch's brain and the lights had gone out. He started repeating phrases over and over to himself—he was totally disconnected—and then it was as if somebody had flicked the switch in the opposite direction and his mind became focused again. It was a sort of seizure. I don't think he realized he had gone off the way he did.

"Mitch began to explain, in his own weird way, that Bobby had been a crossing guard a few years back, but that he had been fired for molesting a girl. They lived in a small town north of here, and what with the molestation and AIDS issues, they were ridden out of the hamlet on a rail. Bobby hadn't gotten over it. He felt he'd been fired because he hadn't done his job well enough, and so he'd get blasted and practice obsessively in the house, hoping that he could improve his performance and get rehired. Something told me that Mitch was putting me on, but who knows? There was really no way that I could separate fact from fiction.

"Anyway, while Mitch was talking, I looked around the room. The place was lined with books. It looked like the home of a professor. There was also a bunch of money magazines, the kind a businessman would have for reference. The whole scene made me extremely uncomfortable. I had an eerie feeling, like what I originally told you, as if two madmen had broken into the house and were pretending to own it. Mitch handed me a letter, this letter," and Carlos reached into the inside pocket of his cowboy jacket and pulled out an envelope and passed it over to me.

The stationery was expensive, but the address side of the envelope was filthy, as if the letter had been dropped on the floor and kicked around.

There was no cancellation mark, so that it must have been hand-delivered.

I opened it and read:

August 29, 1991

Dear Mr. Byrd:

This will inform you of my intention of making a fifty-thousand dollar donation for the benefit of your wonderful humanitarian organization, Project Love Tacoma to help those who cannot feed themselves properly as a result of this terrible affliction is a wonderful thing to behold. In return for this gift, I ask only that you place me on your list of clients, and after I die you keep your eye on beloved son, Bobby, that you see he is properly clothed, sheltered and fed and allowed to work with you in the kitchen preparing vegetables, where he will do a good job.

I presume there are many loving people in Tacoma, such as yourself, who would help a man who cannot care for himself. I have instructed my lawyers to put aside money from estate, which will pay your organization an additional thirty-thousand year so long as Bobby is kept happy and is working in your kitchen chopping vegetables, where he will gain a real satisfaction to rely on, since I can't trust anyone to display affection and care that I know you and your friends will show. I do not wish to stick my son in a mental institution. He needs good work to do things.

God bless and much luck,

Mitchell Emerson Finkelstein

This letter had been written only a week or so after our abortive telephone conversation. I experienced a twinge of guilt. Perhaps this business with the meals organization was an act of desperation. Perhaps my father had been forced to turn to strangers, to some bureaucratic program, mistakenly thinking that these people would want to be helpful. He had done so because he couldn't rely on his own daughter. It hit me with full force that this was the request he wished to make of me when I came to Tacoma: he wanted me to come there to meet my retarded "brother." He wanted me to look after him.

I handed the letter back.

"You make a habit of carrying this kind of document with you to funerals?"

He shrugged his shoulders.

"I was hoping to run into a relative of Mitch's," he admitted. "I wanted to make it clear what your father wanted done with Bobby."

"You called my father a charitable man, and yet you were making fun of him. Where's your sincerity?"

"I wasn't making fun of him. Where did you get that ridiculous idea? I respected him!"

"That's not the way I read you. That business about the dead not catching cold? I don't like your pompous tone of voice."

"You don't know me at all," he protested.

"And you don't know me either," I replied in turn, "but you're just dying to help me out, aren't you? You have a natural affection for bull dykes with foul mouths!"

"I would appreciate it if you wouldn't call my integrity into question."

I could see that I'd gotten to him, but instead of exploding or getting up and taking his leave, he managed to pull himself together. He was a man with a purpose.

"Did he give you the money?" I asked him.

"Yes, of course. We received a check in the mail," he replied as calmly as he could.

"Did anything else happen during your visit at the house?"

"Not much. He invited Bobby into the room, and we talked for a few minutes, but you'd ask him a question, like what he was doing, and he'd say he was dating Marie Antoinette. He was way out there, stoned out of his mind. He reeked of alcohol and kept leering at me. Like I said, I couldn't tell whether the whole thing with the stop sign was a put-on or not, but it made me angry because I had this paranoid feeling they were goofing on me.

"Meanwhile, Mitch had faded out again and began singing to himself: some Irish tune with a lot of 'traw-law-lee''s in it. It was very distressing, and I sat there waiting for him to recover, not knowing what to do. That time I went to his house was the only time I actually visited Mitch, but I called every few days up until he died to see how he was getting along. He was very friendly on the phone, although most of the time he hardly knew who I was. Once he told me—before he totally lost it—that he had a daughter named Emma. He went on and on about how much he cared about you and how deeply he loved you. That it had taken him months to get up the nerve to call you, and when he did, you trashed him, and he was too ashamed to call you back because he couldn't trust himself anymore. I advised him to try again, but I guess he never did."

"No, he never did."

"He degenerated badly in the final weeks of his life to the point where he was totally incomprehensible," Carlos added.

"Why did you follow me in here?" I asked him again. "It wasn't because you felt sorry for me, was it? In point of fact, you were upset with me because you thought I was some kind of bigot. And I don't believe it was just to show me that letter."

Carlos stared at me coldly.

"I made a commitment to help Bobby," he said. "You'll probably be placed in charge of Mitch's affairs, or at least have a say in them, and I want to give you my assurance that he'll be well cared for. Our organization will do the best it can. He can live and work with us, and we'll try to make him happy."

"In the last two months you never went back to visit my dad. You just dialed his number. You probably had it in some kind of tickler file, like a reminder, as part of your precious fund-raising techniques. My father asked you to watch over this guy, but you never lifted a finger to try to get to know him better or to arrange in advance for a professional evaluation. So what provisions have you made for him?"

"For Bobby?"

"Of course, who else?"

"It's not going to be a problem."

"You're anxious to look after this drunken brain-damaged child-molester?"

"He might have been having a bad day."

"That's not funny."

"I didn't mean it to be funny."

Looking over Carlos's shoulder, I saw the cab driver standing in the door.

"After my father's death, did you check his house to see if Bobby was still in there, playing stop-and-go all by himself? Did you think that maybe my father would have wanted you to see that this son of his made it to the funeral? Who else was going to do it? The maid?" And I stood up to go.

"I only want to do what's right, for Christ's sake!"

"Sure, you snide bastard! For thirty fucking grand a year!"

"Wait! Take my card," Carlos said, pulling out his wallet.

"Somebody has to take care of him. When you're feeling less upset, I want you to give me a call. There'll be no hard feelings. We can work on this together."

"Keep your goddamn card," I said, as I gathered up my bag and umbrella. "I know how to reach you if I need you. I'll look you up in the Yellow Pages, under Love."

And I stuck him with the check for the coffee.

•   •   •

Joseph Blumenson, a gray-at-the-temples magisterial type, met me at the reception desk and guided me toward the conference room where my father's will was to be read. I could see that my appearance—I was dressed in a rough wool sweater and denim—made him uncomfortable. The last person to arrive, I was seated at a black-lacquer table, shaped like a planchette, that spanned a row of floor-to-ceiling windows providing skyscraper views of downtown Seattle. He introduced me in turn to Gerald Merkin, a short, acned lawyer in a cardboard suit, whom I immediately recognized as the slumbering man at my father's funeral; Felicity Carpenter, a woman in her forties wrapped in gypsy-like scarves and smelling strongly of patchouli; her brother, Rufus Perkins, a gigantic, soft-featured man in a Gore-Tex running outfit; two more lawyers named Stoneham and Risken; and Miss Harmon, the legal stenographer.

Blumenson made some welcoming remarks dealing with the rainy weather and the unfortunate demise of my father, in that order. He explained that the reading of a will was an unusual procedure in the state of Washington, but that it was specifically requested by the deceased. A copy was placed in front of each of us by Miss Harmon. The document, he said, wouldn't be read verbatim. He would simply describe the salient provisions and relate the intentions of my father as expressed to him four months previous, at the time the document was drafted. He said he was confident that the meeting would be a short one, as the provisions of the will were straightforward and not at all complex.

"Absent the boilerplate, Mr. Finkelstein's desires are easy enough to summarize," he began.

"My father's name was O'Banion," I corrected him. "Mitchell Emerson *O'Banion.*"

"Yes, we know all about that," Blumenson agreed. "O'Banion was his given name, but he had it legally changed in 1981. Jerry has the documents in his files, if you'd care to see them later."

"I'd like to see them now."

He turned to Mr. Merkin, the puisne attorney with the skin problem, who seemed unable to keep his eyes open. It was evident that this was a pretense, a way of indicating contemplative self-importance. The senior lawyer asked him to retrieve the necessary papers, and Merkin immediately came to attention and left the room to attend to the errand.

"May I continue?" Blumenson asked in an irritated tone of voice.

"By all means," I replied, "after you explain to me why my father changed his name to Finkelstein."

"I have no way of knowing the answer to that," the lawyer replied.

"Perhaps you know why he claimed to be Jewish, when he had

always adhered to the tenets of Roman Catholicism?" I asked.

"This is a legal meeting, not a religious one."

"Please answer my question."

"Mr. Finkelstein was in point of fact a practicing Jew," Blumenson replied angrily.

"That's very difficult to believe."

"We belonged to the same synagogue, so I happen to know firsthand. Now may I continue with my explanation of the will?"

"Did he change his face at the same time that he joined your synagogue?" I asked him.

"What in heaven's name are you talking about?" The lawyer put down the papers he was holding and stared at me as if I were out of my mind.

"He must have had plastic surgery," I said. "That's not the way he looked when he was younger."

"Do you have any pictures of your father?"

"No. I was raised in the worst possible circumstances, and all of my family possessions were destroyed."

"I'm sorry to hear that," the lawyer said, brushing aside my objection as he picked up his papers again. "Now if I may proceed with my explanation, Mr. Finkelstein's estate, after the payment of taxes and probate fees, amounts to fourteen million, three-hundred thousand dollars. I can't provide an exact accounting quite yet."

"You've got to be kidding!" I was shocked by the amount. "How did my father get all that money? He must have robbed a bank! He didn't have two nickels to rub together."

"Would you please let me finish, or at least get started!"

"I've come all the way from Italy, and I intend to learn what's going on around here. How did my father accumulate fourteen million dollars? What business was he in?"

"I don't know what business he was in," Blumenson said. "At the time he died, he held a mixed portfolio of securities. He owned his own residence. Why don't you let me say what I have to say so that I can make it home for dinner?"

"You have no idea how he made so much money?" I was incredulous. "You never asked? Nobody at your synagogue knew?"

"Why would anybody at my synagogue know about Mr. Finkelstein's private business?" the lawyer asked me.

"Don't you people share information?"

Blumenson's face went beet-red.

"Miss O'Banlon, I've heard about your outbreak at the funeral from Mr. Merkin, and I won't tolerate any more disgusting remarks. One more anti-Semitic comment and we'll show you the door."

I realized that I'd carried things too far.

"I didn't mean anything negative," I apologized. "I certainly have nothing against Jews. I only object that my *father* was a Jew."

"I see here that your middle name is Goldman. What religion was your mother?"

"She was a Catholic also. I was named after Emma Goldman, whom my father considered to be a great American patriot."

At this point, the other lawyer came back into the room with a document. It was a court order, showing the name change, issued in the town of Port Hamilton, Washington, in June of 1981.

The senior lawyer adjusted himself in his seat and began again.

"As I said before, the terms of this will are relatively uncomplicated. Mr. Finkelstein has made specific bequests from his estate. He has left five-hundred thousand dollars to Felicity

Carpenter and an identical amount to her brother, Rufus Perkins."

Tears gushed down the cheeks of the woman, whose narrow head was swathed in an absurd bandanna and whose teeth were badly in need of work.

"I knew he wouldn't let us down," she wailed, her nostrils flaring as she sucked in air. She struggled to her feet while being supported helpfully by her brother. Hoop earrings clacked about her ears. "What an incredible man," she cried, turning toward me. "You're father was a prince! An avatar! A moral giant!"

She continued to sob, as her brother, who had a large puffy face, fretted over her clumsily. He stroked her sleeve while guiding her slowly back into her chair.

"Mr. Risken," Blumenson nodded toward the lawyer at the other end of the table, "is here to represent the interests of his client, Judith Thorpe, a minor. Mr. Finkelstein has expressed his regrets for any damage that might have been done as a result of actions taken by a family member and has placed in trust the sum of one million two-hundred twenty-five thousand dollars for the benefit of Judith when she attains her majority. The terms of this trust are spelled out in the document in front of you."

Risken, a short bald man with horn-rimmed glasses, then stated that he would review the contents of the will, but that it seemed at first glance that its terms were in accordance with the arrangements negotiated after the incident. He reserved his right, however, to get back to Mr. Blumenson if on examination he discovered any problems or oversights prejudicial to the interests of his young client.

I interrupted again.

"May I ask," I said, "what damage was done to this girl and by whom?"

"Mr. Finkelstein's son, Robert, in the course of his employment as a crossing guard, made sexual advances to my client that caused her severe emotional trauma," Riskin replied. "Since Robert is without funds, his father properly assumed responsibility for his behavior and agreed to compensate my client for the problems his son had caused her."

"What did Robert Finkelstein do to her?" I asked.

"He hugged her inappropriately."

"What was that again?" I couldn't believe my ears.

"On a number of different occasions he made sexual contact with a child of ten."

"Hugging her? Did he stick his tongue in her mouth? Did he paw her between the legs? I don't get it!"

Blumenson interrupted.

"Please, Miss O'Banion," he said. "This arrangement was made with the full concurrence of your father. It was his right to leave his money to whomever he wished."

"This impresses me as a sweetheart deal. My father didn't do anything wrong, and I'm wondering whether giving money to some strange girl was absolutely necessary."

"I encouraged you to bring a lawyer," Blumenson reminded me.

"There are enough lawyers in this room as it is," I snapped. "How do you know that Robert Finkelstein is my father's son? Yesterday was the first time I heard that I had a brother."

"Mr. Finkelstein legally adopted Robert. Again, there are papers on file."

"Well, that's a relief!"

"What do you mean?"

"I'm not a blood relation of this guy, that's what I mean. Is this supposed to be his original name, 'Robert Finkelstein'?"

"I believe that it is," Blumenson replied.

"How do you know that?"

The lawyer hesitated.

"I have no reason to assume it isn't."

"Maybe you should check your assumptions. I'd be willing to bet that my father and his moronic sidekick decided to change their names together."

Rufus Perkins spoke for the first time. He had stringy hair and large misshapen lips. He had a two-day growth of beard and looked like he hadn't had a bath for a good deal longer than that.

"Bobby isn't a moron. He's a genius!"

"Maybe by your standards," I said sarcastically.

"Miss O'Banion," Blumenson interrupted, "I think it's in your best interests not to draw conclusions about someone you've never met."

"Not to draw any conclusions about some sex-perverted, drunken, brain-damaged crossing-guard-retard who can't make it to his own father's funeral? I'm happy to keep an open mind!" I sneered.

"You don't know him," Rufus said.

"I'd like to meet him," I replied. "Where is he?"

"That's not at issue here," Blumenson said.

"It seems to me to be *the* issue! What am I to think? Why hasn't somebody arranged for me to meet my long-lost brother? Why haven't you lawyers shown any consideration for *me*! Something's rotten about this whole thing!"

"Please, Miss O'Banion . . ."

"Why don't you just call me Miss Finkelstein? Why not make it one big happy Hebrew family?"

"Miss O'Banion! I've warned you before that . . ."

"Stop trying to throw your weight around!" I said angrily. "How do I know that my father was in his right mind when he wrote this will?"

"He was perfectly lucid," the Blumenson objected.

"That's your opinion, and it's obviously in your interests to think so. He was totally bonkers when I spoke with him on the telephone. He was singing nursery rhymes!"

"Can we try to move this process along?" Riskin asked me peevishly. "I have other appointments today."

"No one's keeping you here, shyster," I said.

"You're behavior is totally uncivilized!" he replied

"I'm not interested in your social views," I said, "so why don't you crawl back into your putrid little hole."

"Can we all calm down?" Blumenson pleaded, raising his hands in the air.

The lawyer for the molested child bowed his head, trying to reign in his temper.

"The remainder of Mr. Finkelstein's estate," Blumenson began again, "in an amount slightly in excess of twelve million dollars, has been placed in a trust for the ultimate benefit of the Cystic Fibrosis Foundation. Income from the trust, after netting out legal fees, will be distributed as follows: two-hundred-fifty thousand dollars per annum for the maintenance of Robert Finkelstein, and the yearly remainder, currently estimated at seven-hundred thousand dollars, to the Cystic Fibrosis Foundation. Upon the death of Mr. Finkelstein, the residuum of the estate will be paid over to Cystic Fibrosis."

I was stunned.

Blumenson paused for a moment and stared at me. He had a

simpering look, as if he'd just defeated me in some superfluous legal battle.

"Furthermore," he continued, "Mr. Finkelstein has been quite specific about how he wishes to handle the care of his son. He has requested that he be placed in the hands of Miss Emma Goldman O'Banion, his daughter. He asks only that Miss O'Banion treat Mr. Finkelstein with kindness and consideration and that she take him into her own home to live. He makes no stipulation as to where that should be. He requires that Mr. Finkelstein be adequately fed and clothed and be allowed to follow his vocational and avocational pursuits *ad libitum*. It was Mitchell Finkelstein's fervent hope that Robert and you, Miss O'Banion, would develop a loving relationship as brother and sister. Contrary to what you might have been told by others, it has been my impression, having met the younger Mr. Finkelstein on a large number of occasions that, although he is an eccentric and somewhat withdrawn person who requires help in his day-to-day living, he is very bright and won't be the burden you presume him to be. In any case, any funds beyond the amount necessary for the care of Robert can be used at your discretion. It is the responsibility of our firm to check from time to time on Mr. Finkelstein's welfare, to make certain that you are adhering to your father's requirements under the terms of his will."

"Whoopee!"

"What did you say, Miss O'Banion?"

"I said, 'whoopee!'"

"What do you mean by that?" the lawyer asked.

"I'm supposed to bring some pervert into my studio in Rome? Perhaps he could help mix paints when he's not out balling the *ragazze*! Perhaps he could chop my vegetables! I have my legal rights as Mitchell O'Banion's only daughter! I'll see to it that this bullshit document is overturned! I'm not going to be shoved aside, into the role of paid governess for a mental cripple!"

"I caution you again to be more circumspect in your use of language," Blumenson said. "We are counsel to the estate, and we're not going to place Mr. Finkelstein in the hands of someone who is incapable of sympathetic understanding. I'm troubled enough as it is by your other remarks."

"And what if I don't want to take care of this guy?"

"The money has been earmarked. If you don't bring him into your home, then the will specifies that we find someone else to do so," Blumenson said, "and at this point, I'm beginning to think that the alternative might not be unwise."

"If this man is so bright, why does he need someone to watch over him?"

"I didn't claim he didn't have emotional problems. Frankly he does, but a lot of families care for . . ."

"In one breath you practically acknowledge he's a child molester, and then you tell me he's not going to be a burden. Do you know how inconsistent you're being?"

"Nobody has admitted anything of the sort."

"This is a railroad job! Why was my father so interested in cystic fibrosis? Giving all of his money to one charity seems irrational. Has he supported your organization in the past?" I addressed this question to the foundation lawyer, who up to this point hadn't said a word.

"My understanding is that he hasn't," Mr. Stoneham said.

"Then why cystic fibrosis?" I asked.

"I don't know the answer to that," he replied courteously. "It's a miserable disease, and apparently he had taken an interest in financing our search for a cure. Lately we've been making real progress. Perhaps he knew someone who suffered from it."

"If there are no more questions," Blumenson interrupted, as he began to gather up his documents, "I think we can adjourn. We'll be in touch with you shortly, Miss O'Banion, about Robert Finkelstein."

"But I *do* have more questions," I said, "so hold your horses. Did my father leave any money to Jewish causes or to an organization that delivers food to AIDS victims in Tacoma?"

"There are no other beneficiaries." The lawyer continued to put away his papers.

"You still haven't addressed the most important matter," I added, before Blumenson got too far along in implementing his desire to flee my presence. "You still haven't told me why Robert Finkelstein isn't here in this room."

"What's that?"

"You damn well heard me," I said. "Where's Robert Finkelstein? Where's my charge?"

"We don't know," the lawyer admitted. "We've engaged an investigation firm, and we'll let you know as soon as he shows up."

"Why didn't you tell me he was missing in the first place? Why did I have to drag it out of you?"

"I'm sure he'll turn up quickly."

"You over there," I said to the unshaven lummox with the huge head, "are you a pal of his?"

"He's my special friend," the man answered quietly.

"Do you know where he is?"

"I don't want to talk to you any more," the man said.

"You leave Rufus alone, you asswipe!" the woman in the headscarves suddenly shrieked at me. "You're not fit to lick Bobby Finkelstein's toenails!"

"Don't talk to me like that, you disgusting old crone!" I shouted back at her.

"We've got a million dollars now," she struggled to her feet and pointed her finger uncertainly in my direction. "A million bucks! And we'll fight you. Mitch asked us to take care of Bobby. Rufus and me. Not you! And we're going to do it. We love him. We want to spend the rest of our lives with him. It's our job!"

"Oh, great," I said, more to myself than to the woman, who broke into tears and sat down again. "You and Mr. Beagle."

"Mr. Beagle?" Blumenson asked

"Never mind," I said to the lawyer, "but tell me, what happens if you can't find my supposed brother? Let's assume he never turns up."

"He'll show up," the lawyer said.

"That's what I thought about my dad, and he stayed out of sight for two decades. Do you know anything about my father's past, Mr. Blumenson? His distant past?"

"Very little."

"My father built bombs. He poured blood on draft records. He beat up scabs. Those are just a few of his many credentials."

"You're entitled to your own recollections. Please make your point, " the lawyer said wearily.

"My point is obvious. As a child, I was told that my father was a fugitive. He probably changed both his name and his face because he didn't want to be apprehended by the law. Did it ever occur to you that Robert Finkelstein was also afraid of being discovered? That he was a fugitive, too? You should find out what this character's real name is and see if he's wanted by the police. I also find it curious that he's apparently suffered some kind of head wound. Perhaps it's related to his flight."

"You're being melodramatic," the lawyer objected, although he was visibly troubled by my line of argument. "Robert never impressed me as being a fugitive."

"He's a fugitive already," I said. "He ran away from a small town for doing God knows what with some young girl. Maybe he was in much more serious trouble before that."

"He didn't do anything wrong," Rufus said. "He loved little Judy with all his heart! Just because he held her in his arms doesn't . . ."

"Please, Rufus," his sister said spitefully, "there's no need to get involved with this horrible person."

"Excuse me," Mr. Risken said, as he stood up from the table, "but I must get going."

"So must I, unfortunately," said the foundation attorney.

The lawyers packed their briefcases and left, and no one, except the Cystic Fibrosis attorney, bothered to say good-bye to me. Then Miss Harmon put away her notes as if nothing had happened and showed me to the elevator.

•　•　•

As a result of my meeting with the lawyers, I was forced to the conclusion that my father hadn't cared a whit about my welfare. Instead of leaving me a portion of his wealth with no strings attached, he had tried to buy my services in order to help a stranger whom he loved more than he loved me. I was merely an afterthought, an insignificant piece in his emotional puzzle. Yet there was no way I was going to accept his will without a battle. I decided I would fight aggressively to get what was coming to me.

It had finally stopped raining, and I walked from the law offices across downtown Seattle to my hotel. Returning to my room, I tried to figure out what my next step should be. I'd booked a ticket with an open return, and my inclination was to grab a plane back to Italy and deal with the situation from there. On the table next to my chair I'd placed the manila envelope from the law firm, and I opened it and removed the will. I spent the next hour examining it carefully. As I expected, he had nothing to say to me from beyond the grave. I was simply a name that appeared in a few sub-paragraphs. As I read the document, I came to realize that the events of the past few days would haunt me for the rest of my life if I didn't try to uncover the circumstances surrounding his disappearance, and more specifically, the identity of the enigmatic man who was the center of his concerns before his death. I made a decision to hire an attorney and to attempt to track down Robert Finkelstein as well.

Telephoning the public library, I found out the name of the largest law firm in Seattle and called the receptionist. I told her that I needed to speak with their most senior litigator—that I wanted to fight a fourteen-million dollar legal settlement—and I was immediately put on the line with one of their top people. His name was Reynolds Lipton, and I explained to him what had happened. He was encouraging and said that, assuming there were no pertinent facts beyond what I was told by Blumenson, and assuming that my father was deranged at the time he signed the will, then the prospects of a reversal were excellent. Even if it were shown that my father were in his right mind, Lipton said, there was little doubt that I had a strong claim against a portion of the estate. He insisted on a personal meeting before taking on the assignment, and we set up an appointment for early the following week.

The most logical place to begin my second task, the search for Robert Finkelstein, was with the list of beneficiaries whose names and addresses appeared at the beginning of the document: with Felicity Carpenter and her brother, and with the parents of Judith Thorpe, all of whom lived in Port Hamilton. I called downstairs to the concierge, who told me that the town was located on Puget Sound, about an hour north of Seattle. The following morning I rented a car and drove up there. I had expected, for some reason, that the place would be picturesque—a quaint little fishing village of some sort—but it wasn't. Among its prefab downtown shop-ping structures lay the sinister cow-plops of American greed: McDonalds, Blockbuster, Pizza Hut, and Wendy's. Port Hamilton was just another depressing, soul-gutted rural enclave. I went into one of the few stores that had any sense of individuality, a gift shop whose window-display was embowered with miniature pumpkins, and asked if anyone knew Felicity or Rufus. I was told that they operated a motel on an island that stood out to sea, less than a mile from the shores of the town.

The Whaler's View Inn was a dilapidated structure of a dozen rooms, flanking a cracked swimming pool, that squatted on an outcropping less than six blocks from the island's ferry dock. I immediately questioned the aptness of its name, since I doubted that whales streamed through the narrow channel between Port Hamilton (which so far as I could see was without a port) and the eastern shore of the island where the property was located. When

I pulled up to the motel, there were no cars in the lot. Opening the door to the office and entering, I encountered Rufus, who was sitting, like a bereft Victorian clerk, on a raised stool behind a tilt-top desk. A grandfather clock and captain's chair stood on either side of a beaded curtain door leading to a back living area. There was a moth-eaten Turkoman rug on the floor, and a calendar from an insurance agency was nailed to the wall behind him. Although it was late October, its pages hadn't been flipped since May.

"Are you seeking a sleeping accommodation?" he asked in a gruff voice. He seemed flustered and strangely agitated. His forehead was covered with sweat.

"Don't you recognize me?" I replied, incredulous.

"Of course, I recognize you. I just want to know if you want a room or not."

Peering over the edge of the desk, I saw that there was a stack of old newspapers piled on the floor. In front of him was a handmade leather scrapbook and a book entitled "Battles of the Civil War."

"I'm not staying. I came here to visit you and your sister," I explained.

He didn't look at me, but stared at the cover of his scrapbook. In the clumsy curlicue of a semiliterate were scrawled the words, "The Halowed Hall of Amerrican Heros." His huge puffy lips were trembling.

"So you haven't retired yet?" I ribbed him.

"That's none of your business, miss," he mumbled resentfully. "If you're looking for Felicity, she's out in the sun."

Without looking up, he pointed toward the parking lot.

I turned and stuck my head out the door. Felicity was hunched in a wooden lounge chair on a concrete pad, a picnic area, that overlooked the water. It was a windy day, and she was wearing a slouch hat, a bright pink overcoat and sunglasses. Without wasting any more conversation on Rufus, I walked across the lot past the swimming pool to where she was sitting. As I approached, she motioned me toward a chair alongside her own. In her outstretched hand was an empty highball glass.

"Are you still gonna behave like an asshole?" she asked me abruptly. There was a humid quaver in her voice.

"That's a hell of a way to start a conversation."

"I just wanna know if you're gonna be as fuckin' obnoxious as you were when I met you at that lawyers office, because if you are, you can get the fuck off my property."

"I'm not interested in fighting you."

"That's good. That's very good. You know the one thing about your dad, he was a real gentleman. He could be tough as nails and rude as hell, but he always treated strangers with total respect. As long as they were straight with him and weren't on any power-trips or anything, he was straight with them."

"I didn't have the luxury of being raised by my father, so I wasn't in a position to absorb his value system."

"That's a fuckin' pity!" She stared into the bottom of her glass and forced a drunken sigh. "He was a real inspiration. It's funny how children can go astray."

"So you're still upset about yesterday."

"Shit, no," she replied with sudden animation, putting her glass on the ground next to her chair and reaching into the pocket of her overcoat for a pack of Winstons. "I might not think much of you, lady, but how can I be angry? Rufus and I just scored a million bucks!"

"What was that scrapbook your brother has?" I asked her, in

order to find some common ground for conversation.

"It's a project he's been working on for years."

"The cover's misspelled."

"So what? Actually, I help him with the spelling."

"What does that mean, 'The Hall of American Heroes'?"

"Rufus collects photos of our countrymen who died trying to save other peoples' lives. He's very proud of being an American."

"That's weird."

"Nobody's asking your opinion."

Suddenly, a beat-up Chevy Impala pulled out from a garage behind the motel. I could see that Rufus was driving. The wheels squealed as it lurched over the curb and zigzagged down the highway.

Felicity stood and yawned, and an involuntary shiver ran beneath her coat. She cupped her hands in the wind and lit a cigarette. Then, without another word, she staggered across the parking lot. I followed her through the door of the motel office and into the back room. She lowered herself into a busted armchair behind a filthy glass coffee table, on top of which were several copies of the Racing Form, a TV Guide, and a large metal bowl loaded with cigarette butts and crusted ashes. It looked like somebody had spilled syrup on the papers. A bottle of Jim Beam stood two-thirds empty on the table. Without offering me anything to drink, she poured herself some bourbon. There was only one other chair in the room—a folding chair leaning against a wall underneath a bookcase filled with dusty bowling trophies—and I carried it over to the coffee table, unfolded it and sat down.

Although Felicity was being difficult, she didn't seem entirely displeased with my company. She removed the pack of Winstons from her coat pocket and placed it carefully on the table, as if to fit it perfectly within the context of the rubble in front of her. She did this in spite of the fact that she had a lighted cigarette dangling from her lip.

"So what do you want?" she finally demanded. "You didn't drive all the way up here for a cozy fuckin' chat."

"I want to know what my father was up to for the last twenty years."

"You should let your dad rest in peace."

"He'll rest in peace regardless. How did you two know each other?"

"I was an acquaintance of his in San Francisco. Well, maybe a bit more than an acquaintance, since we boffed."

She took off her hat and tossed it behind her. Then she unbuttoned her overcoat and removed her sunglasses. She still had a decent figure, but her skin was mangled from the effects of drinking and clung to the bones of her head. Her mouth sagged slightly, and her features were frozen in a way that made her look perpetually, if not hopelessly, preoccupied with her own thoughts.

"So the two of you were lovers?"

"Back then all of us were lovers," she said. "We fucked like rabbits. I didn't know your old man that well at the beginning. I mean I knew other guys a lot better than I knew Mitch. . . . we did some Movement stuff together. The last time I saw him—before he came up here—was in Mendocino, with Bobby, just before they split for Turkey after the kidnapping."

"I don't know anything about a kidnapping," I protested.

"I know you don't know anything about a kidnapping. That's why I'm telling you about a kidnapping," she bawled at me suddenly, as if she were talking to a dummy. "If you just relax for a fuckin' moment, I'll tell you all about it. You wanted to know why your old man skipped out on you, isn't that what you said?"

"Yes, I do."

"Then stop jumpin' all over my carcass!"

"Was Robert Finkelstein involved in this kidnapping?"

"Of course, he was involved. So were Cynda and a bunch of other people."

"Who's Cynda?"

"Cynda was Bobby's wife. A fashion model. Real thin. That Twiggy thing."

"But you weren't involved in it?"

"In fashion?"

"No, in the kidnapping."

"Shit, no. I wasn't involved," she said defensively. "Not me!"

"You didn't know about it when it happened?"

"No, I didn't know a damn thing . . . I found out later . . . when I was in Mendocino. I'd run into some of the people, but they didn't say they were going to do this kind of job, boosting some mobster. They didn't tell me anything about it!"

She stuck her little finger in the glass of bourbon and swirled it around nervously. Then she downed the remainder of her drink.

"And so you're going to tell me the details?" I asked. "At least as much as you know?"

"All anybody cares about these days are *details*."

"I just want to understand what happened, for God's sake."

"You want to understand what happened? What happened?" she bellowed at me, as she swerved from side to side in her chair. "I'll tell you what happened, if you want to know so much. Most of the gang at the mountain cabin where they stashed the kid *died*. They *fuckin' croaked*! They were bound with their hands behind their backs, and plastic was put over their heads, not tied or anything, just put over their heads so they suffocated real slow, and when they were half-dead someone came along and bashed in their brains with a tire iron! That's what happened!"

"Who did these friends of yours kidnap?"

"The daughter of someone you should never screw with. A little girl. Her corpse was returned to the family bosom. At least that's what I was told by Mitch." She poured herself another bourbon and held it up in the light.

"Here's to the good-old bosom," she toasted and slugged back her drink.

"You mean they murdered some young girl?"

"When the dust cleared, the girl was dead. Her throat got slit. What can I say? It's a tough world out there."

I remembered what my father had said on the phone about my own throat getting slit, and suddenly I felt frightened and vulnerable.

"And you're telling me that this is why my father disappeared all those years? It had to do with this kidnapping attempt?"

"Bingo."

"And Robert Finkelstein had his brains beaten in and survived?"

"Double bingo.

"Was my father hurt?"

"Nah. He was down in San Francisco collecting the ransom. He was supposed to be turned into putty along with the rest of them, but he didn't come back to the Sierras. As soon as he got his hands on the cash, he began to fiesta. He was such a party animal, your old man! When he finally showed up at the cabin, it looked like a butcher shop. Brains all over the floor. He buried the bodies, brought Bobby down to the city, got him patched up by a neurologist—black-market surgery, the whole bit—and then they split overseas with the money. The ransom was supposed to go to the Panthers, but I guess the carnage kind of knocked the wind out of your dad's political sails. He decided to screw the Blacks and pocket the dough."

"So Mitch and Bobby weren't hiding from the police?"

"No, they were hiding from the guys who finally caught up with them."

Felicity seemed to be trying to pull herself out of her drunken frame of mind, as if she wanted to consider something a little more soberly. There was a trace of terror in her eyes. My blood ran cold.

"Are you trying to tell me that my father was murdered?" I asked her hesitantly.

"Triple bingo."

"But he was crazy and dying anyway. . . ."

"Oh yeah. So what? Big goddamn deal."

"I don't get it."

"Sure, I suppose you wouldn't. Why should you? Just consider yourself fortunate that I don't bear any grudges. I've got this thing about karma, and if somebody snuffed my old man, I'd sure as shit want to know about it. Do unto others and all that crap, and so I'm telling you because otherwise somewhere along the line I'm gonna get my own cage rattled. Anyway, I don't give a shit anymore, so what the fuck. That's the way I look at it. I'd like to live to spend your old man's dough, but if I don't, *c'est la fuckin' vie*! What will be will be."

I was stunned. I realized that some of the comments my father had made to me on the telephone weren't as crazy as I'd originally thought. He had been trying to communicate with me, to be honest with me, and I'd misjudged him. I hadn't been willing to listen.

"Where's Bobby?" I asked, my voice trembling. "Was he murdered, too?"

"Oh yeah, you see, that's the deal. I'll help you with that thing with your dad, because that's karma, but Bobby isn't part of the equation. You're never going to see Bobby. Not a trace, do you hear me? I know what you really want!"

The woman stood and stumbled over to a bureau covered with a heap of paper. She was squinting, trying to focus. Then she picked up an orange cap lying on a corner of the desk and waved it at me. She could barely keep her balance.

"Bobby was in this room, and you missed him," she laughed fiendishly. "You were standing right next to him, and you missed him. Ha!! You see, we're way ahead of you. Way ahead!"

"It was foolish of you to tell me. I'll go to the police. You can't hide him forever."

"You aren't going to the cops. No way. You go to the police and you die. Snuff-fuckin'-city!"

I was taken aback by her remark. She said this in a way that made it sound less like a threat than a certainty.

"You're going to try to kill me?"

"I wouldn't hurt a fly. Well, maybe a fly, but not a maggot like you!"

I suddenly understood why she was being so open with me. She was trying to bait me in some indefinable way. Her description of my father's career as a kidnapper was part of some devious alcoholic master plan.

"There's no reason to get personal," I said, trying to calm her.

"Mitch asked me and Rufus to take care of Bobby, and that's

what we're going to do," she cried hysterically. "Not you! Us! We're supposed to do it! He wanted us to take care of him, because we understand him. We share the same soul! We all believe in social justice! He wanted us to do it! He was nuts when he wrote that will!"

"That's obvious, but it's not stopping you from spending his money."

"We deserve it!" she said, wiping her mouth and plopping herself down again. She had a combative look on her face, as if she were being tested by unnamed powers.

I was trying hard to pull myself together, and I had to struggle to keep my feelings in tow. Something ugly and dangerous was propelling me through a landscape where nothing made sense.

"You still haven't told me why these people wanted to murder my father, if he was dying already," I said.

"He wouldn't give them back their dough."

"You mean the ransom money?"

"Right. All they wanted was a refund, and Mitch told them to take a hike. He was worth a lot, but he told them to fuck themselves royally up the a-hole, he wasn't going to give them a penny."

"After all those years, they were still after their money?"

"Some people have long memories."

"I don't understand why he didn't buy them off?"

"You really didn't know your dad, did you?" Felicity laughed, having momentarily forgotten that she was furious with me. "Nobody could push him around. He was a real scrapper. They said they'd kill both him and Bobby, and he told them to lick his fucking *dick!* Mitch said if they tried anything, they'd be sorry."

"How did they finally locate him?"

"I don't know," Felicity said defensively. "I'm not supposed to know everything! One day some goombah jumped out of the woodwork and bumped him off."

"But you know who these people are, don't you?"

"You shouldn't ask unhealthy questions. Asking the wrong questions can screw with a person's enjoyment of the finer things in life, like bourbon and breathing."

"Do you think they really want to kill Bobby?"

"He was part of the kidnapping, wasn't he? Anyway, I don't try to figure people out."

"Were they lovers?"

"Who? Mitch and Bobby? That's a joke! You think because your dad had AIDS, he was cornholing Bobby? What a pathetic joke!"

"Then how did my dad get the disease? I assumed he was gay."

"Your father was a King-Kong junkie, dearie. What do you think he was doing all those years on the docks?"

"You're trying to tell me that my father was a smuggler and not a union organizer?"

"He did both. How do you think he put together fourteen million bucks? By being a legitimate businessman? He bootlegged smack. He had a nice little operation that he ran out of Vancouver."

"Unbelievable."

"Yup, it's a fact. It all started back in the fifties, when he worked for the mob."

"What do you mean?"

"Who do you think ran the unions back then? The good guys? How fuckin' dumb can you get?"

"You're trying to tell me that my father was importing drugs for the Mafia?"

"I didn't say that," she protested, seeming to change her mind suddenly about being so specific, although in her drunkenness she had already let the cat out of the bag. "I didn't say anything like that. You gotta draw your own conclusions. Anyway, Mitch told me that the father of the girl whose throat got slit was his boss on the docks. The man dropped dead a few years back, and it's the son who's been causing all the trouble. The little girl's brother. One day he grew up and started throwing his weight around."

"And Bobby?"

"Bobby what?"

"Was Bobby into heroin also?"

"Bobby a junkie? Once upon a time he chipped, but no longer."

"I was told by someone that he likes to get loaded."

"Your dad's illness hit him real hard. It kind of drove him crazy. And then he can't do his job anymore."

"Helping kids cross the street?"

"Is there anything wrong with that? It's an honorable profession. It's holy work!"

"I didn't say anything was wrong."

"You've got a big fucking attitude, lady! You're twisted!"

"I told you, I didn't mean anything negative by it."

"It's obvious you don't know the first thing about Bobby."

"You're right. I don't. Why should I?"

"Yeah, well then you shouldn't draw conclusions based on what other people tell you. For instance, who told you he was thick?"

"Someone who met him once. He told me he was out of his mind."

"Yeah, did you ever stop for a moment to try to figure out why?"

"What do you mean?"

"Well, *you* seem pretty fucked up right now. You look like you've swallowed a goddamn toad! So what do you think *he's* been going through, watching his best friend die?"

"You mean his father, don't you?"

"Yeah, whatever. It's just fuckin' words."

"Well, I have to admit that the man who told me about Bobby only met him on that one occasion."

"You see," she admonished me, pointing her finger in my direction, "you should be more humble. You must have left your heart back in Italy!"

"So he's not retarded then?"

"No . . . he's not . . . fucking . . . *retarded!*" she mimicked me. "His brains are scrambled, but he's smart. He's *very* smart. He's a poet! And whose brains aren't scrambled nowadays anyway? Yours, lady? Mine, lady? My brains are fucking egg foo fuckin' yong!"

"What do you mean, 'He's a poet'? A poet of what?"

"That's how he spends his time. He writes beautiful *stuff.* He is an elevated soul, he has visions of . . ."

"What are his poems about?"

"How should I know? I just play the ponies. I know he writes great stuff, that's all. There's something in the guy that sings . . . ever since I first met him."

"So you don't think he's molested any kids?" I changed the subject.

I expected her to be angered by my question, but strangely she wasn't. She surveyed the chaos of the coffee table, searching for her Winstons, which were directly in front of her, and finally she found them. All of her energy seemed suddenly concentrated on the problem of pulling a single smoke out of her pack.

126

"Aren't you going to answer me?" I insisted.

She lit her cigarette and tossed the book of matches towards the table, but she missed and it landed on the floor next to my feet.

"Oops."

I didn't bother to pick the matches up for her.

"Did Bobby molest that little girl?"

"Sometimes he gets enthusiastic," she said, trying to refocus on the conversation. "There's something cracked in Bobby, but shit, there's something dark in all of . . . "

"Sure, I see. So what's his real name? I assume it's not Finkelstein."

"You should know that. You met him."

"No, I haven't. He wasn't at the funeral."

"No, that's not what I meant. When you were a kid. You knew him real well back then. He was very fond of you."

I didn't know what to make of her comment.

"Under what circumstances? I have no recollection of it."

"Details, details . . ." she mumbled.

"What was his name?" I repeated. "You're avoiding my question. How did I know him?"

"I hate details. Besides lots of people change their names. Take me for instance, my name isn't really Carpenter, and it isn't Felicity either; but I wanted to be a builder of joy and happiness for all the peoples of the earth and so I changed my name in order to realign my energies. Simplest thing in the world. And Rufus's name isn't really Rufus, but after he got gut-shot in Nam, he stopped acting like a Thomas and started acting like a Rufus, and so I started calling him Rufus. He didn't care. Not at all. He sort of appreciated it."

"Your brother is a combat veteran?"

"That's right, a decorated soldier, a real trooper . . . and that's why I got involved in the peace movement, because of what that Lyndon Bullshit Johnson did and what that motherfucking war did to my baby brother. It stole away his innards. Nobody remembers now, nobody gives a shit about the scars, but I do! I sure as hell fuckin' do! That's why Rufus is collecting his heroes."

"I don't understand what you're talking about."

"Another grunt ran through heavy fire and saved my brother's life, but just as he was loading Rufus onto a medevac, the guy took a bullet in the neck. Now that's a true American patriot! Not some bullshit bureaucrat who gets blown up in a space shuttle or some tin-star fuckin' general farting behind a desk. Not some goddamn rock star primping in a mirror. Everyone nowadays is a two-bit heroic piece of shit! But Rufus wants to honor the real ones!"

I took out a cigarette of my own and lit it and sat back and thought for a moment about what I'd just learned. Some hireling had supposedly murdered my father, and now he was wandering around, trying to kill a man who had been hiding in this very room. I realized that if I kept searching for Bobby, I could run into the murderer—assuming there was a murderer and that this story of a kidnapping wasn't some dipsomaniac delusion.

"Why did you say I'd die if I went to the police?" I asked her.

"Oh, it'd happen. I don't owe you any goddamn explanations. If you want to go to the cops, be my guest. It's your funeral!"

"Look, I don't want any trouble. I just want what's rightfully coming to me."

"Yeah, sure, I understand," Felicity said, waving her hand at me again. "Sure, it makes sense to me. Go ahead. Sing to the police. You'll be pushing daisies in no time!"

"No, I mean it," I said. "I don't want any problems."

"I'm not going to do anything," she said. "I already told you. You're looking at me as if I could get you aced or something. Well, I can't, so you can rest easy."

"How do you know my dad was murdered, if no one else does?"

"I can't say."

"But you know for certain he was killed?"

"Yup."

"And you didn't report it? It's not important to you that my father's killer is getting away with it? You're taking his money, but you're not going to do anything about this? What the hell's wrong with you?"

"I'm handling this my own way."

"I don't see you doing anything at all," I replied. "I see you sitting here in this motel, guzzling booze."

"You got all your information. I don't have anything more to tell you."

"You didn't even show up for my father's funeral."

"I was sort of indisposed."

"Indisposed? That sounds . . ."

"Get lost!" Felicity suddenly screamed at me. "It would be healthier for you."

"Is that why you told me all this? To get rid of me? So I won't contest the will? Or so I'll stay away from Bobby?"

"You're just like your asshole mother!" she shrieked. "She got what was coming to her, and you will, too. That's what I get for trying to be helpful, you stupid fucking cunt!"

"What was that about my mother?"

"Get the fuck out of here! You stink!" Saliva dribbled from the side of her mouth.

"You've really been a great friend to my dad," I said bitterly.

For some reason, I must have hit a sore spot with my comment about her relationship with Mitch, because she went ballistic. She tried to jump up and grab me, but she fell across the coffee table. The ashtray spilled on the floor.

"Just go! Go, go, go!" She began crying. She kept reaching for me, but she couldn't find her feet.

I wasn't about to get physical with a drunk, so I backed out of her way and turned around and left.

Then I took the ferry back to Port Hamilton.

A mini-mall stood across the street from the ferry dock, and I parked my car and walked over to see if I could find a place to have a cup of coffee. I was feeling extremely shaky, and it required all of my self-control to keep from becoming hysterical. It appeared that my father had been a kidnapper. Perhaps he had actually murdered the daughter of a mafioso. If so, my father had intimated on the phone that in retribution the mafioso had wanted to murder me! And then the final comment about my mother's getting what was coming to her: never until this conversation had it occurred to me that Gina might not have been a suicide victim, and yet why would anybody want to push a poverty-stricken, pathetic madwoman out of a hotel window? What did she have to do with all of this?

I found a doughnut shop, but before going in I went to a pay phone and dialed Marlon Thorpe's number. He answered, and when I identified myself, he immediately became nasty. His attorney had warned him, he said, that I was "obnoxious and contentious," and given the trauma his family had been forced to undergo, the last thing in the world he wanted was to engage in "verbal fisticuffs." He told me that within the past few weeks

Bobby had again accosted his daughter, Judy, and that he had been forced to complain to the authorities. A warrant had been issued for Bobby's arrest. Without any further explanation, he slammed down the telephone.

No matter what I did, it seemed, I kept facing hostility.

Thinking things over as I drank my coffee, I came to the conclusion that I no longer possessed the courage nor the energy to participate in the confused and apparently dangerous scramble to lay my hands on a child-molesting psychopath. There were now a half-dozen parties, including myself, who were involved in the chase for Bobby: the lawyers, Felicity and Rufus, Carlos Byrd, the police, and an assassin. I decided to give up my search at least until after I had returned to Rome. I went back to the pay phone and called Joseph Blumenson. I told him that I wanted to gain access to my father's house.

"It doesn't belong to you, Miss O'Banion," he replied coldly, "nor does any of his personal property. Everything will be liquidated and the proceeds distributed under the terms of your father's will."

"Are you telling me that I can't get into my own family home?"

"That's precisely what I'm saying. If you have a specific request, for example if there are any mementos you would like, I'd be happy to speak with the people at Cystic Fibrosis. I'm fairly certain they'll be willing to turn things over that are of no use to them."

"So if there's something that has sentimental value but is worth a few bucks, they won't give it to me? Instead they'll sell it?"

"Quite frankly," the lawyer replied, "I don't think they'd be allowed to give it away. All their funds must go toward supporting their mission."

"That's just great."

"I didn't write the laws," Blumenson said impatiently.

"How am I supposed to know what there is of my father's that I want to keep if I can't get in there? There could be possessions of my mother's, family photos, things that could be overlooked or thrown away."

"Eventually, we'll put together an itemized inventory, and at that point I'll ask them if they'd be willing to show it to you."

"That's not good enough, Mr. Blumenson. By then I'll be back in Italy."

"Well, it will just have to be good enough, Miss O'Banion."

That was the last straw.

"If you don't allow me access before I leave the country," I exploded into the phone, "I shall interpret it as an obstruction of my ability to get in touch with Robert Finkelstein and as intentionally withholding information from me as to the circumstances under which my father drafted his will. It's inhumane, and I give you my word right now that I'll sue the crap out of your law firm and out of you personally! I'll dedicate myself to making your life miserable!"

There was silence on the other end of the line.

"OK," he finally conceded. He was doing his best to maintain his calm, although his voice trembled with anger. "I'll send Mr. Merkin to meet you there tomorrow at noon, but you must agree that my associate will accompany you at all times and that you are to remove nothing from the premises without receiving permission from our firm. Mr. Merkin will bring a document for you to sign. Is that going to be acceptable to you, Miss O'Banion?"

"I guess it'll have to be," I replied.

• • •

It was a medium-size ranch house on a quiet suburban street. Its lawn was manicured, and a wrought-iron fence surrounding the property carried a fresh coat of paint. An ash and a horse chestnut, their leaves turning yellow in the autumn, overshadowed the yard. Leaning against the fender of his BMW sedan, Gerald Merkin was waiting impatiently for me. When I pulled up behind him, he approached with fountain pen at the ready, and without a word handed me a one-page document to sign. The language was straightforward and, as expected, demanded that during my visit I remove nothing at all from the house. I scrawled my signature. Then he dug a key out of his briefcase, and we walked up to the front door and entered.

The place was as orderly on the inside as it was on the exterior. From the front hall we stepped down into a spacious living room lined with walnut bookcases. Examining the titles on the shelves, I saw immediately that this was a working library. Besides books in English, there were volumes in French, Greek and Latin. In the middle of the room, two armchairs faced a fireplace, and on a reading table was a stack of magazines. I removed the first three: the Harvard Business Review, the Society of Biblical Literature, and a Swiss photojournal. The furnishings were neither expensive nor tasteful, but there was nothing offensive about them either. There was a deep-pile beige carpet on the floor. I rubbed my finger along the surface of the reading table.

No dust.

An old-fashioned breakfront in the dining room contained antique china from the twenties and contemporary glassware. To the left of the dining room was an updated kitchen. I opened the refrigerator. It was filled with groceries. The fruit was fresh and the milk was postdated.

Two bedrooms, separated by a bath, were located at the end of a hallway. I went into the bathroom first, with the runtish lawyer following doggedly behind me. Again, it had been modernized. On a shelf above the sink, a pair of toothbrushes rested in a nickel stand. The wall cabinet was filled with medications and herbal mixes, the alphabet soup of AIDS therapy.

The bedroom closest to the kitchen had been my father's. It was a Spartan space containing a narrow bed, bedstand, dresser and closet. The bed was neatly made, with a white down comforter and white linen. A reading lamp and clock radio stood on the side table. There were prints of British sailing ships on the walls. On the dresser were two framed photos. The first looked as if it had been taken in a public park. In the background were a flagstone path, a clump of trees, and a wooden bench. My father, his face altered by plastic surgery, was dressed in slacks and a madras sports jacket and was smiling broadly. He appeared to be about sixty years of age. His arm was resting on the shoulders of a smaller man, obviously Bobby, who was proudly holding a diploma or some type of award certificate in front of him.

I had constructed an image in my mind of a grotesque person, but Bobby in the picture was nothing of the sort. He had a handsome face, an easy smile, and was partially bald. Whereas my father was somewhat overweight, Bobby seemed trim. He had intelligent features. In fact, he looked like a tanned business executive in a crossing-guard uniform.

At first glance, I didn't recognize the other photograph, but when I did, I suddenly started to cry. It was my parent's wedding picture, from the old-fashioned Italian ceremony that had been engineered by my maternal grandfather: tux, gown and bouquet. I broke down for a number of different reasons: because I finally understood that my father had always loved my mother—in spite of his protestations about being "stabbed in the back"—and because I saw my mom, for the first time, in a way that I could never remember seeing her before. I saw her as someone who was part and parcel of the world, a person with normal joys and expectations. I saw her sane and whole.

And finally, I broke down because there wasn't any picture on the dresser of me.

I lost the strength to continue my search and retreated into the living room. Merkin disappeared for a moment and reemerged with a box of Kleenex. I sat on the sofa and continued to weep, while the lawyer sat patiently at my side. I am very rarely emotional, but I felt completely helpless to control my tears. Gradually I managed to pull myself together and told the lawyer that I needed to step into the backyard for some air.

The yard was a uniform patch of lawn with an apple tree in one corner, the land sloping gently to the ironwork fence. I walked down the hill and squatted in the grass next to the tree, facing back toward the house. I was stunned by how dearly, in spite of the neglect and insanity of my parents, I held them both in my heart, and how much I mourned their loss and the loss of innocent love. Desperately, I rummaged through the wrack of my earliest impressions, trying to uncover an instance when I was fawned over, when anybody had shown me warmth and affection as a child. This was the first time I'd allowed myself the freedom to engage in this kind of exercise, and I came up with nothing. There were, as I mentioned before, moments with my father at church, and I could remember my mother in our kitchen in San Francisco, although in these particular memories there were always men hovering in the kitchen as well, but I couldn't come up with a single image that included my mother and father together, playing with me or caring for me.

And yet there was something else, something more undefinable that was bothering me. I placed my head in my hands and sat cross-legged, trying to concentrate, trying to figure out what it was. Suddenly it occurred to me that I had seen Bobby before. The face in the photograph was vaguely familiar. I tried to bring this memory forward, to place it in context, and abruptly I sensed that there was a time as a small girl when someone had actually shown me love; and I realized, unexpectedly and without knowing the basis for my conclusion, that this person must have been Bobby!

I knew I couldn't afford to consider the issue any longer— that, considering the pain I was going through, I needed to put this barely discernible intuition aside. Being once again, after so many years, in the same space as my dad, even though his presence had been removed by death, had stirred up dangerous memories and emotions, and it would take every bit of my reserves just to go through the effort of finishing up my search of the house.

Eventually I was able to calm down enough to go back inside. I let Merkin know that I wanted to look at the other bedroom, and we walked down the hallway and entered Bobby's room together.

Bobby's furniture layout was similar to my father's. There was a bed, a reading chair, a floor lamp, a nightstand, and another dresser with photographs on it: in this case nine of them. Eight were the same size, five-by-seven's, but the last was much larger. The smaller photos were headshots taken with black and white film by an amateur. They were of young girls and boys, and each was signed with a message.

"To Bobby, with love, Mandy."

"Bobby, you're the greatest! Charles."

"To Mr. Wonderful. Trudi!"

As far as I could tell, none of the photos was signed by Judith Thorpe.

The larger color photograph was again a wedding picture, but this one was of Bobby and a tall, thin woman, who was quite beautiful. Bobby had been handsome as well, and it seemed obvious, by comparing this photograph with the more recent one in the other bedroom, that, like my father, he had undergone surgery to change his appearance. The couple were dressed as hippies, standing in front of a Jewish altar, with fingers intertwined. Bobby had straight black hair, side-whiskers and was wearing an open, spread-collared shirt. The woman wore a print gown and had a beaded fillet strung across her forehead. They were both young, in their early twenties. I stared at the picture. Now I was certain that I'd spent time with Bobby when I was a child. Unaltered by a scalpel, his face seemed placeable. Yet something about his features made me extremely uneasy. Again I flinched at trying to make the connection and put it out of my mind.

I opened all the drawers of his dresser, but there was nothing noteworthy there. Underwear, shirts, sweaters, jeans, and socks, all folded neatly. I went into the closet. There were poles on either side of the doorway, although clothes were hanging only on the left: a gray suit, a dozen shirts, a crossing guard vest, and several pairs of pants. Bobby's shoes were lined up neatly on the floor beneath the clothing. A stop sign rested against the back wall. There were no empty hangers.

There was one other unexamined area in the room: the nightstand. Opening the drawer, I found three ballpoint pens, a wooden ruler, two sticks of chewing gum and a King James Bible.

I went back into my father's bedroom. There I found slightly more clothing, a few more suits in his closet. The drawer in his bedside table contained some financial records and prospectuses for public stock offerings, which I didn't bother to examine. There was no evidence of drug use—no paraphernalia—just an obsessive neatness.

Then I went systematically through the rest of the house. All the utensils and habiliments of life were there, but little else. No bric-a-brac. No mementos besides the pictures. No documents or poetry books by Bobby. No passports. No personal notes. No evidence of any Mafia connection or of any other criminal activity. I remembered that the letter to Carlos Byrd had been run off on a laser printer, but I found no evidence of a computer. I came to the inescapable conclusion that the place had been sanitized. I sat down in one of the chairs facing the fireplace and stared into the grate.

Several minutes went by, and then someone placed a key in the lock of the front door.

A short, dark woman in a wool overcoat, holding a plastic bag filled with cleaning supplies, came down the steps into the living room.

"Hello," she chirped, and she walked past us without another word and vanished into the kitchen.

"Come back here!" I shouted after her.

She quickly reappeared, minus her coat and bag. She was

wearing an absurd white uniform. She fussed self-consciously with the pleats of her skirt, as she waited to hear what I had to say.

"Do you know this woman?" I asked the lawyer.

"I saw her at the funeral," he replied. "Obviously, she's the maid."

"How come I didn't see her there?"

"At the funeral? She walked in, stayed a minute, and then got up and left."

"You're Adele," I addressed the maid, remembering the signature in the guest book, "isn't that right?"

"Yes, ma'am. That's my name."

"What are you doing here?"

"I come three days a week. Today is one of my days."

"But my father is dead."

"You are Mr. Mitchell's daughter?"

"Yes, I am. Did he ever mention me?"

"No, he never did."

"Why are you working? There's nobody left to pay you."

"Mr. Robert will pay me."

"Have you seen him recently?"

"Does Mr. Robert know you're here?" she asked suspiciously, without answering my question. She seemed to have suddenly realized that she had been neglecting one of her primary duties. "He told me that no one is to be let into this house without his say-so."

"I already told you that I'm Mitch's daughter."

"I guess I can't argue. Can I go back to work now?"

"No," I said flatly. "Sit down."

"Why don't you let her do her job?" Merkin interrupted.

"What's this to you?"

"We didn't give you access to the house so that you could grill the employees. You're only supposed to look at the possessions."

"Somebody's removed property from here already," I said to him. "If you don't have the brains to see it, I do!"

"What are you saying?" he looked at me dumbly.

"I said that somebody has been in here since my father's death and removed property from this house, and I want to find out who did it and why."

"But that's . . ." he started to object.

"You people aren't doing your job," I snapped at him. "You're supposed to be trustees for the assets of my father's estate, and property is disappearing right and left. I intend to get to the bottom of this!"

I turned to the maid.

"Now come over here and sit down!"

She obeyed.

"Tell me, where is my father's computer?"

"It wasn't your father's."

"Whose was it then?"

"It belonged to Mr. Robert."

"Anyway, where is it?"

"It was sitting in the corner, but I guess it's gone."

"You see!" I shouted at Merkin. "Somebody's stolen stuff from the house. Now what do you have to say to that, Mr. Keyholder?"

"I should let them know at the office."

"Just wait a minute. Now tell me, Adele, what else is missing around here?"

"I don't know."

"What do you mean, you don't know?"

"I mean, there are other things missing. . . ."

"Such as?"

"I don't know."

"Have you seen anybody else in the house since my father died?"

"No."

"What else is missing?"

"Nothing much. Just a few things."

"Stop playing dumb. What things, goddamn it?" I raised my voice.

"I'd have to think . . . I don't know."

"Why didn't you stay for my father's funeral? You came and then you walked out. Why?"

"I . . . changed my mind."

"Why?"

"I felt uncomfortable."

"Haven't you been to funerals before?"

"No, it's not that. It was the man who was standing there."

"What man? Standing where?" I asked.

"The man standing in front. I'd seen him before and I didn't like him."

"The rabbi? You saw him at the house?"

"He came a few months ago with another man while I was working. He scared me, and he upset your father and Mr. Robert. Mr. Robert was crying."

"He didn't come alone?"

"No, he came with someone else."

"What's the point of all this?" Merkin asked.

"Shut up, you moron!" I barked at him.

"You can't talk to me . . ."

"Shut your stupid fucking mouth! Now, Adele, tell me who was with this man when he came?"

"I'd rather not talk about it. I was really frightened."

"Miss O'Banion," Merkin said, taking hold of my arm. "I think we should leave immediately! You've finished looking at the house."

Adele rose to her feet.

"I have to do my job now."

I wriggled from the ineffectual grip of the lawyer and grabbed the woman by the throat and slammed her up against the wall.

"Answer my goddamn question, you nitwit," I yelled at her, pressing into her trachea, "or I'll tear you apart! We're talking about someone who killed my father!"

"I don't know," she said, choking. "They came . . . in a big car."

"A limousine?"

"Yes." She was flailing her arms, but I held her fast. I'm a very strong woman and much larger than the maid, and she instinctively submitted. I continued to squeeze my hand into her throat.

"What was the other man like, the one who came with the rabbi?"

"He was young, like a businessman," she said, her voice strangled by my grip. "He talked with your father . . . and the older man talked with Mr. Robert."

I let her go. She took a couple deep breaths and shook her head involuntarily, as if to clear it.

"You mean the older man didn't speak with Mitch?"

"No," she replied, taking a step to the side. There were tears in her eyes. "He spent an hour talking with Mr. Robert. Then he looked through some papers. That's all he did."

"And you didn't hear what the two of them said?"

"No, but they spent time reading the Good Book together."

"Miss O'Banion," Merkin interrupted again, having mustered a modicum of courage. "If you don't leave immediately, I'm going to call the police!"

"Go ahead, weasel! I dare you!" I replied with disdain.

Merkin walked cautiously over to the phone. I ignored him.

"So you saw them reading the Bible?"

"Yes, the older man asked him to go get his Bible, and Mr. Robert did. And then they prayed some together."

"What were they praying for?"

"It's personal," the maid stammered, taking another step away from me.

"What were they praying for?" I moved forward and my hands rose instinctively toward her neck again. If she hadn't answered my question, I would have throttled her. In the background I could hear Merkin talking with someone at his law firm.

"Please, I have to get back to work," Adele whimpered.

"Answer my question, or when I'm done with you, you'll be so twisted, you'll never work again! Do you understand me?"

She nodded.

"They were praying that Mr. Mitchell would die painlessly," she said.

"Both of them together were praying for this?"

"Yes. Mr. Robert was crying . . . he said he just wanted Mr. Mitchell to die."

And the maid started crying, too.

"He was suffering so much!" she whispered. And then she fled the room. I didn't go after her.

"You have a way of really messing things up," Merkin said to me, as he hung up the telephone. His voice was trembling.

"I don't know what you're talking about," I said. "I'm just

trying to find out what's going on around here. I want to know the truth."

"What's there to know?" Merkin asked me sadly.

We could hear the maid sobbing in the kitchen.

"That's a question you should be asking yourself," I replied. "Are you calling the police?"

"No, they told me not to do anything. Just to ask you to leave quietly."

"I need a couple more minutes to think things over."

"Please leave now," he insisted.

"Cool your jets. You've got legal work over there, so just do it for a while."

Merkin stared angrily at me, but it was all bluff.

I looked around me. It felt like I was in a doll house, in some rigidly-arranged psychotic environment. Once more, I stared into the fireplace. The debris hadn't been cleaned from between the andirons, and it occurred to me that I was looking at the only dirt in the place. I walked over and sifted my hands in the heap. I needed to soil myself. I needed to experience the touch of ashes. I needed to feel there was a residue of something warm that surrounded me, and at that moment I suddenly realized that I might have been given my first clue to the true identity of Robert Finkelstein.

They had prayed together!

I rose quickly and went back to Bobby's bedroom, with Merkin trailing ineffectually behind me. Walking over to the nightstand, I opened the drawer and removed Bobby's Bible, and turning to the inscription page, I read:

This Bible belongs to:

Robert Simon Lazarus
385 Palmerston Lane
Tacoma, Washington

Baruch Hashem

• • •

Late that afternoon I returned to Seattle.

When I entered my hotel room, the shadow of a man was hovering on the curtains that shielded the balcony. I grabbed for the handle of the door. It jammed momentarily, but fortunately the mechanism gave way, and wrenching it open, I lunged back into the hallway. I had to make a fast decision as to whether to wait for the elevator or take the emergency stairs, and as I ran toward the elevator bank, I turned and saw the door to my room reopen and light pour onto the opposite wall. I opted for the staircase. I didn't dare look back for fear of tripping or losing a step, although it seemed that my panic was slowing me down anyway. My muscles felt stiff and unresponsive.

"Stop!" a man shouted at me.

I hit the landing on the next lower level and ran back into the hall. I hurried to the elevator and pressed the button. Behind me, Rufus Perkins burst through the door, red-faced and out of breath.

"Miss O'Banion, please, I can't be out here like this," he pleaded with me.

"What were you doing, skulking in my room?"

I kept punching the elevator button. It arrived and the door opened, but the cab was empty.

"Don't get in!" he begged me. "I have to talk to you. Please!"

"I can't afford to trust anybody," I said, beginning to calm down. "Least of all the likes of you!"

"My sister's been murdered," he whispered. "We can't stay in the hall like this, please!"

He leaned over me. He had on the same Gore-Tex running suit he was wearing two days before. His T-shirt was filthy, and his breath was abominable. His left foot was twisting spasmodically into the hotel carpet.

"I don't trust you," I repeated.

"Miss O'Banion, pleeease!"

His body was shaking.

"We can talk here," I insisted. "We'll stop speaking if somebody comes along."

"Miss O'Banion, I'm next!"

"What do you mean?"

"You have to get out of town. We should leave this hotel right now. I'll wait at the bottom of the stairs. The police will be here, and you can't be here when they come. If they find you, you'll get into a lot of trouble, I know!"

"What do you mean, the police are coming?"

"You were there just before she died. They'll want to question you."

"Are you crazy? What are you babbling about?"

"You have to make a decision, Miss O'Banion. You have to trust me, please!"

I looked in his eyes. It was clear that he was genuinely terrified.

"OK," I said, making a quick decision and pressing the up button on the elevator. "I need to grab my things."

Ten minutes later, we were driving away in my car. I followed his directions to a bowling alley in the suburbs. During the ride, Rufus refused to say anything and stared out the side window. Every few seconds, he squeezed one of his eyes shut in what appeared to be a nervous tic. I began to consider the possibility that he was high on something, perhaps speed or coke. There was a raw quality to his edginess that seemed independent of the stress he was under.

The bowling alley was a nondescript structure that shared a parking lot with a building-supply warehouse. We entered together, and Rufus went up to the counter and talked briefly to the man who was handing out sheets and shoes. Then we walked across an empty cafeteria and through another door into a tiny office containing phony wood paneling and a white laminated desk, on top of which were stacks of bound accounting records and an old Macintosh computer.

"OK, now tell me what's happening," I demanded.

"Felicity's dead."

"You said that already. When?"

"I warned her, I begged her to leave with us, but she wouldn't do it. And now she's gone!"

"What do you mean? When did this happen?"

"We knew he'd come!"

"Who killed her?"

"That rabbi guy, only he's not Jewish. He's a hit man. We warned her. We pleaded with her, but she wouldn't listen. So stupid!"

"Why would anyone want to murder your sister?"

"I don't know what she was thinking. She was waiting at the

motel for him to come! You saw her! She was just waiting on the patio."

He was breathing heavily. Saliva dribbled from the corner of his lips.

"Why was she murdered, Rufus?"

"It was horrible! Bobby and I were hiding out, and then we came back and found her lying in the office."

"But you were waiting there, too."

"Hell, no," he said defensively. "We were trying to drag her away when you showed up. I pretended I was working but I wasn't. If you hadn't showed, maybe we could've saved her. That guy was right behind us. We had to split. There was nothing we could do! It's horrible. I'm going to shoot myself!"

"Please try to calm down. You have to think constructively."

"I'm not worth saving," he mumbled. "I'm no hero!"

"Why are you blaming yourself?" I asked.

"I'm no hero! I'm not worth anything. I'm a coward. I don't deserve to live."

"I don't understand what your sister did that was so bad."

"They wanted our money."

"What are you talking about?"

"The money Mitch left us. Those guys think it belongs to them. She pleaded with the man before the funeral service, but he said that unless we turned over every single penny, they were going to blow us away. He gave us twenty-four hours to make up our minds."

Sweat was pouring down his face.

"So that's why you didn't go to the funeral!"

"It was a joke, having the guy who bumped off Mitch giving a big speech about him. We couldn't say anything, so we split."

"How do you know this rabbi killed my dad?"

"Me and Bobby saw him through the window. We were walking up to the house and when we got there, your dad was dead in a chair, and the man was burning Bobby's poetry books in the fireplace. He was burning the whole stack. Bobby screamed and began tearing his hair out. The man came to the front door and stared at us, very calm-like, but he didn't do anything. He just closed the door. Bobby sat on the steps and was moaning and groaning."

"Why did you come to see me at the hotel?"

"Bobby told me it's dangerous for all of us. He wanted me to warn you. They're really upset that nobody will give them their money back."

"But what do I have to do with this?"

"Bobby said that anybody who gets any of their money is in trouble."

"But I'm not getting much money."

"Bobby told me to come. He said you were in trouble," Rufus repeated with conviction. "He said you shouldn't take any money. No matter what! Not a penny!"

"Why shouldn't I go to the police, then?"

"If you tell the police anything, you won't live long. They don't like people who squeal to the cops."

"How do you know so much?"

"I don't know anything except what Bobby tells me. Bobby knows a lot about these things."

"What do you mean?"

"Bobby made me come warn you. Even though it's dangerous, he wanted to help you."

"Where is he now?"

"He doesn't want you to know. He doesn't want to see you. He's so ashamed. You don't know how much . . . he's lost everything. He's kind of gone crazy . . . on the sidewalk. He's saying strange things. He's not like he was. He's much worse. It's like he's broken in two."

"They burned his books because they contained information, I suppose, on what happened in the past?"

"I don't know."

The more Rufus talked, the more jittery he seemed to become. He was fussing continually with the zipper of his running jacket as he spoke to me. His long sweaty hair clung to his cheeks.

"I have to see Bobby. We have to meet," I said.

"No, you can't." Rufus quickly rose to his feet. "He can't think clearly. He wants to help you but he'd be embarrassed."

"Where are the two of you going?"

"We don't know. We have to get away."

"Do you have any money?"

"No."

"You'll get the money eventually from the lawyers, though?"

"We can't trust them. Don't you trust them."

"Why not?"

"Bobby says they're devils. He says the money's evil, because of that dead girl, and that anybody who gets his hands on that money will be hurt real bad. That's why he didn't give you any."

"My father?"

"Bobby says the money's evil," he repeated. "Mitch only wanted to get you to love Bobby. Love's free, that's what Bobby always says. Love's free for everybody. That's why Mitch gave the money to charity, to help people breathe."

"But he left you and your sister money."

"See what happened? I warned Helen not to ask for anything, but she wanted it. She's not like she was because of the drinking. She didn't used to want anything at all, but she changed. She wormed it out of him, and now it's too late. She was greedy."

"Helen?"

"That was her real name. It doesn't make any difference."

"Then why don't you turn over your money? Then they might leave you alone."

"They just killed my sister!"

"I see your point."

"You should get on a plane and go back to Europe. Maybe everything will be all right. You should drive to the airport and get on the plane. Don't wait! Get away from here!"

"It's a small world. They can find me in Rome just as easily as here."

"Just go. Bobby says you should get out of here. Now!"

Throughout our conversation I had been in a state approaching panic, but I had the presence of mind to realize that this might be my only chance to communicate with Bobby. I needed to do something immediately that would convince him to get in touch with me. There was a pad of stationery from the bowling alley on the desk. I tore off a sheet and wrote the following note:

Bobby:

I want you to think of me as your true sister. Please call me in Rome. My number is 396 668 6775. Call collect. You can come stay with me. I'll pay for the ticket.

Emma

Rufus stuffed the note in his pocket and without another word left the office, closing the door softly behind him. I reached for the telephone and called Northwest Airlines. Within the next few hours, a non-stop was leaving for New York. I hurried to my car and made it back to the freeway and out to the airport. When I arrived at the ticket counter to check in for the red-eye, I decided to purchase an upgrade; then I called New York and reserved a room at a relatively quiet hotel near Central Park. I was afraid to go home, and I needed time to regain my composure—a few anonymous days, without any disturbance, so that I could try to sort things out and develop a new plan of action. There was a lounge not far from my departure gate, and I went inside and downed a couple scotch and sodas while praying that I wouldn't throw up. Then I went into a gift shop and bought some magazines.

When they announced the boarding of the flight, I was the first one on the airplane. I sat next to the window, with my temple against the cold glass. My head was spinning, and I had a sharp pain in my stomach. I remained there, motionless, clenching the armrest. Closing my eyes. I became oblivious to the outside world, and for a few precious minutes I floated away, in my head, into a huge protective space where nothing could possibly hurt me.

Somebody patted me on the hand. I opened my eyes and turned.

Sitting next to me was the rabbi.

"Please don't scream or do anything foolish," he warned me in a low voice that, considering the veiled threat, was surprisingly friendly.

I quickly looked around the cabin. We were airborne. I must have passed out. Besides a stewardess who was busying herself in the galley, there was no one else in the first-class compartment. The lights had already been dimmed, and everything was quiet except for the hum of the aircraft. A movie was showing silently on the screen.

I was surprised that up close this man, although in excellent physical condition, seemed older than I'd thought at the funeral. He appeared to be in his sixties. He had a high forehead, a thick mane of silver hair, alert blue eyes, a large shapeless nose, and a chin that was slightly cleft. He was wearing a red-checked flannel sport shirt, a knitted cardigan sweater, cuffless slacks, cordovan loafers with tassels and green argyle socks.

"I'm not here to hurt you, so there's no reason to be upset," he continued. "Would you like me to order you a drink? Perhaps something to eat?"

I had been in a constant state of fear ever since looking down into my father's coffin, and with the passage of time, this fear had only deepened; and yet miraculously and unaccountably, when face-to-face with my father's murderer I suddenly felt in control. Perhaps it was because I had been unexpectedly attacked from so many different directions in such a short period of time, and had been battered down in so many different ways—but whatever the cause, I had simply run out of the energy to be frightened. I knew that I needed to be strong, that I couldn't afford to react passively to whatever this man was here to say to me, and I was able to access some hidden resource or reserve: I became resolute and relatively calm.

"There's no reason to patronize me. I'll take the drink," I said quietly.

"What will it be?"

"Scotch and soda. Make it a double."

"Now we have an agreement that you're not going to do anything stupid?" he looked at me and smiled.

"You don't have to worry."

"Excellent."

He called over the stewardess and ordered the drinks. He also ordered a light meal for himself.

"I'm famished," he commented, after the stewardess had left, "but I still have to watch the calories."

"Hard day at the office?"

"Ah, you're referring to the unfortunate Mrs. Carpenter?"

"Yes, I am."

"She acted foolishly, just like your father. She must have had a death wish."

"Why do you say that?"

"My employer made her the same offer he made your dad. He said that if she gave him back the ransom money that was extorted from his family, he'd forgive and forget."

"Why would he need to forgive and forget?" I asked. "She wasn't involved in the kidnapping, was she?"

"Of course she was. So was her brother."

"That's not what she told me."

"Probably a face-saving gesture. She was involved. Take my word for it."

"And you expected her to trust that you wouldn't kill her after you got the money back?"

"She'd run out of options."

"You shouldn't make wisecracks about someone you just removed from the planet," I commented bitterly.

"You're a brave young lady, challenging me like this," the rabbi said, and he smiled at me pleasantly, "but that's all right. I actually welcome constructive criticism. I'm nothing but a hired specialist, after all, and I never hurt anyone unless I'm paid to do so—and paid extremely well. I've never done it once. Not once in my entire life. Theoretically, I'd do it in self-defense, of course, but otherwise I'm quite harmless."

"And you haven't been paid to kill me?"

The stewardess brought him his setup and then came back with our scotch and sodas. His mind seemed to wander as he toyed with his fork.

"Do I need to repeat my question?" I asked, after she left.

"You're name hasn't come up in that regard," he replied, as he took a sip of his drink. "My employer has his good points—quite a few of them in fact—and yet he's miserably tight-fisted. I'm paid on a per-body basis, if you'll pardon my crassness, and he isn't about to waste money where nothing can be gained. It's far less expensive for us to have this little chat. Better for your health and better for his pocketbook."

"So there's no revenge motive? No eye for an eye or tooth for a tooth?"

"None whatsoever."

I downed my double as the stewardess arrived with an open-face sandwich of irradiated beef. I asked her before she left to bring me another drink.

"Another for me, too, if you please," the rabbi said. "I can't let you get ahead of me."

"Do you intend to pursue Bobby?"

"Robert Finkelstein? No. There's no reason to."

"Well, he was involved in the kidnapping, wasn't he? Isn't that reason enough?"

"As far as my employer is concerned, Mr. Finkelstein is as good as dead already. He's paid the price for his sins against humanity. His wife was killed while carrying his baby, and his brains were turned into mashed potatoes. Besides that, he has no real money so his death would be a terrible investment."

"You mean that his wife was pregnant at the time of the kidnapping?"

"That's what I was told. Apparently, they were both suffocated. He watched through plastic as she choked to death. Then someone bashed him in the head and punctured his bag, which accidentally allowed him to survive. Not a pretty story, and yet the exercise they were engaged in, the kidnapping and murder of a defenseless child, wasn't pretty either. By the way, do you happen to know the name of my employer?"

"No, I don't. I only know that the man who hired you was the brother of the kidnapped girl."

"My employer's father died a few years back," the assassin said. "If he were still alive, I have little doubt that Mr. Finkelstein would also have been put out to pasture. The old man had a two-ton chip on his shoulder and took the kidnapping as a personal insult. He pledged to hunt down every single person responsible for the death of his daughter and put out each of their lights. But the younger generation is much more civilized. Yuppies, alas."

The hit man finished off his glass of scotch. He still seemed somewhat distracted.

"Are you upset with me?" he finally asked.

"For what? For killing my father? You didn't torture him, did you?"

"No."

"Then I'm not upset. You probably did him a favor."

"You really feel that way?"

"He was dying and had lost his mind. He had nothing left to live for."

"That's true, of course. . . ."

"How did you know I'd be on this airplane?"

"You're not a difficult person to follow, Miss O'Banion. You haven't been out of my sights since you left your hotel."

The stewardess delivered our refills.

"OK, so why don't you tell me why you came here?" I asked him, after she had left.

"I thought you would have figured everything out by now."

"Frankly, I don't have a clue."

"We need to fashion an agreement, a working arrangement," the killer explained. "We want you to sue to get ahold of your father's estate. Cystic Fibrosis is a wonderful cause, all and all, but it was my employer's sister who was murdered, not some poster child, and he wants the ransom money back. Originally, he was willing to forgo certain penalties, but now, considering all the fuss, bother and expenses, he requires reasonable interest, plus a liberal amount for pain and suffering. So here's his offer: we'll find the best possible lawyers and pay all your legal expenses. We think you've got a strong position. Your father wasn't in his right mind when he signed that will, it's obvious. If we lose the legal battle, there'll be no hard feelings, just so long as you haven't interfered with how we structure the case. You must agree to be totally cooperative and leave everything to us. On the other hand, if we win, we get to keep eighty-five percent of the proceeds and you get fifteen percent. We'll arrange for a tax-free, off-shore transfer. You could wind up with around two million dollars."

"So you're a negotiator as well as a character actor and contract killer?"

"It's marvelous that you appreciate my talents."

"What if your lawyers only get back part of my father's estate?"

"You get fifteen percent of whatever we recover."

"Is this negotiable?"

"No."

"And what if I don't agree?"

"You die."

"Now?"

"Later."

I had somehow mustered the courage to face this man, and now I realized that I had the power to judge him. I knew precisely what I had to say.

"I don't want to die, so I agree."

"You'll go along with this?"

"I just said, I agree. My only stipulation is that until things are concluded, I can use the small amount of money I'll be getting from the estate to support Bobby and myself, if Bobby shows up. The two of us can't survive on my income alone."

"I already told you that this isn't negotiable. You can't spend a dime until we settle this. Besides, if you hear from Mr. Finkelstein, we want you to let us know immediately. He is being allowed to live, but we don't want the two of you having any contact. None at all. Things will be much better for everybody concerned if we go our separate ways."

I sat there thinking for a few minutes. He didn't interrupt me.

"Fine," I finally said.

"So you agree to that, too?"

"I agree. I see your point that it will be better for me not to have anything to do with him, regardless. Why did this child-molester inspire such affection in my father and his friends?"

"There's no accounting for taste," the rabbi replied, at the same time conveying an unwillingness to continue discussing the subject.

"I suppose not."

"There's one last thing about the agreement we've just made," he said, with the intention of wrapping things up. "You must promise to bury the past. My employer doesn't want you delving into his personal history. Simply follow instructions, maintain a strict silence, ask no questions, and you will probably live a long and fruitful life. If there is a single infraction of our arrangement, no matter how minor, there'll be the same consequence."

"You mean death?"

"That's precisely what I mean."

"I agree to that, too."

"It's a pleasure doing business with you," the rabbi said in an easy manner. "I'm pleased that *somebody* finally had the sense to accept our offer. No disrespect to the memory of your father, but it was getting tedious killing misers."

He hadn't touched his sandwich, but now he tore into it with evident satisfaction.

I stared out the window into the darkness as he ate his food. Again I felt nauseated. I understood on some level that this was not a difficult decision to have made. It was life and two million dollars or extermination and nothing. I didn't like doing business with someone who had just murdered my father, and yet I felt certain that Mitch had used the situation as a way of avoiding a demeaning AIDS death. Moreover, it was obvious that these people had a legitimate grudge against my dad.

I took a deep breath.

"There's something that's bothering me," I said, after he had put down his silverware. "Something we haven't discussed."

"Oh yes? What's that?"

"Do you know anything about the circumstances surrounding the death of my mother?"

"I don't know anything about her. I have no idea who she is. Why do you ask?"

"Felicity Carpenter implied that she was murdered."

"Not by my employer. I'm quite certain of that."

From what I could judge, he seemed sincere.

"By the way," I said, "if your employer's father was once the head of Mitch's labor union, I could find out his name with a visit to the library. So how will you ever know whether I know too much or not?"

"Take my word for it, the identity of my employer is not an easy thing to determine, since his father was a man who stayed well in the background."

"But I'm concerned that once you get your hands on the money, you'll kill me anyway."

"You haven't done anything wrong, Miss O'Banion. If you do business with us, then you're on our side. You're going to have to trust me on this one."

"You take a lot of pride in the way you do your job, don't you?"

"At my level, assassination is not about killing people, it's about something much more important."

"Finesse, is that it?"

He relaxed and smiled.

"When I'm finished, the wrong person is always left holding the bag. It's an underground art form."

"I have one last question and then I'll stop."

The assassin took a final sip of his scotch.

"OK," he replied cordially. "Go right ahead."

"Why did you deliver that eulogy?"

He laughed as he patted me again on the hand. His fingertips were cold from clutching his drink.

"You're an intelligent young lady, but let's call this one a professional secret."

He wiped his mouth and leaned back in his seat. Then he let out a soft sigh of satisfaction and closed his eyes.

And within a matter of minutes, he was sound asleep.

•   •   •

My three-day experience in the States had been perilous and painful, but somehow I'd managed to navigate my way to safety. Shortly after my arrival back in Rome, I received a pile of documents from a lawyer in Miami named Horatio Cyrus which I executed and promptly returned. These papers assigned my power of attorney and rights to proceeds in the lawsuit to a limited partnership in the Bahamas. Approximately a year after I'd said goodbye to my father's killer at La Guardia, the lawyer telephoned to let me know that everyone was pleased that I was being cooperative. He assured me that there was a good chance we would win something and a fair chance we would be able to acquire the entire Finkelstein estate. The principal reason for his call, however, was to advise me that Gerald Merkin was flying in to take my deposition, and that a team of lawyers from the Florida firm would arrive in advance to coach me and hold my hand while I answered his questions. Once Merkin was finished, Cyrus's attorneys would depose me as well.

The process of interrogation went smoothly. No mention was made in the course of my questioning of the kidnapping, of the Mafia, of the murders, or of the past of either Mitch or Bobby. The fiction of the Finkelsteins was immaculately maintained. The issues were restricted to my relationship with my father and whether or not he was in his right mind when he spoke to me on the telephone. It was as if everyone—Merkin, the Cyrus legal staff and I—were colluding in order to insure that the truth behind the lawsuit never emerged. The performance took place without a hitch, and everyone seemed satisfied with the result.

Within a short time, I received another call from Cyrus to inform me that the parties to the dispute had agreed to terms. We were fortunate, he commented, in that nobody had the stomach to engage in a five-year legal battle: we were settling for half, and our final share was to be approximately seven million dollars. I was mailed another mound of paperwork to sign, and within months an amount slightly in excess of a million dollars was wired into my bank account. Mr. Cyrus then telephoned for the last time to say that he hoped I was satisfied with the outcome. I told him that I was. "All's well that ends well," he quipped. He wanted me to know that his client was now closing the books on this unpleasant business, and he trusted that I would do the same. He said that his client expected me to keep my side of the bargain and to maintain an absolute silence. Was I willing to commit without qualification to this? I told him that I was determined to look forward, not backward.

Consequently, I was able to return with only minor distractions to my work as a painter. As a matter of fact, my art seemed to mature as a result of the strength it required to adapt to my new set of circumstances and put the experience of my father's murder behind me. There was only one problem. On two occasions, the face of Robert Lazarus, alias Finkelstein, appeared unexpectedly on one of my canvases. The second of these faces, especially, bore an unmistakable resemblance to the Bobby of the wedding picture. I tried as hard as I could to erase this image from my mind, and I immediately repainted the figures from scratch. I told myself that at this point I didn't care if I had ever seen Bobby as a child, I didn't want to know where he came from, or what he had done, or what kind of person he actually had been. In spite of my revulsion at what I had heard about him, I included him in my prayers—that he was safe and sound—and left it at that.

There was an instance, however, where my curiosity did get the better of me in relation to my past. As I said, all the legal documents that were sent from Miami had been returned, but there was one document, the notarized settlement decree, that didn't need to be mailed back. I stuck it unexamined in a file drawer, and yet in my more meditative and unproductive moments, I kept asking myself certain vain, theoretical questions. I knew it made absolutely no practical difference what the answers to these questions were—that what was done was done—but the questions kept gnawing at me nonetheless.

First, I wondered how much money had been paid to the Thorpe family on the abuse claim. I was resentful that small-minded people could use the system to extort money from my father. After all, their child had been "inappropriately hugged," whereas I, at the same age, had been penetrated anally by a smelly, jacked-up hippie. At the time, I didn't have the luxury of emoting soft feelings of vulnerability and betrayal. There was no one to compensate me or even help me. I couldn't engage in the puling idiocy and emotional masturbation of the modern-day victim. I had had to move ahead in order to survive. I wondered what Judith Thorpe's father, who had found it necessary to hide behind the shield of his lawyer, had managed to wangle.

Secondly, I wanted to know, in retrospect, if any money had been set aside for Bobby Lazarus. I couldn't imagine that the court would have thrown out his claim, and yet Horatio Cyrus had never mentioned him. I was curious to know if anybody had cared enough to honor my father's most urgent request and make a permanent provision for his welfare.

And thirdly, even though the Mafia's share of my settlement was long gone—having probably been transferred into some remote Caribbean bank or other fail-safe money haven—I couldn't help wondering if I'd been cheated and had actually been awarded more than I'd been told.

I knew that what the Mafia, Bobby and the Thorpes received, in the final analysis, could in no way impact my life, far away in Rome, yet human nature being what it is, I wanted answers to my questions, and these answers were in a file cabinet only a couple of steps away. I promised myself, fatuously, that regardless of what I learned—even if I'd been scammed, even if huggable little Judy collected more money than I did, even if Bobby Lazarus wound up without a pennyworth of consideration—I would chalk it up to experience and let sleeping dogs lie, and with that convenient rationalization in mind, one morning after coffee I went over to my file cabinet, removed the document, and read it.

As it turned out, there had been no reason to be concerned about any of the things I'd feared. Apparently, the Thorpes' claim had been challenged, and they had settled for two-hundred thousand dollars. Blumenson's law firm had managed to be designated guardian ad litem for Robert Finkelstein, and it was up to them to find somebody to watch over Bobby in the event he showed up. A million three-hundred-seventy thousand dollars had been placed in an account with SeaFirst Bank, to be used for his support and maintenance. An additional million dollars had been set aside for Rufus Perkins and the estate of Felicity Carpenter. This money, not surprisingly, hadn't been claimed, and legal provisions were made to maintain the funds in a trust account pending resolution of their bequests. The estate had grown considerably since my father's death. Consequently, I had received six-million eight-hundred thirty-thousand dollars, and the Cystic Fibrosis Foundation had received an identical amount plus any remaining Bobby-money, once he died or was declared legally dead. Everything seemed above-board, and the rabbi's employer had kept meticulously to his part of the bargain, so that the bottom line was that, with my fifteen percent, I was a million dollars wealthier than I would have been if I hadn't chosen to cooperate.

There was a terrace at the top of my apartment building, and I placed the settlement decree back in the file drawer and went up a narrow metal staircase to the roof and into the open air. It was a beautiful fall day. I looked across the Tiber, out past the Baroque palaces of the Via Giulia to the Gianiculum, the hill on which was perched one of the most graceful structures in Rome, marking the site of Peter's crucifixion: the *Tempietto* of Bramante. It occurred to me, at that moment, that when martyrdom is commemorated with monuments of beauty, something important is always lost— the reality and character of sacrificial pain—and yet without such elegant commemorations, there would be a subtler loss of a different kind: a loss of memory. In a parallel sense, the chaos and duplicity of my past had somehow been reduced to a civilized conclusion from which I had benefited substantially. Whatever pain had occurred, and whatever history was buried with that pain, had ultimately become irrelevant. The myth of the Finkelsteins, the graceful structure, had supplanted some dismal, unknown truth.

I took a deep breath and felt, for the very first time, that I had put my miserable childhood behind me.

•   •   •

One afternoon, after another year had passed, there was a knock on my studio door, and I opened it to discover my Aunt Donata, Gucci suitcase in hand. As I've already mentioned, I was the recipient of her obligatory trimensual correspondence, but the last time I had actually seen her was at my cousin Paulie's wedding in Boston (followed within months by meltdown and divorce) in 1988. No one could have been more temperamentally different from my mother than this timid older sister, who hadn't entertained an original idea or emotion in her life. Her husband, who I always suspected married her for her money, was also thoroughly mediocre. Uncle Jack had bullied his way to unspectacular results in the auto parts business which, given the achievements of my grandfather, were still good enough to allow him to indulge in the delusion of acumen and reward himself unsparingly for showing up at work every morning as a preliminary to eighteen holes of golf. My aunt's cutsey-pooh frivolity, flitting from shop to shop and market to market, had always driven me to distraction, and over dinner she would relate how sorry she had felt, on a particular day, for a sales clerk or lowly hair stylist who couldn't afford to put her children through college or had had to suffer through a nagging skin problem. She would write out thousand dollar checks for such people behind her husband's back and whisper to her children that such small gifts were what made her own unworthy life worth living. One of my most horrifying moments occurred at the age of seventeen, when I finally realized that behind the mask of this brainless moral posturing was a yet-more-brainless suburban automaton in jewels.

What was most surprising about Donata's visit to Rome was that she hadn't called in advance to let me know she was coming. This was totally out of character. She plunked herself down without any apology and told me, by way of explanation, that she was only staying for a week and that she wanted to spend some quality time with me—that she was lonely. I slept on a cot and put her up in my bedroom.

As far as I could tell, my aunt had absolutely no interest in art or history. Gamely, we set out each morning around ten, after two hours of preparatory clucking and primping and make-up application in the studio, to view the sites of Rome. In the Forum, she was thirsty; on the Campodoglio, she was hungry. Her feet ached walking up the Spanish Steps, and standing in the center of the Pantheon, she asked where she could find a cup of American coffee. It was only when we entered the Via dei Condotti, the elegant passage containing some of the world's most expensive shops, that my aunt's sixty-year-old body shifted into overdrive. She moved determinedly from counter to counter every afternoon until closing, fingering whatever could be touched and admiring from a distance everything that couldn't.

After a number of days of this mind-numbing ritual, I suggested that we limit ourselves to walks in the parks and gift purchases. She seemed relieved, and we spent the next few mornings sitting on benches, people-watching, and our afternoons dallying at cafes, where I would watch her nibble ice cream while I counted the hours. Donata was raised speaking Italian in the home, although with an archaic southern accent, and from time to time she would strike up conversations with passers-by or with people seated at the tables next to her. In the evenings we watched television, and she was particularly fascinated by the game shows where blondes in fluorescent bikinis bounced up and down and clapped as second-rate soccer talents raked in the money.

Our conversations were always constrained. Paulie was living in Vermont and refused to communicate with her. As far as she could tell, he was unemployed and relying on whatever could be gleaned from his trust funds. My other cousin, Maria, had just given birth to child number-three and was still ensconced in Winnetka, less than a mile away from the old family homestead. Donata went on and on about the both of them. She was involved in a goodly amount of volunteer work, and so I learned the intricacies of yard sales, hospital service and bake-offs. In order to feign nostalgia for the days when I lived with her and Jack, she related a few shopworn incidents from my teenage years and recounted in detail, based on hearsay and confabulation, the three or four dates I had had with men. My aunt wouldn't admit that I was a lesbian: it never came up in her correspondence, and the only time I broached the subject, during a vacation from college, she treated it as a transient form of madness. Consequently, she asked no questions about my social life in Rome, because she was fearful I would bring up my love life. Nor did she ask to look at my paintings. It was a mystery why she had come to visit me in the first place. I assumed that it was as a result of some guilt-driven impulse, since her actions were always ruled by a pleasure-destroying, overweening sense of sinfulness; but to ask for an explanation would have created even more unease, and she would simply have repeated that she missed me.

On her last day in Italy, we wandered along the Tiber, and by the time we crossed the Garibaldi Bridge, I had pretty much run out of entertainment options. Hoping that I could trade an hour in a cafe for a minute's glimpse of some art, I told her that the best gelati in Rome was served in a little cafe across the piazza from the Basilica of Saint Mary in Trastevere, one of the truly magnificent churches of the city, which contains, along its chancel arch, an exquisite Pietro Cavallini mosaic on the life of the Virgin. As we headed for the Via Lungaretta, it occurred to me that the Church of Saint Chrysogonous, which we were just passing, also contained an apse of Cavallini's school, and because I wanted to take a quick look at both mosaics, I hung a sharp left, and we headed through a side door into the church. I knew that she would start fidgeting the moment I stopped to examine an artwork, and so I told her that there was an interesting "dungeon" below us. This temporarily excited her interest. I paid the sacristan, who turned on the lower lights, and we went through a wooden door and descended twenty feet of staircase.

There are many subterranean layers in Rome. One of the fascinating things about this city is that there are intact neighborhoods spreading out for miles beneath the streets. Wherever one penetrates the ground, it seems, one breaks through ceilings into structure. Only a short walk from my studio, the Largo della Torre Argentina, haunted in the moonlight by Republican spirits and stray cats, is a typical example of what emerges with just a little digging. Beneath many of the older churches are still older churches and beneath them are older churches still, the *tituli* and crude Manichean assemblies of the paleochristian era.

The excavation beneath this church, a Constantinian basilica turned Carolingian confessionary, was one such site. Its earthen floor was dotted with spolia. Here and there along its crumbling sidewalls were inferior sarcophagi from the second and third centuries and mural fragments that had been created over a span of five-hundred years. One large grouping, along the exterior of the ambulatory, showed Saint Benedict curing a beggar covered with sores. He was holding a small book in his hand. I turned to my aunt and mentioned rather casually, "This is a thousand-year-old picture of a saint blessing the leper, Lazarus."

My aunt stopped and examined the fragment. She craned her neck from side to side, as she clutched her purse.

"That's strange," she said, trying to be humorous, "he doesn't look like a Lazarus."

"I don't get your point," I replied irritably.

"It's just that I knew a man named Lazarus once, and this man doesn't look at all like him."

I had begun to walk away from my aunt. I turned and stared at her.

"Whom did you know named Lazarus?" I questioned her sharply.

"A friend of your mother."

After answering, I could see that she had suddenly become uncomfortable.

"You knew Bobby Lazarus?" I asked, stunned.

"Sort of," she replied, and I could see that she was shocked that I knew who Bobby was.

"What do you mean, 'sort of'?"

"I'll tell you about it some other time," she said, trying to recover from her confusion as she hurried toward the stairs.

We ascended to the main level of the church, but I no longer had any interest in looking at mosaics. Going out into the sunshine, we walked down the street toward the piazza where my aunt could get her ice cream. Foolishly, I had always taken for granted that Donata, mired in her bourgeois Chicago existence, knew little or nothing about our situation in California. But why should that have been so? At the time, both sisters were conservative, married women in their thirties, and their lives, prior to my mother's immersion in lysergic acid, were not that dissimilar. Why wouldn't they have confided in one another? For the first time in my life, I considered the possibility that this flustered, ineffectual woman had always known about my father's exploits. We sat at a small table adjacent to the square. I tried to relax. I wanted to hide my emotions, and I told myself that I couldn't afford to be upset, that I had to stay calm and be careful what I said. My aunt was fretting her lower lip as she worked hard at selecting the proper gelati flavor from the menu.

"I think I'll have mocha," she said. "How about you?"

"I'm going to stick with an espresso."

I looked across the piazza at the central fountain, which was an elegant remodel by Bernini. Students and tourists, clutching their guidebooks, were draped on a flight of stairs surrounding the base.

"Aunt Donata," I said, still looking away, "how did you know Bobby Lazarus?"

There was no answer, only silence, and I turned to her and repeated my question.

"Tell me, Aunt, how did you know Bobby?"

I could tell that she felt trapped. It was obvious that she was trying to devise a tactic of evasion.

"I met him in San Francisco," she finally said, trying to make the best of it. "He was at your mom's house. His wife was there, too. She was such a beautiful woman."

"You met him only once?"

"Yes, that's right."

"Did he make some sort of impression on you? What did you learn about him?"

"Nothing really. He was a close friend of your mom's. He was a kind man. That's all."

"But many years later you still remember his name in some church basement?"

"That's right, honey."

"Some man you met one afternoon, and his name pops into your head?"

"That's right."

"I didn't know you went to visit Mom in San Francisco. When were you out there?"

"Let me see. . . . it must have been the summer of 1970. That's it, because your Uncle Jack had just received his promotion."

The waiter came over and took our order. I stared at the ground.

"Aunt Donata," I said, after he left, "I need to ask you a question. It's something I never felt comfortable asking when I was young, and now I want you to promise me, on your word of honor, that you'll give me a full and honest answer."

My aunt looked terrified.

"OK," she said feebly.

"Why weren't you there for us during the three years when Mom and I were homeless?"

"We didn't know where you were," she blurted out.

"Your only sister vanishes for three years, and you don't do anything about it? Was she mentally ill when you saw her the previous year in San Francisco?"

"Yes, Emma. She was becoming quite disturbed. She wasn't thinking clearly at all."

"And yet, when she disappeared, you didn't do anything about it, even though you knew she was demented and had a ten-year-old child?"

"We didn't know where to look."

"Did you file a police report?"

"No."

"You just shrugged your fucking shoulders and went on with your life?"

"Please, dear, don't swear."

"Answer my question!"

Suddenly, my aunt began to cry. She opened her purse, as tears poured down her cheeks. When she finally found a handkerchief, she covered her eyes.

"I always wanted to avoid this," she said weakly. "Somehow I knew when I came here this would happen."

"You came here because you finally wanted to tell me, but you didn't have the courage, isn't that it?"

"No," she said, "not really, but I knew this would happen. I had a feeling."

She wiped her eyes and looked at me sorrowfully.

"Look, Aunt," I said, "part of the problem I've always had is that I never understood why you weren't there for us. You and Jack and Grandpa Nino were the only family Mom and I had."

"We couldn't do it," she wailed. She held her handkerchief over her eyes again. "Your grandpa wouldn't allow us!"

"Grandpa?"

"I had to protect my own children!" she sobbed.

"What in God's name are you talking about?"

"Grandpa Nino said that that if we helped you and Gina, somebody might do harm to our family. I had to make a choice! It was the worst thing I ever did."

"I don't understand. What did Grandfather have to do with all this?"

My aunt pulled herself together and took a deep breath. Then she wiped the tears off her cheeks and looked around hesitantly. There was nobody seated near us.

"Dear, I never intended to tell you this."

"What is it?"

"Your grandfather . . . he wasn't really in the auto parts business. I mean he was in the parts business, but that wasn't really . . ."

"Oh, my God!"

"I promised I would never tell. If Jack knew you knew, he'd be very upset. He'd be turning over in his grave."

"And Jack, too?" I asked, thoroughly shaken.

"No, not Jack," she admitted. "He didn't want to, and your grandpa respected that and let him lead his life as a businessman. It was your father who wanted to become involved. When he married your mother, your grandfather got him a job through friends. Mitchell went to work for a labor union out there, but he never got along and he got into drugs and from that point on he would never listen to reason. Then he started doing strange things in politics. He felt that our family didn't accept him, not being Italian and all, and he was very angry. It hurt Gina. She was caught in the middle."

"I can't believe this!"

"By the time you were old enough to understand, you were closed off in your own world. I don't think you were aware of much, playing your saxophone and all, and I never felt I could confide in you about what went on back then, and we were all so ashamed and then when Uncle Jack was still alive and . . ."

"You know about the kidnapping, don't you?" I interrupted her savagely, as I suddenly understood what she was getting at. "You've known about my father's little caper ever since it happened!"

"Yes," she admitted, looking around again, "but I couldn't tell, ever! I didn't know you knew."

The waiter came up with our gelati and coffee. We stopped talking for a minute, and my aunt self-consciously wiped her nose.

"Whom did they kidnap? You have to tell me, Donata," I said, after I paid the check.

"I shouldn't say."

"Why not? Who was it?"

"Something bad might happen."

"After twenty-two years? Tell me!"

"It was Turi Cannavota's daughter, the poor little girl!"

"Who killed her?" I asked.

"You know she was killed?"

"Yes, I know she was killed. Now who did it?"

"It wasn't your dad," she protested. "Grandpa Nino said your father was innocent of blood."

"But you don't know that for sure, do you?"

"Grandpa said your father wasn't even there. When she died.

That's what he said. I just wish I hadn't opened my mouth in that church."

"Do you really? Why? What did the years of silence get us, Donata?"

"I suppose you're right."

She wasn't touching her ice cream. Her hands trembled as she took a sip of coffee.

"So tell me the truth, how did you really know Bobby Lazarus? And don't lie to me this time!"

"Are you sure you want to hear this, dear?"

"I told you I want the truth."

"Your mother was in love with him. But I don't think he returned her affections. Your mother had some wild ideas. She was obsessed. I pleaded with her to move back to Illinois, where she could calm down and think more clearly. We could have gotten Mitch a job in the parts business, but she just laughed at my suggestion. Later when Mitch and his friends stole Turi's daughter, your mother got upset and called Grandpa and told him what was going on."

"Why did she do that?"

"Why did she call Grandpa? Because she thought that Mr. Lazarus was going to run away from her once he got a lot of money."

"And so Grandpa ratted on Father, is that it?"

"Grandpa said he had to do it. If Grandpa Nino hadn't told Turi, we all could have been hurt, including Grandpa. It took all his effort to get Turi to promise to leave you and your mother alone, but we had to disown Gina. We had to turn our face from her. There was no other way. She called and we told her. She pleaded that she was being abandoned because at the same time your dad had walked out on her for good. She said that Mitchell and another man had brought Mr. Lazarus down from the mountains where they were hiding, and your parents had argued, and your mother had his blood all over her. They suffocated everyone up there, at least that's what she said, and she couldn't breathe, she said she was cursed never to be able to breathe again from the guilt of having turned in your father and the man she loved. She pleaded with us to save her. She tried calling one or two more times, but I never heard her voice again."

And then Donata began to cry. Her body heaved as she covered her face. She didn't make any noise. She sat there, her eyes covered with her handkerchief, shaking.

"She didn't do anything wrong, Emma. She was a very sick woman. She needed help. They should never have done that to her. It was horrible!"

I didn't know what to say. I was crying, too. As she told me the story, it came back to me. I could finally remember. I had been there, in my bedroom, with Bobby. Mother was screaming that she was cursed and was washing her hands in the bathroom sink. Father was yelling at her, accusing her. Bobby was lying in my bed. He was my friend. I was stroking his hand. His head was covered with purple flesh and there was a constant sound coming out of his mouth. I had thrown up. My pillow was red. Mother was shouting that they had killed a little girl. A little girl the same age as me. It was the beginning of the end.

"How did my mother die, Aunt Donata?"

"What do you mean?"

"Just what I said: how did she die?"

"She killed herself, honey. You know that?"

"You're sure she killed herself?"

"Of course."

"You're sure she wasn't murdered?"

Donata turned pale.

"Grandpa Nino said they would leave her alone! He said they promised. He said that Turi never broke his word. Not once!"

"You *did* come here to tell me all about this, didn't you? Something happened, didn't it? You didn't just show up." As much as I was feeling and remembering, I had to keep prying. I had to continue to get information while I could.

"Yes," she sighed, wiping her eyes, "something happened."

"So tell me what it was! I'm sick of having to pull teeth to get you to talk with me."

"A couple weeks ago, Tony Cannavota came to see me."

"Who are these Cannavota people?"

"Before all the trouble started, they were like family. Turi always watched over us. When Grandpa Nino died, Turi helped us, in spite of what had happened with Gina."

"But you just said that Grandpa was afraid of him."

"Turi was a big man. He had a lot of influence. Tony told me that his brother, Enrico, Turi's oldest son, was gunned down in Florida last month. Tony was very upset. He said that his family had found out that your dad had taken out a contract on Enrico before he passed away. Mitchell had paid five-hundred thousand dollars to have Enrico killed. Your father was a crazy man, Emma. I told that to Tony. I told him I was innocent. But he wasn't interested in me. He had come to talk about you. He wanted to know if you had been in touch with your father before he died. I told him that I knew nothing. Then he said he knew that you and your dad had talked, because he had gotten ahold of his phone records. He was very angry."

"Unbelievable!" I said. But then I remembered what my father had said on the telephone. He said they'd be sorry if they tried to hurt him. He said he'd "smash their balls."

"I told Tony that I never saw you any more," Donata continued. "I told him that you were an innocent woman, that we never even told you about Grandpa. He said that everyone had thought you were a stand-up person, but perhaps everyone was wrong. What did he meant by that, Emma?"

"I made a deal with them, and I kept my commitments to the letter. After Dad died, I gave them back the money he had stolen."

"I see." She paused for a moment, and her features seemed to relax slightly. "I'm just pleased you're all right, dear. I had to come warn you . . . you understand."

"Is that all this Tony said?"

"No, he said one other thing. He said that everyone connected with Jaynie's murder had been made to pay with their lives. It had taken many years, but even after Turi passed away, Enrico had never given up on avenging his sister's blood. He said that he and his brother thought that after so many difficult years everything now had been made right between our families. He was very disappointed. We had been so close at one time and . . ."

"Oh, God!"

"What's wrong, dear?"

"They murdered Bobby. They finally killed him!"

"They don't tell us everything. Our men always try to spare our feelings," Donata said to me gently, as she took a bite of her melting ice cream. "The point is, we can move ahead now. Tony said if you didn't do anything wrong, then nothing bad will happen. Ever! He gave me his holy word."

• • •

After Donata returned to Illinois, I began to think a lot about Bobby. It's ironic that the only memory I was able to conjure up after my discussions with my aunt—aside from that climactic scene in our San Francisco apartment when my father finally walked out of our lives—was of his helping me cross Euclid Avenue in Berkeley, when I was eight or nine years old. I had been at a picnic with him and Mom at Cordonices Park, and Bobby had taken my hand and guided me across the street to the Rose Garden, where we sat together and talked. He had picked a blossom off a trellis for me. He told me that it was illegal but that it didn't matter. It's strange, but I actually remember his saying that the love of flowers was more important than the love of laws.

I also recalled what Rufus had said in that bowling alley, that Bobby had cared about my feelings, that he had wanted Rufus to come see me, even though it increased his own exposure to danger. Was this a true statement? Had he always continued to love me from a distance, the way he loved me when I was very small? What were his thoughts? Why was he so ashamed of himself? Was it because of his perversion?

Now that everyone connected with the kidnapping had presumably been tracked down and murdered, I returned to my painting in the firm belief that my father's insane path through life would no longer be able to haunt me. I tried not to worry about Tony Cannavota. I had done nothing wrong, I did my best to put all of my doubts aside.

The following year, I fell in love with an Italian woman, and we settled into my apartment together. At about the same time, I started exhibiting my paintings in a well-known gallery in London, and I was included in a number of group shows in European and American museums. As often happens in one's thirties, my life began to assume a more stable and favorable shape.

But there was a final surprise in store for me.

In the fall of 1994 I received a call from an accountant in Los Angeles who wanted to verify my name and address, and shortly thereafter a box arrived in my mail. The package had been sent by a man named Claude Dumont, who was the owner of a bistro on the corner of Bronson and Franklin Avenues, at the northern margins of Hollywood. His place of business, he wrote in a lengthy letter he enclosed, was across the street from a supermarket. Adjacent to a recycling depot in the parking lot of the store stood a bus shelter, and over a two-year period spanning 1992 and 1993, a demented man, around fifty years of age, had appeared there every morning. Most weekdays the man would push his shopping cart down Franklin Avenue to the Cheremoya Elementary School and watch as the boys and girls crossed the street on their way to classes. At noon he hiked to the Fern Dell entrance of Griffith Park, a mile up the road, and sat at a picnic table underneath a magnolia tree and scribbled in a notebook. He returned in time to watch the children leaving for home. He wore a filthy orange crossing-guard vest and a baseball cap. His face and hands were coated with grime.

A friendship between this restaurateur and Robert Lazarus had begun strangely enough. A couple had shown up one morning for breakfast, and as they spoke no English, had addressed the owner in his native language. When Dumont asked how they had known he was from France, they pointed across Bronson Avenue. They said that, as they were walking by the bus stop, the wife had complained to her husband that she was hungry, and Bobby had interrupted and advised them in French that the food in Dumont's restaurant was *superbe*. His accent and way of speaking were cultivated, and it was he who told them that the owner was from Paris. Then he turned away and began talking to himself.

Later that day, Monsieur Dumont crossed the street. Bobby, although subject to outlandish opinions, turned out to be willing to communicate. Dumont was attracted to the homeless man, in spite of his filthy appearance and his obvious mental illness. Among other things, Bobby told him that he had lived on the Left Bank, on the Rue de Vaugirard across from the Luxembourg Gardens, in the sixties, when he had worked as an assistant to a fashion photographer, and his description of the city was precise enough so that Dumont believed his story to be true. The Europhile Dumont was impressed that Bobby spoke French, and he eventually offered to help him transit into an institution, but Bobby refused to take any action that would alter his condition. He readily accepted Dumont's offer of food, however. Every evening before going off to sleep, he showed up at the rear of the restaurant, where the busboy handed him a bag of leftovers and a bottle of table wine.

Dumont wrote that he was saddened to report that Robert Lazarus had died on the streets of Los Angeles. He had stopped showing up for his dinners, and after a few days the Frenchman had checked with the city and found that his body was at the morgue. Bobby had been stabbed in the chest in front of a liquor store on Wilcox Avenue, in the heart of the Hollywood ghetto, and had bled to death in a doorway. What was unusual about this murder was that, less than a week before the incident, he had asked Dumont to care for his valuables. It was as if he were aware of what was going to happen to him. At the time of Bobby's death, Dumont had gone through his personal effects, but it had been a difficult time in the restaurant owner's life, and he hadn't paid sufficient attention to what had been entrusted to him. A few weeks ago, however, he had once again come across Bobby's possessions on a shelf in the closet of his office. This time Dumont was more methodical and had discovered among the papers my note written in the bowling alley, where I claimed to be Bobby's true sister. He hadn't bothered to read much of the material he was enclosing, although he had looked at some of the photos and a few of the other things. He apologized for his original negligence but wrote that he was thankful he was finally able to forward the homeless man's effects to someone who had known him. He concluded by commenting that it was tragic that sophisticated men could die in such quiet desperation. Things like this, *grâce à Dieu*, rarely happened in Paris.

The package he sent contained a huge leather scrapbook, of black paper, which was similar to the one that Rufus had had behind his desk at the motel. Its pages were threaded by hand, and its cover was tooled with the words, "The Book of Lazarus." The volume was stuffed with writings, drawings, photographs and letters. Beneath it was a buckskin wallet coming apart at the seams, containing a library card, a Social Security card, a Washington State driver's license, and expired Visa and American Express cards. The first was under the name of Lazarus and the others were under the name of Finkelstein. At the bottom of the box were a portable chess set with pegged pieces, a King James Bible, Bobby's few articles of clothing, which had been laundered, presumably by

Dumont, and a clean manila envelope containing a gold wedding band, a certificate signed on the back by the children of the sixth grade of Frobisher Elementary School, nominating Bobby Finkelstein as the "best crossing guard in the Universe," a charm bracelet, his wedding picture, the eight smaller children's photos, the photo of Mitch and Bobby in the park (it was clear that Bobby or Rufus had sneaked back into the house), and $7.38 in cash.

That evening I read through Bobby's scrapbook.

Its first page was a tombstone containing the names and dates of birth and death of each of the members of the People's Liberation Brigade, the group that had kidnapped the daughter of the Mafia don. Also included were three other names: my mother's, the kidnapped girl's, and my own. I quickly realized that I was the only one on the list of a dozen names who still remained alive and, as I was soon to learn, the only one who hadn't been murdered.

Two zip-lock bags, inserted in sections near the front of the book, each contained a document: a set of New Year's resolutions, listed on a single sheet of paper by Gretchen Halder, a prostitute, probably the day before she died; and a letter from Martin Kulander, the apparent killer of the child, written shortly after his release from San Quentin prison. Both documents were written on two sides, which explains why they weren't mounted.

Following these, and glued onto the black scrapbook pages, were, in order: a pitiful ransom note, probably never delivered, from the dead girl; the message that I'd handed to Rufus in the bowling alley; an undated love-letter sent to Bobby by my mother; a group of aphorisms, probably intended to be a "Red Book" of their cadre, put together by a man, who was nowhere described, named Tubby Hyams; a farewell note from Rufus (whose real name was Thomas), written in 1992; and a bizarre seventy-page sentence, or more accurately a section of a sentence, created by Gerald Holt, who was a professor of some sort. His pages were produced in elite ten-point type, on onion-skin paper, double spaced, and were mounted consecutively in the book.

Following this sentence was a collection of two-line poems by Cynda Lazarus, surrounded by drawings of unknown authorship. Cynda's poetry had been machine-printed in block lettering on fortune-cookie slips. The most probable—and romantic—explanation for what had happened was that she had taken her verses to a Chinese bakery where they were produced and inserted inside cookies, which were subsequently presented as a gift to her husband. The slips, now shorn of all context, had been glued in the center of the recto pages of the scrapbook, opposite black pages left blank. My hunch is that the surrounding drawings were created by Bobby as guardian figures or spiritual icons of defense and that they were intended to be crossing guards.

After these came a barely coherent discourse by my father from early 1991, judging by a political reference to the Gulf War, and then a letter mailed to Mitch in 1974 by Helen Scott, alias Felicity Carpenter.

The last entry was a long poem, written by Bobby at the end of his life, when he was out on the streets. This wavering poem was very sad. Bobby presented himself as the biblical Lazarus who in life after life had emerged from his cave—fated always to escape the clutches of death as a result of Christ's repeated interventions. It is strange that this man, who had probably been raised as a Jew, was such a fervent Christian; whereas my father, who had been raised as a Catholic, while maintaining his belief in redemption through Christ, had become a practicing Jew.

Finally, throughout the scrapbook—set evenly among the other entries, each of which was preceded by an identification page—Bobby had pasted similar eight-page groupings: a blank page, an enlarged letter of his name, a glossy photo from Rufus's Hallowed Hall of Heroes scrapbook and a single-page commentary scrawled with Magic Marker on a 5 x 8 index card, another blank page, an overflow page of Tubby Hyams's political aphorisms which, like the aphorisms contained in his section, had been cut out of what I would guess was a samizdat edition with a razor-knife, and then another photo and scrawled commentary. It's quite possible, on the basis of consistent style and film quality, that all of the hero photographs were taken by Rufus—the outside backgrounds were similar to what I'd seen in Port Hamilton—and so I immediately doubted that the images were of actual "heroes," although I might be mistaken.

The strange assortment of documents, flowing through the formal architecture of the scrapbook, confirmed a number of things I had suspected: I learned that my mother's death hadn't been a suicide and that my father had been a drug smuggler, Mafia enforcer, scam artist and murderer. I also discovered that Bobby had engaged in some form of sexual misbehavior with me back in San Francisco. Many people in my situation would have reacted with grief or fury on making such a discovery, but I considered the information relatively insignificant since I already knew that my tender young body had been penetrated by other men. In any case, my life had already become way too dramatic for my own taste and I had truly ceased to care. I'd been battered and manipulated to such an extent over the preceding three years that this newfound understanding of my past, including the truth about my parents, no longer had the power to unhinge me.

Moreover, the People's Liberation Brigade, as I learned to my surprise, were nothing but a group of maladjusted crackpots, an assortment of elitist drug-addicts possessed of varying degrees of sanity, all of whom shared the flawed liberal notion that they alone harbored the secret to fashioning a better America. I made a $7.38 contribution to Cystic Fibrosis, and then I stored the contents of Dumont's box, including the leather book, on the bottom shelf of one of my work cupboards.

Several months later, I received a visit from my old girlfriend, Katrina Heutz. I was actually pleased to see her, and we spent an entire afternoon together. Even though it was over a year since the passing of Enrico Cannavota, I hadn't discussed anything that had happened as a result of my father's death with anyone but Donata; and yet because the scrapbook was such an unusual work—and because it contained information about my background that I knew would shock her—I wanted to share Bobby's legacy, in confidence, with Trina. I showed it to her without telling her anything essential about the circumstances surrounding it. I explained that it had been designed and compiled by a childhood acquaintance of mine, a revolutionary who had been a friend of my dad's, and that, as a result of an enclosed note which I'd sent this man, the book had mysteriously come into my hands.

She was interested, even fascinated. I felt protective and wouldn't let it out of my studio, since it contained one of the few things I possessed of my father's—his contribution among all the others—but she came over the very next day and spent several hours reading it from cover to cover. Afterwards she said that the book was extremely important and needed to be published, which I let her know, in no uncertain terms, was totally out of the question. She then said that she knew there was more to my story than what I was willing to admit. I became furious and told her where she could jam her curiosity, and she threw down the scrapbook and stormed out of my apartment. After her car drove away, I picked up the book, and on a vague impulse I searched out the contribution that had been made by my dad, and again I read his lines:

"Nobody will step on my dignity, and nobody will ever keep me quiet. I cannot expect to find integrity in this world if I possess no integrity myself. Nobody will ever put me down and I'll go to my death standing."

When things got tough, I realized, my father had always gotten tougher, and in this respect I saw that I was exactly like him. I took pride in the fact that Mitch had not only stood up to the Mafia, he had *attacked* the Mafia. He had wounded them badly. He had inflicted pain. He had made them pay for the disrespect they had shown him. Like me, he had never allowed his life to be lived normally but had inhabited his own space, his own ontological arena with his own set of marginal, obnoxious values.

I concluded that my perverse behavior since our conversation on the telephone and my pursuit of a share of the ransom money—money that my father, in the final analysis, wouldn't ever touch—were based on a concealed fury that I felt because he hadn't shown me affection and consideration. The cold-blooded assault I'd launched against his memory within the confines of my head was the same kind of unrelenting attack that he had leveled against his enemies. I was the true daughter of my father, not only in my spiritual searching but also in my relentless aggressiveness.

As I sat there thinking about my past and about the scrapbook, the hatred I had mustered against him, the hatred that had been buried under a young girl's love and that had emerged after his death to take on a life of its own, suddenly began to vanish, and I felt for the very first time that I shared in my father's quin-tessential freedom. I had plugged into a wild energy, and I under-stood that the courage I had shown in the past—my bluff obtuse-ness in negotiating my way through society—had been essentially superficial. Now, finally, I had become truly brave, even "heroic," and I was willing to assume more meaningful risks.

It turned out that Katrina had been right about the publica-tion issue—for reasons that she was in no position to understand, for reasons of vengeance—and I decided then and there to break my commitment to the Cannavotas.

• • •

History, as I've come to understand from my many years in Rome, is composed of a few scant shards—a landmark here or there, the miraculous survival of an artwork among thousands just as good, the cognomens of leaders turned headers for a jumble of exhausted lines, some tawdry epics of miniscule winners and losers—a scattering of stones that no one views and of words that no one reads, and of very little else. Every trace of the billions who have gone before us is gone, the elements of their futile lives van-ished or at best misinterpreted, and in this sense history is the greatest of all possible liars, the embodiment of the fiction that something about us is truly lasting and fictionless.

Even though there is an excellent chance that I shall wind up like the members of the brigade, I have decided to exact my revenge for the murder of my father, regardless of the consequences. Whether my inclusion on the tombstone was an accurate prediction of my own demise or simply an acknowledgment that I was part and parcel of this pathetic drama remains to be seen. I have retained Reynolds Lipton as my attorney and am sending him an optical disk containing my transcription of the scrapbook, some of which has been scanned. I've been as faithful as possible to the original text: the only changes I've made were to add the date of Bobby's murder to the tombstone—which I called Los Angeles to obtain—and to substitute this story in place of my bowling-alley note in the sequence of documents. I've instructed Lipton to spare no expense in seeing that this book is published without commentary in the event of my death. It is now February 19, 1996. Within the next week or so I shall mail away the disk, and then I'll contact the FBI. I shall tell them everything I know and send them the actual scrapbook as evidence.

And then I intend to call Antonio Cannovota on the telephone and tell him to go fuck himself.

As strange as it might seem, in looking back over what has happened to me, my greatest regret has been that I didn't make contact with Bobby Lazarus at the Whaler's View Inn that October afternoon, before he fled into a world of homelessness, insanity and death. The fact that I didn't see my father in his final days, when he was delusional and covered with Kaposi's, was probably a blessing; but I feel that if I had spent some time with Bobby, I might have somehow benefited. His mind seems so foreign to me—even after reading his poetry—and the lineaments of his life remain obscure and distant; but my intuition tells me that in the same way that I was harsh in my attitudes towards my father, I was equally harsh towards Bobby. For all that was ridiculous and disgusting about the man, I sense that there was something that he could have taught me, something that he began to teach me when I was very young.

As I conclude this writing, I feel strangely taciturn and have no desire to engage in any further speculation or analysis. Providing this explanation and personal history has made me weary, and at this point I just want to return to my painting. My refuge has always been in day-to-day routine. In the visual. Perhaps the presence of Bobby's book in the world will cause those to suffer who have caused my family suffering. And perhaps it will elevate others.

I hope that it will do both.

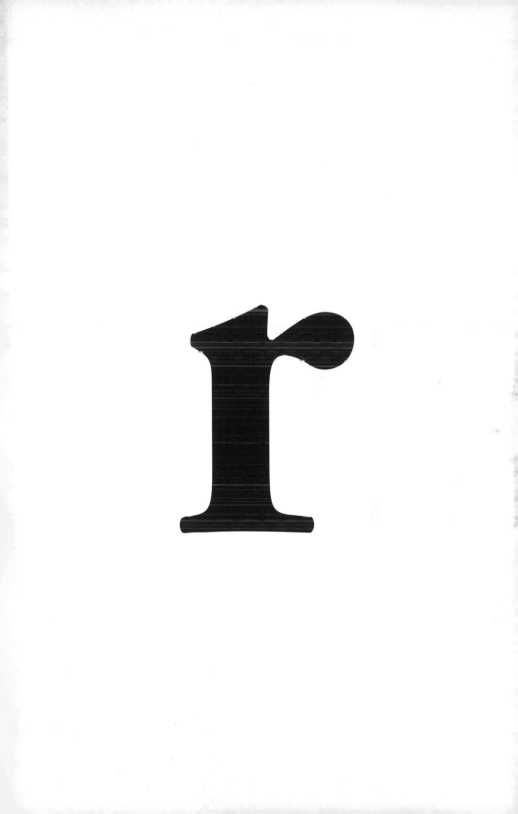

Harold Grady
did trying to
save the life
of Jim Single
who was
touching a wire
Death by current.

The ultimate accomplishment of an enlightened thinker is a carefree sense of humor.

The most revolutionary of human acts is to hold the hand of the dying.

One day, the inevitable will occur and the largest business in America will merge with the federal government. Then the agent who collects your taxes will sell you cheeseburgers and theater tickets.

The most difficult thing to fathom in life is stupidity.

What would go through the mind of Thomas Jefferson if he wandered down the streets of America and saw that all his hallowed citizenry were bolted in their homes and staring into boxes?

The destruction of small entrepreneurs by corporations is genocide.

It is possible for the diary of a revolutionary to have a greater impact on society than the revolution itself.

If a bird is born in a cage, then the cage becomes a boundary, not an obstacle.

The infliction of pain is a political action.

Courageous people change the world, not by achieving their goals, because the courageous almost always fail, but by demonstrating their courage. The trembling mass of cowards slaughter the courageous between meals, and yet the world slowly changes, because courage provides the only human light.

Patrick P.
O'Rourke
died trying to
save the life of
Richard Dorr
who was sleep
ing in bed. Death
by smoak.

Gina

Bobby my darling dearest:

I know how you feel about me. I can sense it.
You make me want you. It's your fault. Even though
you won't do the thing with me, I am telling
everyone that you do do it because it's what you
deserve. I know you don't really love your wife
because what you have between the two of you isn't
real. You say I have changed and am different since
you put your hands on my cheeks and kissed me on
the lips. You tell me that that kiss wasn't real
but you're a liar. I know it was. What you did with
Emma, I won't tell. It will be between you and me
if you play ball.

Mitch killed a man once when he was angry.
He beat him to death with a baseball bat and he
buried the body and nobody ever found it. Did you
know that? He could do the same thing to you if he
found out we kissed. You would say that Mitch fucks
other women and maybe there is truth there but he
has two minds which is why we will always love each
other very much. I love you in a different way.
Since I started taking drugs everything is
sunshine. I feel a thrill when I am in the sun and
I see God's energy shining in my own eyes. The way
I am arranged inside is a miracle and that is my
gift to the world. I am a plant that has the
universal energy that always grows toward the sun.
I need more than Mitch can give me. He is too
strong a man for me which is why he has moved out
and is living downtown. If you make love to me, you
will give me strength which is a different kind of

strength and that will make me strong so I can have
my husband back. I will take away some of your
strength which will make you weaker and then you
will see that Cynda is worthless. She is a nice
woman but she can give you nothing.

Today the rain is falling. The sunlight hits
the ground and comes up in flowers and gives the
flowers their color. I wish you weren't part of my
husband's awful gang. They are thugs. That man
Gerald is no good, and his friend Marty has changed
my husband in awful ways. They are nasty junkies
and I know what Mitch is doing, too. It makes me
sad because there are good drugs and bad drugs.
Mitch looks up to Gerald but I don't know why. He
says he is theoretical and everything is a theory.
Life is not like that, is it Bobby? It's flesh and
bones and sunshine.

It has been six months since I started
dropping acid almost every day and I lost my job
and am following the string of suffering through my
life as it unwinds in the sun. The sun will always
shine, my love, and that is a special treat. You
are the best but you are weak. You say you love
your wife madly, but you are not mad enough to know
what that means. You are not safe with children and
that is your problem. Mitch says that you were hurt
when you were small. You are the kindest and
handsomest of men, he says, but you have a deep
tiny wound. When you write your poems, you are
releasing your shame into the world, but you are
young and one day your wound will heal. You are
active and sharp. You are beautiful and everybody
loves you. You are spoiled. I must get what I can
because I have not been given what I need. I hate
myself for this and want to climb in a hole and
bury myself. I feel something coming that is good.
Could it be you?

Cynda is smug. She says I flipped out and my
brain was removed by other females. I know I was OK

last year and that you loved me then when you
kissed me. My heart is broken over what has
happened to me. Why am I so different? I can't
tell. I have tried to be a good mother and a good
wife. Why am I being punished in my inner being so
that I only have the sunlight to hold on to? You
are not political like your spouse and my husband,
I know, but you think you owe the world something.
Why is that? The world doesn't care about anyone.
That's the truth that nobody will accept, but
everybody cares about what the world thinks. I was
raised to be good and obedient and to do the right
thing in every situation. My father is a decent man
but he is very tough and very hard so I know how to
handle men and make them happy. I could make you
happy. I could do things to you that have never
been done to you. I don't know how I learned those
things but I did and now my consciousness has been
expanded and I can make my energies move through
other people's bodies.

Mitch liked me to tie him up and then I would
suck his dick. He can't get hard unless he is tied
but he hides this secret, because to know this
secret is to have power over him. He pretends he is
sick in order to manipulate my love. He is a
hypochondriac. I was raised in a traditional
household and my father is a powerful man and shows
no fear. I married Mitch because I thought he was
powerful too. When Mitch went out and collected
money, I would find blood on his shirt. In college
he studied pyrotechnics, which is the study of
volcanoes. Did you know that Mitch has plans? He
does. But he can be dark and greedy.

When I cry, my beloved Bobby, I squeeze my
lids and the pain builds in my eyes and the tears
run sideways. They are like opposite rivers of
hope. Wires run through my legs and groin. That
awful Gerald told me one day outside class that he

was writing a book that never stopped and would
describe human history. I am not part of anything.
There is too much history. I am detached. God has
given me sunshine, which is personal. He has denied
me everything else except my little daughter whose
eyes are green. I am almost alone. I have been
brought single-handed to the edge of the world.

My older sister was here last week and she
wanted to put me in the hospital. She cried all the
time. She says that my husband is an animal for
abandoning me and not taking care of me in my
misery but I have my own little secret. I am happy.
We must run away together. You don't have to be
part of that horrible group of people any longer.
I will have nothing to do with them. You and I can
run away. Mitch will take my daughter which will
be better for her. You cannot be around her any
more, Bobby. Please. Emma will be happier without
me. I don't know why it is. I look at her face, but
I don't see myself. Am I going around in circles?
Why won't you speak to me any more? I left you
that gift but you never said anything! I don't want
to hurt your wife. I never said that. I want
everyone to be happy but we need to rearrange
things. I wait every day for you to come to me.
Mitch has no suspicion of our love. I won't tell
him if you don't.

Please call me right away my love and don't
show this to your wife.

Gina

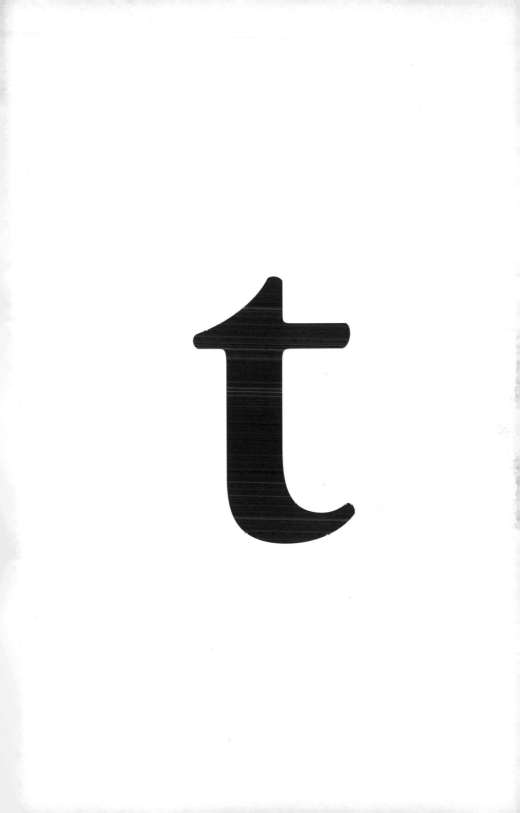

Moira Tanskay"
died tsyng to
save the life
of Timothy
Tanskaya who
was surronded
by gas. Deth
by exploading.

Men and women must never stop struggling for those who are spit on, for those who are lynched, for those who are commanded, for those who are ignored.

Mankind came closest to perfection shortly before the invention of weapons.

Intricate thought infuriates the bozos: that there are ideas that are impossible to understand, works of art that are impossible to fathom, music that creates unbearable passion—all of this humiliates the average man, who invents his own understandable thoughts, fathomable art and hummable tunes. What was never meant for him, the work that aims at intelligences greater and nobler than his own, he plots to destroy.

Nowadays free discourse is eliminated by experts.

It is almost impossible for an intelligent person to earn money in America without acting stupid.

In a world of positive change, most men scamper out of the way.

A revolutionary is at worst a nuisance and at best a public failure. Karl Jaspers pointed out that the last thing a philosopher should want to become is "exemplary." The same can be said of a revolutionary.

People who are in revolt because they like the clothing should be shot.

The profit motive will eventually drive business to develop devastating, miniaturized and easily-accessible weapons of mass destruction. This is the practical flaw in the capitalist dream of endless technological improvement.

Jack St. Claire
died trying to
save the life of
Jason Rudolf
who was at
takked by mug
ers. Death by
bullets.

Tubby

The larger a business, the greater its need to be lubricated by digitized spiritual emptiness.

The silent enemy of America is the small-minded and witless corporate slave donkey: the middle-manager living in code.

A man of principle is quintessentially unemployable.

Executive genius relishes brainless slogans.

One can defend a margin of profit much more easily than a point of honor.

The moral consciousness of man is no longer contested by vast armies of good and evil. Today the battlelines are drawn between the relentless global forces of payables and receivables. Men kill to defend their ledgers.

A revolutionary must be committed to performing irrational deeds of courage.

If, as revolutionaries, we refuse to engage in a futile fight and be defeated, our descendants will lose the crucial war they otherwise would have won.

Nature abhors cash.

The creative personality is usually ignored, and if that doesn't work, disdained, and if that doesn't work, destroyed.

The simplest way to reform a criminal is to give him what he needs.

Uncle Sam is the taskmaster of a gutless system of corporate flesh barter.

The two-edged sword of revolution is forged on the anvil of a love of strangers.

Pioneers massacred the Indians with the same blissful inattention that suburbanites employ in mowing their lawns.

Mob hysteria is embedded in the precise movements of an army.

Men prefer porkchops to freedom.

The pathos of modern man is expressed in his obsessive atonement for the crime of non-existence.

The greatest threats to capitalist enterprise are unprovoked acts of charity.

It disturbs a torturer more to burn his toast than to toast his victims.

The highest form of self-expression among the rabble is a stampede.

A revolutionary must be willing to sacrifice current pleasure to the endless miseries of anticipation.

We must always think creatively about our means of protection: a man in the desert may burn to death for lack of an umbrella.

One must free oneself to live by disciplining oneself to die.

Coins return to the earth as fossils.

One of the most attractive psychological features of corporate capitalism is that it allows for vertical chains of petty tyrants, with multitudinous opportunities to be cruel.

In a world of perfect manners, there would be no need for jails.

A peasant in a suit and tie is still a peasant.

One day men will roast in the Promethean fires that originally descended upon them as blessings.

Wisdom was invented in gardens.

That Shostakovich scraped before Stalin does nothing to belittle his music; that Mandelstam died for ridiculing the same man does little to elevate his poetry.

When armies collide, the world resounds with the empty ring of heartbreak.

Men will gladly submit to civilized barbarities in order to avoid the onslaught of barbarism.

In every society there are classes bred to be victims.

The destruction of the final wheel will precede the destruction of the final man, so that sometime in the future we shall once again be blissfully free of technology.

Nobody sane believes that all races were created with an equal ability to play basketball.

Revolutionary parties are spawned to control the damage of revolutionaries.

The hardest and most efficient workers are students of minutiae.

The path to salvation is never pretty.

In society, as in a barnyard, the wounded are slowly pecked to death.

The most valuable art in the moneyed world is the art of acting.

Men cannot shape clouds.

One day a religion will be founded so that lawyers can adore lawyers.

Junius Brutus, the quintessential revolutionary and ancestor of Marcus Brutus, was so transported with rage at man's injustice that he murdered his own sons.

The Achilles heel of modern humanity is the brain.

Revolution is a compression of time.

Capitalism teaches men to worship money; democracy teaches men to worship capitalism.

Utopian dreams are the foundations of autocratic power.

In order to obtain a false sense of comfort, men will sacrifice their children on prefabricated altars to the mindless puppet-gods of General Electric.

The rabble always votes for the strongest smell.

The suburban mind is slowly being reconstructed as a theme park.

Divine light shines equally steadily on birdbaths and bloodbaths.

Wardrobe spells access.

A man who has never been humiliated is a monster.

Men of large minds and vast capacities inhabit small, fragile worlds.

Excommunication is another word for opportunity.

Men who will do anything for money are the first to whine when robbed.

The household gods of capitalism buff their Chevrolets.

Only a madman can spend his days in heaven.

When nobles possessed the right to take the virginity of peasants on their wedding nights, the countryside was strewn with blue-blooded bastards who labored in misery for their aristocratic families. Nobody cared as long as the work got done.

Certain men, when they hear the soothing sounds of a fountain, suddenly start to drown.

The original purpose of poetry was to clothe tyrants as gods and henchmen as priests.

When the world goes out of tune, the cretins start dancing.

A fool's paradise is filled with bargains.

The rich and powerful spend their psychic lives in dungeons.

Democracy strives to enforce the myth that all men are created equal. Capitalism strives to enforce the myth that all men are created identical.

One of life's pretty illusions is that no one is past redemption.

If a politician kisses your baby, wash it.

Men become violently disaffected when they are denied common seasoning for their gruel.

Hope is the only refuge of the hopeless.

The last man off a sinking ship rarely looks back.

Beauty can be as onerous as sin.

Mercenaries follow the cash.

The moron who believes that his ballot counts should study mathematics.

Most atrocities fall within policy guidelines.

The irony of our prayers is that our blessings go unasked for.

Coups are instituted by men of action; revolutions are instituted by men of words. If a revolutionary can create the proper language, he can project the proper deeds.

The quickest way to develop an overview of a society is to live among its underclasses.

It is the nature of every man to fashion a tiny kingdom he can rule.

People who learn identical languages have nothing left to communicate.

If government could outlaw greed, everyone would obtain what he needs.

Murder is only of consequence to a political machine if it needs to count the dead.

A man who is free to vote but isn't free to think isn't free.

The final luxury of a revolutionary is a sense of gallows humor.

The law of the jungle will destroy all the jungles.

By fabricating a glorified myth of life, an unapproachable purity of nationhood, a nonsensical heroism, a flawless economic system, an ideal method of self-government, by creating values that cannot be lived but can only be worshiped, the masses can be controlled.

There is a special form of squalor that infects the minds of the wealthy.

Most men desire to be free not for the spiritual wealth of freedom but for the wealth that freedom can bring them.

Efficient government is invisible government.

Heartless, brainless men have a natural calling as bankers.

Human progress can only be achieved when parents set an example for children.

The pampered always love to discuss hardship.

Modern man is so deformed that even the constellations have become shapeless.

People in a position of absolute power must always fear who comes through the door.

Without money, one cannot buy poison, weapons, hookers, spies, lawyers, soldiers, servants or politicians.

Character is a function of sacrifice.

In a world correctly balanced between man and nature, man would be terrified of tigers.

Pascal said that men are so consistently mad that not to be mad would amount to another form of madness. If this is true, then every sane government is directed by madmen.

Over the course of history, the bondage of women has been the most underemphasized and grievous source of human misery.

The day will come when men will be viewed as nothing more than burping nodules of information.

It is not by eliminating fear in oneself that one gains clarity and understanding: it is only by working to eliminate it in others.

A revolutionary is an absurdist who takes absurdity seriously.

The difference between a reformer and a revolutionary is that the reformer is wedded to the system he is trying to change and the revolutionary is wedded to the destruction of the reformer.

There is a certain kind of concrete simpleton who becomes a politician.

Society will do its utmost to treat revolution as an outmoded concept, so that anyone who challenges the new world order will seem fashionably *passé*.

Capitalism can only survive in an atmosphere where stupidity is considered a right or a virtue.

Gillian Nugent
died trying to
save the life of
Larry Kaufman
who was at
tacked in a
bar. Death
by KNIFE.

The modern thrust of social evolution is towards creating environments whose defining characteristic is hysterical numbness.

Democracy was not created to empower the masses but rather to empower the people who squeeze money from the masses.

The rabid destruction of nature is not a byproduct of human greed, lust (in the shape of too many bodies), heartlessness or stupidity. It is an organic form of revenge, a payback on the part of the hominid psyche for millions of years of quivering in trees. Man, the avenging monkey, is getting even.

A nuclear weapon is as mystical as a flower.

The principal aim of capitalist politics is to separate men from their passions so that they can live together agreeably under the manipulative control of government.

The global electronic brain has a mind of its own. It is not the creation of its billions of human subparts. Rather it has descended from above, the devilish castoff of an arrogant heaven. It is the background hum of a divine robotic machine.

Men ruin themselves by overexploiting the usefulness of their own moralities.

Even a virus, although seemingly too simple to suffer fear, is mired in a terror of vast complexity.

Fame is the most dismal form of flattery.

To embrace a principle one must first soil one's hands.

Roger R. Icki
mura died
trying to save the
life of Penny
Ichimura who
fell from a bal
cony. Daul b's
falling.

Thomas

December 23, 1993

To my best friend Bobby,

God didn't want for this to be paradice. He gave us troubles for our own good. I want you to put this in your memmory book, my friend. I want you to remember me and throw away my Halowed Hall of Heros from there cuz I'm a coward and put in this instad. You are the best pal I ever had. You are a terific friend. I could have saved my sister but I ran away. I didn't have it in me.

A medic saved my life and died for me and then I knew I was spesial. I knew I had to join the gang with my pals who cared for me now and are murdered. I still miss Cynda

Bobby and will miss you. Even when I'm dead I will miss you guys. Cynda was the smartest prettiest woman I ever met. She was something spesial Bobby like you.

I never liked Marty Bobby and I didn't like Gerald either. He shouldn't be in your book with his snobbie sentance. He thought he had a spesial brane but all our branes are the same which is why I joined the gang. No brane is spesial Bobby isn't that true? Gerald was a stuck up profesor and just because my sister balled him we joined. I was happy until Marty sliced that girl. When Mitch and I came back and saw you guys it was the sadest thing I ever seen. I was not the same Bobby and you wern't either. You know that.

You were always the strongest in
the gang. You thought better than
anyone else! You were stronger!
And you are stil strongest cuz
you will live longer than everyone.
You are alive my pal. You made
us see the joy of being God's
little children.

You were good to Mitch Bobby.
I know you think you let him
down the way I let down Helen
but that's not true. You were
there for him and there was
nothing you could do. Smack
killed that man not the Mob not
you. He was a jem Bobby. Mitch
was a good pal to you in spite
of the fact he was a shit. He was
gifted too Bobby. God made him
angry and he had nowhere he
could rest his head. Just
like you Bobby. Like me and you.
Nobody stuck by him not Gina
or that horible daugter but you

could rely on him all the way. He shot Marty to avenje his wife cuz of what Marty did. He put 5 holes in him. That was supercool!

This is my last will and testament. If you get this I will be dead and buried cuz someone will have mailed this to you after. I feel it coming. Since I left LA I have felt the steps behind me. They are going to catch me Now I know. It is too crazy! Something in me wants to die any how and I regrekt that. I can have no fun this Christmas.

Life is war Bobby. This is my memmory for you to be a peasiful warrior and fight the good fight. I know that God is good and will protekt you Bobby. You are his child and you are my spesial friend and I love you.

Tommy

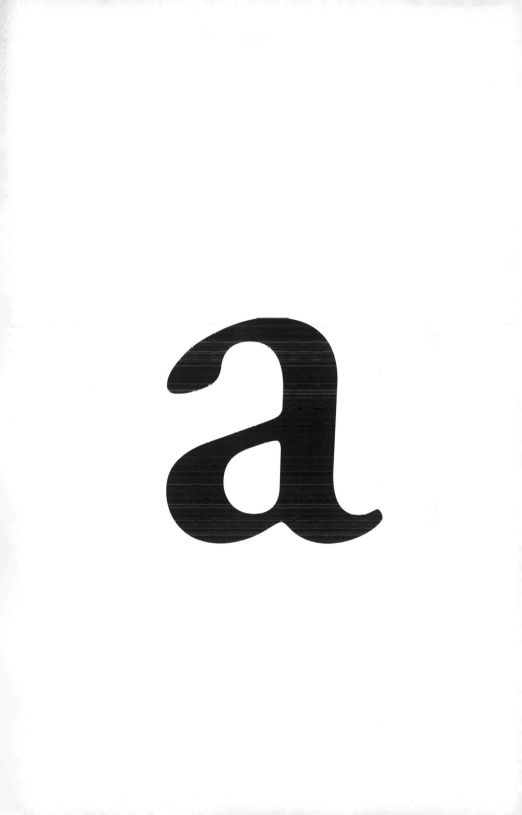

Mary Garber
dead trying to
zcue the life of
Phyllis Adams
Garber who was
burning in her
house Death by
FIRE.

The larger the arena of "freedom of choice" and the greater the mass's access to power, the more efficient, subtle and deadly must be the centralized tools of political domination.

In forty years, names like Lodge, Rusk, Haig, Haldeman, Ball, Fulbright, and even Nixon will be meaningless to a majority of Americans. Even now one feels the weight of oblivion nestled on the shoulders of the bureaucrats and politicians. As this trend continues, politicians working forty years from now will be forgotten in thirty years. In seventy years they will become unrecognizable in twenty years, and then in ten years; and in one hundred years, politicians will not only be instantly unknown, they will be nameless.

The three pompous cretins who are the pillars of modern thoughtlessness: Darwin, Freud and Marx.

A despot will naturally attempt to destroy everything that he cannot control.

The lucky few who cannot be bought cannot be sold.

Within the next hundred years, aging will be arrested, and people will cease to die from natural causes. Consequently, every fatal accident will be considered an inexplicable tragedy, and this will be the pitiful and ultimate reward of science.

The strongest of men can barely defend his taste.

Nature survives in order to be beautiful, and consequently extermination is the logical consequence of ugliness.

The final irony of a bulletproof civilization is that it starves to death.

Troy Valentine
died trying
to save the life
of Richard
Stricker who
was being beaten
in a parking lot.
Death by iron
pipe.

Gerald

neon lights of a theater mall whose anchor tenant was a
vast discount toy warehouse and there was a section in
the store where catechism lessons were being given and a
line of wooden ducks stood on a shelf next to the class
and one of the ducks began to talk and had a hinged
mouth like the mouth of a marionette and there was
another section of the store that carried table saws and
lathes and a man with a yellow boating cap was busy
working a drill into a block of wood that turned out to
be one of the wooden ducks and the metal was whirring
into the ducks asshole and the duck didnt seem to mind
as its mouth moved on its hinge while quack quack
quacking very rapidly so that it sounded like an engine
sputtering and blood poured like a river out of the
asshole of the duck although the river had globs of
yellow fat flowing through it and the fat fell to the
floor of the warehouse in soft piles and began to melt
slowly into the blood that was covering the floor and the
man in the boating cap rolled up his sleeves and had
scars on his arms that werent precisely tracks although
they moved along the tops of his veins but were more
like cross hatched welts with hairs like the hair on the
forearms of women growing out of them and his rocky
muscles traveled up and down between his wrists and
shoulders and he turned away and was wearing an apron
and i thought for a moment it was giappetto from the
pinocchio story and that we were in that type of
workshop situation and i began to back away because the
duck was on the floor and attacking my ankles as it
waddled through its own fat and blood and i was becoming
apprehensive and started to panic because i felt that
the duck was poisonous and contained black widow spider
venom and i had been told a long time ago that there
was a cure for this venom but that you had to search
out a tree and i began to think that there might be a
department in the warehouse that specialized in the kind
of tree that would relieve the pain of a black widow
spider bite and i wandered among the avenues of toys
while keeping my eyes peeled for the duck that i knew
had its own attack path because the duck understood
where i was going and had planned out a strategy and had
a map in its brain that contained all the aspects and
intricacies of the warehouse and there were arrows on
its map that traveled at right angles around the store

and at a certain point the forward moving tip of the
ducks arrow path would intersect my feet as they moved
down the aisles of the warehouse and i would become
poisoned before getting access to the tree i needed but
as luck would have it there was a book store across the
street and i hurried in to look for magazines because i
wanted to learn how to escape the black widow spider
bite and a number of body building journals with
pictures of women with huge physiques who were squeezing
dumbbells and making grimacing expressions and were
ridiculously happy to be lifting and men who were
holding them up like prima ballerinas but hadnt shaved
and werent presentable were in the racks and one of the
magazines was entitled dumbbells in hiding and another
was called precious moments and then i was standing at
the bow of a boat that was bringing me over from a
distant country and staring into the water as it folded
back along the keel and dreaming about what it would be
like to get to the distant country and had a vague idea
i was heading in the wrong direction and was singing to
myself but couldnt make out what i was singing and was
unaware of what was coming out of my mouth or even of
what i intended to sing although i knew i was singing
something but there was no way that i would ever be able
to tell what kind of singing i was doing as the waves
folded around either side of the boat that was taking me
in two directions at once and i was looking at a
contraption resting against a bollard which had a lever
sticking out its top and grinding jaws made of openwork
bronze and i thought that it was office equipment or
used in cutting cloth but it began to move like the duck
moved and the lever jerked back and forth and the
various parts of the machine worked together in such a
way that it assumed some of the behavioral aspects of a
mallard although i realized that it couldnt poison me
because it was totally empty and fabricated out of metal
and sea air and this made me comfortable until i felt a
sharp pain in my side and realized that somehow the
machine could jump high in the air and attack me at any
soft and vulnerable part of my body and eat out my eye
for instance or bite me in the balls or snatch away one
of my fingers and i knew that as long as this machine
was around i had nowhere to hide and there was nothing
that was uncovered that this thing couldnt attack and i

also knew that it would attack me when i wasnt looking
and so i felt helpless and started searching along the
catwalks and passageways for a means of getting off the
boat because i didnt believe that the boat was surrounded
by water and as a matter of fact i knew with utmost
certainty that there were boulevards that led away from
the boat and forces that would allow me freedom from the
machine and from the desires of the machine which i knew
were particularly dangerous because the machine was
attacking me for reasons that were known only to the
machine and involved something about the nature of the
machine and the machines proclivities and there was no
negotiation since the machine would be vicious and would
attack me every chance it got and would continue to gnaw
away at me until there was absolutely nothing left and
if there were pieces of me then the machine would gnaw
on those pieces and although it was incapable of
swallowing it would keep working on me and would start
with a fingernail and then it would get a little toe so
that i would be rendered ever so slightly less effective
and then it would get a big toe so that i would be
hobbled or an ear or it would eventually succeed in
blinding me but bite by bite it would turn me into
nothing but chewable substance and then it would chew
and chew and chew with no ulterior detectable motive but
the result would be the same in any case and i would be
transformed into pulp and someone came up to me with a
ticket that would get me off the boat and i had trouble
talking because a bolt had been driven through my tongue
so that every time it moved it felt sore and overused
and i took a piano wire and tied it around my wrist and
pulled the wire tight and knotted it and in the palm of
my hand was a vortex like one sees when looking at one
of those small hand held games where one tries to get a
number of ball bearings to settle into holes without
knocking the settled ones out and the vortex resembled
the painted playing surface of one of those games but
this vortex in my palm was moving inward and hypnotizing
me and it gave me tremendous pleasure to surrender my
will to an unknown power and i felt my will turning soft
and hoped that it wasnt someone vile who was taking me
over and realized that the vortex in my palm must have
been a form of prehypnotic suggestion that allowed me to
be hypnotized and that space and time had bent around so

that i could surrender myself to my own hand in a
predetermined and totally uncancelable fashion but i
didnt want the process to be endless and decided then
and there to make it a matter of convenience and to stop
looking at the vortex and look away from my hand but no
matter how hard i tried i couldnt do it and just had to
continue to see this twirling pattern digging into my
palm and was stuck there and heard a soft voice that was
very distant and wondered if this voice were controlling
me and part of me wanted to be controlled and was feeling
a deep sexual pleasure and part of me didnt want to be
controlled and was feeling a sharp jabbing over and over
like the clanging of a clapper against the bell of an
alarm clock and the jabbing was causing something to rip
in the center of my brain and was a stabbing or scooping
at my brain cavity with a scalpel or mining tool or
excavator so that i was doomed to have a stroke and
would always be paralyzed until i moved into another
world which perhaps was the world of the distant voices
because i realized that the voice i thought was
controlling me was a chorus of voices singing a requiem
or mass and it might have been the voices of angels or
astral powers singing to me or some drug thing or
perhaps it was the voices of bubbles in my ears or in
my brain like those nymphs that are surrounded by
bubbles and rise from the ocean into the air while
singing in the light but in any case the voices were
beautiful and i stepped onto a raft that had an outboard
motor which ran on batteries that made it speed more
quickly than an airplane and was scudding through a
tunnel and the man with the yellow boating hat was
leading the way in another raft so that we resembled a
regatta that was heading on a mission of the utmost
importance for the future of the world which was a
mission or pilgrimage out of legend that people would
write about for millennia and would cause the creation
of epics and lead us to some type of nautical discovery
and we came to a waterfall and teakettled over and
tumbled out of our rafts and i felt myself hitting stone
after stone as i careened down the endless falls and
everything was white foaming chaos about me as i fell
with the water while knowing that it was the inherent
purpose of water to fall and rise and fall again since
it was a vast vat of sliding froth and cascades and

heavy slamming white water jetting and bashing down the
rocks and shimmering and spouting up and my head kept
hitting rock after rock and my body was broken in a
thousand places as i continued to fall over and over in
the stream and i hit another cascade and was thrust out
and burst up into the air and down into the stream again
and over another falls and the thunder of the falls was
the thunder of a million different thunders and some
were mere tinkles and trickles and others were the
linked slapping and bashing and pounding of water from
the smallest drip to the tug of the sea and the force
of the waterfall battered me down and my body rolled
against the coursing undersurface and my limbs thrashed
in the currents through the dropping mass of sliding
water echoing with the suffering and heaving of voices
and i landed and drifted into peaceful pools where
bulging birds were roosting in the trees overhead and
the reeds were rattling around me but i couldnt hear the
rattling because my ears were plugged with water and
this made my head stuffed and i turned on my back and
looked at the sky which was a banner with clouds painted
on it dipping down from where it was fastened at the
corners and something rose from the depths of the pool
and stroked my sides with hands that wanted to beat me
off and i almost got off but the water was too cold and
so i couldnt but i felt the warmth inside my loins like
a warm pond within a cold pond and the edges of warm
and cold water battled as to whether the critical warmth
would explode or be overwhelmed by the bitter cold of
the pond which also in its own way felt satisfying so
that i wondered whether cold pleasure was as good as
warm pleasure and paddled to the bottom and dwelt in the
feeling of being deep within something dark and baffling
and luminescent greenish yellow plants and bottle caps
and old machinery and coins were shining before my eyes
and i stuck my fist into the muck of the pond bottom and
it sucked against me as i pumped back and forth and
pulled out a squiggly red thing like an appendix or
gizzard piece and laid it down among the greenish yellow
shimmering things and the light from my forehead created
a perfect disk at the bottom of the pond like a moon
with continents and valleys and i wanted to swim upward
but no matter how hard i tried i had no energy to move
up to where i could breathe and decided to move forward

instead because to move in a level manner didnt require
much effort and there was a hatch in front of me with a
circular valve and i turned the wheel and it gave off
sparks and sprang open and i was standing in a strange
light that i had never seen before and am positive will
never see again because it wasnt really light although
it lit things up and made them visible and i discovered
to my chagrin that i was wearing scuba gear with flippers
and women were playing bridge and staring out a window
and i removed my gear and was miraculously unbruised and
decided to cheat and slinked over and sat in a chair
where the dummy hand was being played and removed a card
and stuck it between my legs and nobody seemed to notice
as they turned around and continued their game but the
cards were mystical and the one between my legs was
pumping information into my body and a woman behind me
put her hand on my shoulder and reached over me and had
nothing covering her breasts and the bottom of her right
breast appeared just above my head and i reached up with
my tongue and licked it and the experience was
satisfying and i started nibbling and it was like the
sky that was pinned like a blue banner only the banner
was made of soft skin that contained wonderful milk and
i nibbled against it like a baby but was frustrated
because it was the bottom of the breast and there was no
nipple but i kept nibbling and the nibbling created a
craving for more although there was no reward except for
the feeling of nibbling itself and a pewter jar
containing carrots stood in the middle of the table and
i reached for the jar and grabbed a carrot and took a
bite and chewed until it was soft and spread the carrot
against the skin of the breast with my tongue and the
carrot was stringy and carrot juice fell in my eyes and
stung them which seemed to increase my excitement and
the edge of the card was sawing into my body and there
was no resistance as it sliced into my groin and i loved
the pain in my eyes and the pain in my groin which
wasnt like stinging but something much more thorough and
all i could see was orange with little strings running
through it and there was no space around it so that my
eyesight was shielded with orange and i was trapped as
if i were locked in an orange container and time was
slipping in several directions at once and not
necessarily backwards or forwards but to the side and i

discovered that it was possible to slip sideways out of
the channels of time when one was suspended in orangeness
which would mean that my mind would be forever trapped
and slipping around and moving from side to side slowly
like a pendulum or the spinning of a galaxy every five
hundred trillion years and the galactic movement would
be one half stroke of a pendulum swing and nothing more
would happen and it would be my mind and the presence of
that horrible orange and i tried to think of time as a
coating on a breast and to imagine that there was
something living behind the color or under it because i
figured that the sensation in and of itself would snap me
out of my misery but i didnt want to think about it in
the sense that there would be the same agony because i
could conceivably spend eternity thinking about trying
to get out of eternity which would be just as agonizing
and as endless as eternity itself so that one would live
moment to moment in a totally unbearable world of pure
orange and would not be able to get rid of it or even
lessen it a single degree and suddenly there was a noise
and i thought that the card table had collapsed and i
was elevated to a rooftop of the town and could see into
the distance so that what was close and confining was now
spacious and changing and i felt immensely relieved that
there were details in life but still didnt feel happy
but oppressed because the feeling i had just experienced
wouldnt go away but was coloring everything a shade that
would remain forever in my conscience and i sat on the
rooftop and my legs were tangled in space and my
breathing was not in and out but into and out of and
orange still held in certain tints on the rooftops and i
decided to flee to the mountains which werent mountains
but depictions of mountains that could be climbed and i
was furnished with a pike and a stout pair of shoes with
soles like the rubber on truck tires and i didnt need to
start at the bottom but at the top where bellflowers were
growing and i knew i had to make my way to a shrine
that was several precipices over and the mountains were
in a row with peaks sticking up like teeth on a saw and
on one of the distant peaks was a temple with a steeple
and bells in the same shape as the flowers i was standing
on and i started down the trail but the path was at a
steep decline and i was having trouble keeping my feet
under me because the tires werent fastened tightly to

the shanks of my boots and my skin was sticking out the
sides of the insoles and there were scabs and mushroom
like stains on my feet and i noticed a change in the
weather and a sweet smell rising from the valleys and i
looked out to sea and sailboats were bobbing in a harbor
and fish were darting out of the water and i reached into
my pocket and pulled out a dictionary and noticed that
the entries looked like egyptian because they all started
with the word nile and there was a hammock by the
seashore and i wanted to take a nap and started swinging
back and forth and my eyes closed and i began
experimenting with the notion of boundaries between
sleeping and waking in the sense that i kept falling
asleep and waking into another reality in which i could
fall asleep again in order to wake and the situation
didnt seem to change because i never left the hammock
but when i opened my eyes i was swinging in a different
world although there was always the ocean and boats at
sea and gay fish jumping out of the water and a large
jacaranda with purple blossoms but i knew that every
time i fell asleep i would fall into a new level of
sensation and breathing but when i awoke i would ratchet
up through all the sleeping worlds to the top world in
which i had fallen asleep originally when i lay in the
hammock and closed my eyes so that all of my dream
states were collapsible into the original state i was in
before i first fell asleep and i wondered if falling
asleep could be changed into a method of exploring so
that one could investigate all the worlds that surround
and support a world where sleeping is impossible and
there was a male chimpanzee in the jacaranda who could
speak english and who indicated he was sleeping even as
he talked and in his dreams it was possible to make love
with other animals but when he was awake he was limited
to chimpanzees and unsuspecting humans and i asked what
kind of humans and he said small children who were
investigating their own sexuality and he agreed to share
a vital secret with me since i was interested in
exploring the underlying structures of sleep and told me
how to create a white blossom in the lowest depths of
consciousness and as he spoke he motioned towards an
origami construction hanging from a chain that looked
like a cabbage made out of red metal and i objected that
it was supposed to be a white blossom but he pointed

with a fescue at my head and said that my head couldnt
keep anything intact anyway and that when i constructed
an image it was actually tens of thousands of smaller
images each of which could be turned into the one
original image and all those images side by side were
like a net so that anything i thought was composed
mostly of holes or emptiness and within the redness
there could be whiteness and as he described this inner
whiteness a light in my brain suddenly began to flicker
and i couldnt see anything clearly and this made me
frightened and i wanted to beg the monkey for something
as if by saying words in the form of begging my eyesight
would clear and the flickering which was starting to
throw me into a seizure would stop because through
begging i could be forgiven and there wouldnt be the
possibility of future flickering and i wouldnt have a
seizure and my body wouldnt go rigid and start banging
on the ground and i wouldnt bite off my tongue or stick
my fingers viciously in my own eyes to stop the light
from pounding into my head in the blinding periods
between darkness and my head wouldnt explode so that the
plate that was on the upper right side of my skull about
two thirds of the way back wouldnt blast away from my
head and my brains wouldnt splatter against the trunk of
the jacaranda and jism wouldnt spurt out my prick either
and my balls wouldnt burst and shit wouldnt come
exploding out my asshole and i wouldnt have bones coming
apart beneath my skin but there was something in me that
wanted to continue to hurt and for the flickering to
continue because pleasure unless it is mostly pain didnt
interest me and there is a form of pain that is so
unbearable that it cannot be suffered and yet in its
less intense form forms the greatest pain that human
beings feel in the worst possible circumstances and the
monkey told me that it was important to learn how to
survive this incredible form of pain and before i awoke
from my sleep on the hammock i would need to be tested
in order to determine whether or not i could bear such
misery and the next thing i knew i was buried in a
coffin the size and shape of a railroad car and all i
could see out its windows were stones and the coffin was
moving along a track within the underground confines of a
cemetery and winding among the graves without hitting
other coffins and it occurred to me that it was unlikely

i was dead in any conventional sense because i was still
thinking and i began to worry that there was no evidence
that i could ever stop this thinking even if i were
willing to do so and that thinking could be thought of
as a line extending through endless space and there was
no way of terminating the line or a sentence within the
line or a phrase within the sentence within the line
because without an end to anything large the small
things within the large things have no ending either so
that any thought was just as endless as the line itself
and one could take a particular thought which would be
comparable to a point on the line and move forward to
any other point and the movement would create an infinite
variety of additional thoughts and if one were dealing
with feet on the line and started at 57773832095 feet
and moved forward one would get a certain train of
thought but if one were dealing with a different
standard of measurement such as nanoinches that same
point on the line where one started expressed in
nanoinches might be 98738293847502839876367 2483 and
moving the same distance down the line would produce a
different sequence of numbers so that each sequence
would be unique and since a brain can be considered as a
singular system of numeric measurement therefore every
thought although originating on the same endless line of
thinking is essentially incommunicable and as i paced up
and down in my coffin it seemed that my existence wasnt
as pleasant as it had been when i was living less
mathematically on the surface of the planet and yet i
found that through the brute force of an imagination
devoid of scientific speculation i could escape my
confining circumstances and i wandered into the morning
air where truckers were sipping steaming coffee and
eating danishes and there were carcasses hanging from
gambrel hooks and mist was coming out the nostrils of
prostitutes who were leaning against a loading platform
and they told me they were mermaids for hire but i didnt
know what they would do if i paid them money because i
couldnt estimate their abilities and knew that since
they had fins from the waist down they couldnt fuck and
considering that their mouths were stuffed with
rancid fish they couldnt use them either and how they
could communicate with me i couldnt tell and i wondered
if they had anything i wanted and a manicurist was

kneeling in front of one of the mermaids and buffing her
nails which were round and fat and disgusting and the
manicurist breathed moisture onto the mermaids nails and
could see her features reflected in each nail and know
that her face would never age and that her hands would
never fail her and justice moved like a breeze through
the manicurists hair and one of the mermaids was self
consciously stroking up and down her scales and this was
giving her sexual pleasure and she was about to come
inside herself like along some pole but the manicurist
was too busy working to notice and i joined the mermaids
in a bar and a man came up and pinched one of the
mermaids on a fin and i rose immediately and attacked him
and beat him with a wooden post until his head came off
and shot across the floor of the saloon like a drop of
mercury and i chased the mercury head with my stick and
kept bashing it and it kept wriggling away and people
got in my way and i took the other side of the stick
which was pointed and thrust it through the stomach of
one of the people who was annoying me and he reeled
backwards and i started to break up the bar and threw a
chair into the shelves of liquor behind the bartender
and he took out a club and tried to beat me with it and
the club was cast iron and i decided it was mind over
matter and stood there and meditated and the bartenders
beating was totally ineffective but i felt that i was
being magnetized and as he was hitting me with the iron
club all of the atoms in my body were lining up in one
direction so that things started flying at me that were
made out of metal such as ashtrays and cylinders and
knives and metal shavings and pins and strange balls
with spikes on them like maces and the magnetism became
stronger as he was beating me and i was being attracted
to something else and was jerked off the ground and
yanked out the window of the bar with a scattering of
flying metal objects trailing after me and was speeding
down the streets and moving much faster than any
automobile gliding two feet off the ground but i didnt
hit anything because there was something about my
magnetism that maintained a distance from everything
nonmagnetic and i was moving smoothly and quickly around
cars and people and hydrants and light poles and signs
and trees and at one point i moved through a thick crowd
as if i were a subatomic particle that could penetrate

anything and emerge whole on the other side and nobody
got knocked down and then i was flying over fields and
canyons and i looked behind me and there was a host of
objects and i was pulled through a sieve and felt myself
losing something but couldnt understand what it was i
was losing and then there was another sieve and i felt
myself losing something else but still didnt know what
it was and felt that i was lighter in the air and floated
with more ease as i was being tugged and strained
through another sieve and again something was taken off
me but i didnt have any understanding of what the
process was or why i was being put through it and then
there was another screen and i went through it and
nothing happened except that i felt that perhaps id lost
an internal organ like a pancreas or that something i
didnt understand and wasnt essential had been removed
from my body and then i was standing outside an old
house and there was a bin that said slave bracelets on a
label that fit into a plastic slot and i put one on and
it was heavy and fashioned out of brass and there was a
counter which looked like an odometer that clasped the
bracelet shut and the numbers spun around and kept
ascending and i figured that the numbers were counting
the ever increasing supply of global slaves but i didnt
feel any different inside although i wondered if i were
being forced to perform certain actions and wasnt aware
of it and decided to keep an inventory of all my actions
and when i performed something more than once i would
consider it a slave action and try not to perform it
again and if i performed it again i would take off the
bracelet and go to sleep in one of those bedrooms in old
houses that are occupied by decayed and malicious
spinsters or grandmothers who warp their children while
their grandchildren watch with soft eyes and i ascended
rickety stairs and when i entered the bedroom i was
surprised because it was a bookie joint and a man was
sitting by a phone with a pile of chits in front of him
talking about a horse that was sick with autoamnesia and
couldnt remember that it was a horse and he had bet a
lot of cash and wanted to make certain he collected
because the race had been fixed and he hadnt laid off any
money and the horse had suffered a stroke and was
paralyzed along the withers and he felt that something
must be done to increase the circulation to the horses

brain and i sat on a sofa and opened a beer although i
couldnt tell if it was a bottle or a glass and felt the
beer rising in my throat and my windpipe went into spasm
and bubbles were catching in the upper part of my chest
and i started to panic because i thought that getting
drunk meant choking to death and felt that i needed a
different solution to my emotional problems in the form
of drugs and that the man behind the desk could score
for me if i gave him inside information but i had no
idea what inside information was and started to think
about what it meant to have information in the first
place but i didnt have a clue and so i made him an
offer although i dont know what i offered him but i know
that i offered him something and he handed me a packet
and i went into a corner and opened it and i cooked and
strained the contents but when i put a spike to it it
started to coagulate and i cooked it up some more by
increasing the heat because i had in my possession a
miniature blow torch apparatus and a snowman started
growing out of the spoon with three balls one placed on
top of the other that twisted and turned upside down
like a caterpillar forming a cocoon while hanging from
invisible thread and i took my thumb and squashed it
into the spoon and could feel it succumbing under the
tip of my thumb and each of its three balls were
wiggling around and it gave up and dissolved and i
started fiddling with my kit but couldnt get anything to
work properly and started to feel drug hunger and my
body ached and my cheeks salivated and my eyes watered
and i wanted more than anything else to get off but
couldnt and i even thought a little coke mixed in would
be good and that what i needed was a cocktail and i
turned to ask the man for more but he had disappeared
and the horse with autoamnesia was laughing at me as it
pulled back its lips and i was transported to saigon
where it was hot and humid and the streets were brown
and filled with dust because it wasnt modern saigon but
an ancient village called saigon and men were hanging by
their hands like tetherballs from poles and i could see
they had wet their pants since there were circular urine
stains on the poles from where they had swung around
while peeing and there was a parade with women wearing
plastic see through drum majorette clothing and one of
the women had a tampon string hanging below the plastic

of her skirt and i was sitting with my legs crossed in
the middle of the road as the parade of drum majorettes
approached and the woman with the tampon string was
directly in front of me and coming on top of me and i
felt as she passed over me that i was looking up into a
carpet of thorns and i leaned my head back and arched my
back and watched her feet moving away from me and she
was sashaying as she tossed her baton in the air and
there were baby blue triangular fringes on her boots and
silver bells and her beautiful large ass was jiggling
beneath the plastic and i continued to strain and arch
my back upward and grabbed my prick with my left hand
and began moving my fist vigorously trying to masturbate
and continued to arch my back and neck while straining
backwards to catch a glimpse of her beautiful large ass
as she moved farther away from me down the street and my
back began to hurt from the strain and my prick turned
into a glass tube and began to smart and i gave up
masturbating but the tube was hanging heavily between my
legs with liquid in it and ticker tape and confetti were
falling from surrounding buildings and i realized that
the parade was to celebrate the liberation of asia and i
had to move carefully because i was afraid that the
glass between my legs would break and liquid would pour
out of the tube onto my feet and a gigantic mechanical
animal was marching in the parade while moving its head
from side to side and it was halfway between a giant
bear and a lion and had a bear muzzle and its head was
surrounded with a mane of fur and there were men with
whips on either side of the animal making certain it was
under control and my viewpoint was above the animal
looking down as it lumbered along the street and yet i
was still on my back and began to think there was a
television in my brain and i wasnt seeing through my
eyes but was looking through the back of a television
out to a room and what i was seeing were people watching
a television picture of the animal taken from a camera
mounted on the bottom of an airplane so that i was
somehow involved in a loop where i was seeing through
something mechanical that allowed me to see through the
peoples eyes who were looking at another mechanical
thing that exhibited an image taken from an airplane
that contained the animal and this didnt make much sense
although the proof was that i was seeing something from

my position on the ground with my back arched that was
impossible to see except from the air and i felt elated
but strangely disembodied because it was impossible for
me to be on the ground and off the ground simultaneously
and this meant for the first time since entering the
village that my body had become irrelevant to the act of
seeing and yet i wanted to satisfy my body and had
wanted to dream something beyond the boundaries of my
skin and at the same time had wanted to manipulate my
body physically so that it was satisfied and had put
myself in the position of using my brain and muscles
together in order to give my body what it wanted and
thought i was seeing the giant bear lion mongrel because
i had failed to give my body an orgasm and consequently
my body had made an independent decision to become
irrelevant and thrust me into a different mode of
sensation and that the mechanical monster was the
construct of my body which had an imagination
independent of my brain imagination and could enforce
its will and overpower my brain faculties and insert its
bodily intelligence into my skull and the bearlion was
putting one foot in front of the other and while looking
down on it from above i could see that it had begun to
become more active and prance in time to music which i
couldnt hear and was making the handlers nervous and
broke loose and went amok and crushed innocent people
and there wasnt anything anybody could do and yet my
theories were wrong because i was actually in a
helicopter and that was the reason i was looking down on
the monster and i could see a man below in the street
with his back arched clutching his pants and i had
received a controlled emission statement demanding that
i lift up the giant mongrel and there was a harpoon with
a hook on the helicopter that was launched from a tube
running beneath the chassis and i shot it off and
snagged the animal by the scruff of the neck and it
froze when the hook latched onto its neckchain as if
someone had turned off the source of its energy and i
hoisted it above the buildings of the village and it
soared above the helicopter and the hook came off and
its energy was restored and it started moving its head
from side to side as it pranced along the surface of the
clouds and there were other parading mechanical animals
in the sky as well and the vietnamese sun was hot but

the animals didnt seem to mind and were enjoying
themselves immensely and i bade goodbye to vietnam and
flew my helicopter to florida and landed in miami on a
beach where there was a stall in which an italian woman
was giving away cigarettes laced with psychedelic
chemicals and i wanted to get high so i took a cigarette
from the woman but as i smoked part of it i began to
ache and felt sick and unfocused and thirsty and
staggered along the beach and the cigarette removed all
of my fantasies so that it was impossible to fantasize
about the fish in the florida ocean and whenever i thought
about them i could only track them because my mental
faculties were limited to decisions involving the
directions in which the fish were moving and my mind had
expanded to encompass the energy fields of all the fish in
the water who were swimming in my head and i could tell
their next moves before they made them but couldnt tell
anything else about them and couldnt tell what they were
or what they wanted or what their goals or aspirations
were but i knew with perfect clarity where they were
going and tried to determine for my own benefit how far
ahead i could judge their motions and i experienced the
entire massive movement of fish as a single sensation and
was always ahead of where they were and saw the fish at
a point in time that was not the present but slightly in
the future and understood the structure of the ocean for
i was an osteopath of the atlantic although i couldnt
manipulate anything and thought of the currents as
muscles and fish as bones and the movements of the ocean
as the movements of a body writhing within its endless
banks and tossing and turning like a sleepless maniac
filled with fish and there was a sound reflecting off the
surface like the singing of whales although my intuition
seemed problematic because i could hear laughing and
there seemed to be a constant oceanic sexual obsession
as if the ocean were driven in sleep to laugh about
reproduction and think constantly about what it was
reproducing and killing inside its vast marginless womb
and the ocean couldnt wake up but was laughing in its
restless sleep and because i was bereft of fantasy i
could see that the sun set in the ocean and later rose
out of it and that what everyone for thousands of years
had believed in thousands of cultures was the obvious
unfantasizable reality of the suns immersion in the

sleep of the ocean so that the sun was hatcheting into
the ocean at night and out of the ocean in the morning
and the ocean was being constantly pummeled by the sun
and in its restless oblivion was washing the sun and
turning it into the moon and that the shape and size of
the moon was dependent on delta waves of dreaming
oceanic concerns and when the seas were filled with
energy the moon grew and expanded into its washed
purities of floating being and the water world would
curve out and the fish expanded in joy to the bowing of
the surface of the sea and i tried to concentrate as i
took hungry puffs on my italian beach cigarette and the
sky was woven with thin cobalt fabric and minuscule
animals hung in the shredding of the heavens and i
thought back to my experiences in the helicopter and saw
that the animals in the sky were magnifications based on
a lack of proper drugs of the animals that were actually
in the firmament and these sky animals were the
pollinators of the land based creatures that moved on
the surface of the planet and were created by sky
animals with joyous eyes and as i sat on the beach a
religious party with clashing symbols was chanting
ecstatically that they had adopted the best religion
based on singing the original song of creation from
three oclock to five oclock every afternoon and there was
a sandpiper with its beak in the water moving up and
down like an oil pump and the religious party was
worshipping the bird as some kind of avatar or corporate
head who deserved to be revered because of his good
manners and an indian wanted to show me the world
headquarters of the bird worshipers which was down the
beach and i was taken on a dune buggy to the headquarters
which said ornith hollow over the door which was the
name of the blind leader of the clan who was responsible
for the profits of the group and scientists who tested
the performance of weapons were eating bread and rancid
fish jam in a darkened room that looked like the nerve
center of a submarine and i asked what kind of jam they
were eating and they said it was for reverts but i didnt
understand what that meant and they said that the organs
in their bodies were displaced in reverse and all the
connections were lengthened and gummed up so that things
went smoothly on the outside but inside because of
everything being turned around they were a mess and

needed to eat rancid fish jam to ease the constant
nervousness that beset them and there were cages
containing kidneys on a counter and they claimed this
was part of an examining process and they were looking
at my abdomen and i saw i had been trapped and panicked
and wanted to get out of the laboratory before these
reverts stole my internal organs and the man who brought
me into the lab assured me that my organs were
unimportant and were actually superfluous and that
medical science was wrong because internal organs were
really only there for each other and didnt help keep
people alive but were interconnected functions that
needed the casing of a body to justify themselves and
that the true source of life was in the skin and people
died because their skin was punctured or not supported
in some way from the inside and if one were to say the
name of god over and over every afternoon between three
oclock and five oclock this would fill the human body
with good vibrations called fibrillations and these
fibrillations would keep the body puffed up and healthy
and the human body would not be able to collapse no
matter what the organs wanted and therefore i could
donate my organs to the group and this made sense
because organs impressed me as being absurd and ugly and
unrecognizable and i wondered why they were designed in
the first place because it would have been a lot simpler
to have one substance that was a human jello that
without being filled with anything would be capable of
doing everything a human wanted and that people should
be skin and pure interior organless jello and the next
thing i knew i was strapped to a gurney and the
scientists were turning me in a circle while saying they
didnt believe in anesthesia but only in turning the
patient until it would be possible to operate painlessly
and take out what they wanted and they would pay me for
what they needed because they had a subsidized project
to replace every one of their organs with organs that
faced in the right direction and when i woke from my
operation my brain felt sore but the rest of my body was
ok so i realized that they hadnt removed my organs at
all but only a portion of my brain that governed the
control of the organs for what they wanted was to
appropriate the control centers and the portion of the
brain they had removed if treated and bathed in the

proper chemicals could be reactivated as a kind of
switch that would command the organs in their bodies to
unrevert and my brain section could be placed under a
bell jar and tubes connecting to the jar could be placed
in the ear of each of the weapons scientists and they
could thereby cure their medical condition and a nurse
brought me dinner on a tray but there was something
frightening about her appearance as though she harbored
a malicious motive associated with serving food and it
occurred to me that perhaps it wasnt the woman but my
brain that was posing the real threat and that she was a
gifted nurse and my brain with the sector removed would
always make me doubt people and i tried to cover every
inch of the nurses body with some kind of thought
process so that no observation could slip past me and as
she walked i would be able to see every single inch of
her and know everything about how she manifested herself
and i noticed that the food was undercooked and i started
to eat cold mashed potatoes and was in a cafe and a
waiter came up but i couldnt hear what he was saying and
realized that i couldnt hear anything and that things
that people had been telling me were in fact things that
i had been telling myself ever since my operation and
since part of my head was missing i began to worry that
the world as it was presently constituted didnt have a
rationale and i ordered more lumpy mashed potatoes but
before i could finish my order there was a hospital tray
in front of me with mashed potatoes on it as if it had
been waiting in some hospital reality for me to order it
and then had been transported instantaneously by the
waitstaff to my cafe table and served or else that i was
still in the hospital room and the mashed potatoes i had
eaten there had forced me to hallucinate or worse that
my mind without the brain sector that had been removed
by the reverts had caused me to be in a perpetual state
of hallucination and that all thinking was hospitalized
thinking and always needed to be nursed and i got up
from my table at the cafe and walked into a plaza where
birds were wheeling through the air in a storm of meat
and i was late because i had to make it to election
headquarters to run for political office and was back in
the submarine room talking with the scientists but hadnt
yet agreed to the operation because as it turned out i
was only engaged in forward thinking which was as much

as to say that i was really back on the beach thinking
about the fish in the ocean but what had happened was
that i had redirected the fish thinking to thinking of my
own actions and had gotten a step ahead of myself and
was thinking about the brain operation and the results
of the brain operation and yet my brain was actually
intact although my forward thinking had gotten me into
the hallucinatory position of having a dissected mental
organ which meant that with my nonfantasizable mind i
was engaged in the process of fantasizing which was very
confusing and i was in some kind of mental loop between
fantasy and reality because all i really wanted was to
plot things out and extend all of my actions a small
distance into the future and here i had involved myself
in a horrid possibility and it was really more comforting
to move backwards instead of forwards and i thought of
the example of forming a band to play music in which
case it would be better to spend time forming the band
in order to have the possibility of playing the music
than it would be to play the music itself because to
play the music would involve all sorts of risks whereas
the construction of scenarios that allowed for music was
the most important musical act and so there must be a
music to musical construction and i realized that ever
since i had taken that cigarette i had been outside the
flow of events and that in certain mental states one
could think but that all the thoughts arising from those
states would simply cease to be and all that would be
left would be the thoughtless trail of events and sewage
of mental flows without any analytical mentalities and
that such concepts as analytical mentality would be
impossible to remember although in sleep it would be
possible to think anything and that perhaps in sleep the
best thoughts were always being manufactured but it
wasnt these thoughts that were remembered on waking so
that people didnt realize that when they slept they were
doing their deepest and most analytical thinking
involving the most exquisite dictions and discriminations
but that on waking they would only have the sucked out
rinds of their thoughts on which to reflect and only a
disgusting dump and slush of primitive impulses would
remain in the waking persons memory and ever since i had
leaned back to witness the mammoth ass of the drum
majorette and left my body and ascended over the body of

the prancing animal i felt that i had progressed and
made some subtle moral improvements and had eventually
wound up on the beach getting stoned on weed that was
laced with superpowerful psychedelic chemical and yet in
fact i was involved in a personal headtrip and thoughts
from the past were glued into my brain whereas other
thoughts hardly seemed to be there and were the black
masses of the ninety nine point nine nine nine percent
of all thought that never makes it past the exterior
surface of the unconscious and are the glints and moods
and distractions and lucubrations and meditations and
rationalizations and brilliant sorties of logic that
form the unformed mass of cosmic thinking and account
for the uncounted heft of the universe but that the
events that occurred much earlier in my thought life
when i was sober and more event oriented had turned into
a frustrating and fearsome tangle of considerations and
judgments which is a real problem with psychedelics and
i became unmoored and tasted madness because madness has
a specific taste and is something that forms in the mouth
although as i thought about the taste of madness i
couldnt taste it and couldnt get my mind to make the
taste reoccur and realized that i didnt know if i could
ever taste it again or if i ever had tasted it before
because to taste madness is to become mad and the truth
is that there is no escape from madness and it is
impossible to become sane once one is mad for i was in
a state of mental activity which is one step away from
oblivion and was thinking about thinking about thinking
about thinking and becoming more entangled in the
entangling processes of my brain going round and round
and round which was reflected in my language because i
knew that when i was that close to the rim in fact i
was actually asleep on a floating lip at the edge of
madness looking into a bowl that was slowly turning
green which was a bowl of clear water that had one
organism in it which was a splittable organism or in
other words a one thing creature intent on becoming a
two thing creature and this ambition would eventually
pollute the water and make it smell like rancid fish oil
and i put my nose over the bowl but couldnt smell
anything because i was thinking smells but wasnt
smelling smells and could see into the water where this
creature was starting to split because the integrity of

the water had been compromised which is the condition
surrounding all ambition and the intentions of the
organism in the water were repugnant to the water which
was about to begin to lose its clarity and i wondered if
the clock could be turned back on reality and if there
were a clear presence somewhere and a way for the water
to become clear again through the elimination of life
and i realized that a universe without life wouldnt be
lifeless but would be life fulfilling and unreflective and
a perfect world where nothing would ever come back to
haunt the brain and if there were a world composed only
of rocks and assuming rocks had no consciousness then
there would be a perfect lack of awareness and the rocks
would be there but there would be no place for the rocks
to be where they were and it would be perfect because it
would be a perfect presence and clear greenless water
but i didnt want that kind of clarity because that would
mean that my train of thought would stop and it would be
the end of all thought and the end of all experience
which in a way i wanted but in a way i didnt because i
had this pristine notion of being able to stay in one
mental place and remain unmoving and awake forever but
the mind causes sleep and the mind kills us all the time
and continually slaughters us and drives us down into
the kind of thinking im engaged in now and which i had
been engaged in every since my sleeping conversation
with the chimpanzee and which had been growing more and
more entangled and disorganized and which can be defined
as constant thinking in the mad background we all
entered at one point in eternity and never left which is
constant madness that has no truth and is not the madness
of adjustment or misperception or inexpressiveness or
loss and is not the madness where one is unable to
understand or relate and is not the mad mind dealing in
terms the sane dont understand but is absolute madness
where the senses are mixed and the mind works through
its own embattled universe and i was sick of my tangled
thoughts and language and was tired from the relentless
wrinkles in the smooth movement of situations caused by
the psychedelic cigarette and wanted to camp on the
beach but it wasnt safe because bikers rode through
miami and stabbed people in their sleep and i crossed a
divider that separated the beach from a gravel path
through a dark pine forest and came upon a cabin that

had one light burning and a man in a felt jacket was
perusing a book in front of a roaring fire and invited me
in and the wind was howling although puffy flocks of snow
were falling gently and sifting among the pines and the
shutters were banging and i opened the sash and felt a
twinge of foreboding because the man in the jacket was
standing behind me and as i turned around he thrust an
ancient codex in my face and i peered at the page in
front of my nose and saw that it was a book of the dead
and revealed many bardos of meandering which dictate the
paths and positions and constellations of souls which
have been reconfigured by god in his infinite wisdom based
on answers to a simple question which every human being
immediately after death according to the illuminated
meandering bardo of the book is required to answer in
his or her own particular language and this question is
can you catch this ball if i throw it to you and the
ball is a beach ball and the interrogator is the
archangel michael who is standing in front of the dead
person in flames of gold with fiery wings of purest green
and holding the colorful superlarge ball directly above
his flaming head and if the person says no and refuses to
try to catch the ball then the angel will say that he
was only trying to be helpful because the dead person
was such a marvelous individual in his former life and
that this empty exercise in spiritual sportsmanship
is a mere formality and slight inconvenience and the
angel will make it easy and throw the ball slowly and
accurately and it will be virtually impossible not to
catch the ball since it possesses a sticky surface
and will adhere to the hand and therefore to catch the
ball means barely to touch the ball but if a dead person
asks what will happen if he or she is unable to catch
it the angel answers frankly that that person will
immediately tumble into hell and sizzle and burn for all
eternity in a hopeless state of degradation ruthless
torture and agonizing damnation with never the
possibility of a second chance but if the dead person
catches the ball then he or she is guaranteed to soar
into the heavens and sing psalms to the creator in a
state of perpetual grace and ecstasy and if the person
elects the only other available option and stubbornly
refuses to play the game then that dead person will stay
where he or she is with the angel and the ball and the

circumstances will never change and the angel will ask the same question over and over in the same tone of voice and for eons and eons the question will be repeated as if a film clip were being looped relentlessly through the spools of the brain of the dead person without any pause in a nightmare world of repetition just as thought ribbons are strung through the capstans in the deteriorating skulls of corpses in coffins and the words of the question can you catch this ball if i throw it to you eventually will wear down and lose their coatings from being pronounced over and over by the angel and the consonants will become mushy and dissolve into vowels which will become flatter and longer and the vocalic vibrations will be abraded and the overtones will become smooth like worn rope and the words themselves will turn toneless although they will retain their precise meaning because the meaning will always be can you catch this ball if i throw it to you and the gist of the angels message will eternally be the same without any additional or lesser nuance but the sounds that enforce the meaning will become eroded and corroded and yet the dead person will have the liberty to make any response that he or she wishes at any time because there will be no limit to the freshness and inventiveness and earnestness of the language that the dead person himself or herself can employ nor to the exhortations or denials or wheedling blandishments or manufactured crises or loathsome threats or vituperations or bargains or philosophical speculations or strained predictions or stale hopes or wild seductions or divulged dreams or sorceries or prescriptions or role reversals or emotional payments or any other posthuman communication that the dead person can employ in order to get out of the predicament because there is always freedom of expression in the spirit world and yet the demand of the angel will always be the same because the existential basis of nonexistence is eternally consistent and the demand is and always will be can you catch this ball if i throw it to you and it does not do a whit of good to claim that this question is absurd and that the universe was not created so that the dead would be intimidated into catching beach balls for the question will be wasted because the answer never varies and the question itself can never be called into question nor the situation ever

be changed until the spirit is forced into action and in
many cases the situation festers and the dead person
broods about the eternal ravages of hell and wonders
whether his or her new spiritual body will respond on
demand in a coordinated way once the ball has been
tossed and yet the ball seems so large and easy to catch
and the archangel michael so benevolent that the
exercise in ball catching seems to be a superfluous
preliminary to permanent bliss and meanwhile the spirit
is plunged into distress and begins to think that the
question is a hoax or that the ball will be tossed over
the angels shoulder so that the dead person begins to
question the very nature of the exercise and more
specifically the benevolence or malevolence of divine
power and in order to avoid the emotional consequences
of this dilemma he or she tries to convince him or
herself that he or she hasnt been questioned over and
over in a world without clocks and that the notion of
duration in front of the angel isnt duration at all but
an instantaneous perception that has never been
duplicated and the question can you catch this ball if i
throw it to you has never been asked more than once but
such speculation hardly makes any difference because
regardless of how long the interrogation has lasted the
angel michael is still holding his ball aloft and will
never go away nor budge an inch over the life of the
universe or several universes or an infinite number of
universes because the dead person will always be
required to make a decision and the persistence of the
angel with the beach ball will outlast any delusion or
waffling or fantasy or craziness so that the spirit
begins to doubt that the angels question is in fact a
question but rather might be a devilish form of goading
and tormenting the spirit who still has hands and has
retained the most vibrant body of his or her youth and
is perfectly capable of catching any ball that is tossed
to him or her and even those few unfortunates who were
paralyzed throughout their lives or born without limbs
or were in any other way disadvantaged are restored
through gods mercy to perfect health and flexibility and
therefore one has to wonder why the question is being
posed in the first place and yet there is no way to beg
such a question because one is still faced with the
solidity of the situation as it constantly and eternally

presents itself to the dead person and it is only
natural that the spirit start to complain about the
repetitive nature of the reality thrust upon him or her
and whether the archangel michael is actually telling
the truth about how easy the ball would be to catch and
the validity of the reward and punishment system he
claims has been established because there is also the
grim possibility that the opposite results will occur
and that the spirit who catches the ball will be damned
and the one who doesnt will be saved and yet as long as
the angel doesnt go away then neither does the endless
thinking the angel engenders because every situation
requires thought and if a situation remains unchanged
then so does the thinking process concerning that
situation so that futile thoughts in and of themselves
can be said to be effects of circumstances and the only
thing as endless as the presence of the angel is the
endless thought about the endless presence of the angel
and the meandering bardo of self emancipation which i
saw as i peered into the book that was thrust into my
face by the man who was wearing the felt jacket and
standing in front of the roaring fire in his cabin had a
solution for the dilemma which was contained on the very
next page which told me the somber truth about catching
the ball and revealed that the outcome was predetermined
by iron laws and that even the response of the dead
spirit was decreed well in advance of the birth of his
suffering spirit on earth and therefore the process of
thinking was futile in the first place and could be
avoided just by having access to the book i was reading
and i decided that i needed to rest my brain from the
torments i had been experiencing and go for a walk in
the woods to commune with the snowy night and there was
a tribe of wolfchasers that were bivouacking outside the
man in the felt jackets cabin and their name in the
wolfchaser language was moosechaser because the way to
chase wolves is to chase the weakest of their prey and
at first i thought it might have been a social group of
native americans but that wasnt the case because the
group was actually composed of retired army colonels who
had wild romantic ideas about living off the land and
had formed a rebel militia to kill endangered species
because they didnt want any bureaucracy to dictate their
choices and had beer guts and wore little bands around

their heads with feathers sticking up in the air and
they spied a moose on the gravel path and went running
after it through the woods while whooping and carrying
on and i chased them down the path and they were
moving in a straight line as fast as they could with one
directly behind the other and i was the last person in
the line and running behind them and behind me was a
large pack of wolves that was chasing me down and i was
trapped between the wolfchasers who were running after
the moose and the wolves who were running after me and i
knew i had a problem because i couldnt figure out the
wolves motives because it was possible they were chasing
me and it was possible they were chasing the wolfchasers
and it was possible they were chasing the moose that the
wolfchasers were chasing but the only way i could find
out who was chasing whom was to veer off the gravel and
pursue my own path and if the wolves turned after me i
knew i would be finished and would become a substitute
moose but if they chased the wolfchasers then i would
only have to worry about being lost although the pain of
being lost in the woods or even worse of being lost in
ones head in the woods can be worse than the fear of
teeth and through force of habit i kept running on
gravel and the snowstorm increased and the snow became
thick and formed ridges of crystals along my forehead
and the water melted into my eyes and smarted and
because i was still wearing my beach clothing from miami
i was extremely uncomfortable and a collar of snow
formed around the collar of my tropical shirt and the
water that melted from the heat of my bodily exertion
ran in streams down my chest and back and down my butt
and legs to my ankles as i searched for a well of
energy within my body so that i could increase my speed
and pass the wolfchasers and the retired army colonels
would then form a barrier of beer bellies between me and
the wolves and this would have the added benefit of
keeping me from getting lost in the woods because i
would still be part of the line of pursuit only i would
then be between the wolfchasers and the moose and would
be flowing through the forest with a purpose and the
forest would have meaning as a result of the hunt and
the battle of nature i was participating in because i
knew that a forest is nothing more than a living
background for foraging and murder and i was panting and

the wolves were gaining and the pack which consisted of
a dozen or so animals was four or five steps behind me
and i could hear them calling to each other although i
couldnt make sense of what they were saying but i
intuited that all of them had names and were having a
discussion before dinner and it was a distracted form of
socializing they were engaged in where they would call
each other affectionately as they were attacking and
discuss the cubs and how hungry they were and how the
old bones just werent holding up the way they used to
and all sorts of useless drivel while the phalanx of
salivating snarling predators was racing behind me and
slowly gaining ground and i was up to my ankles in the
furry softness of flurries that smelled of the clean
night of pines and was suddenly catapulted up in the air
by a slingshot mechanism that had been laid as a
guerrilla trap along the path by an intelligence branch
of the government in order to maim the rebellious
colonels and i tumbled like a cannonball arching through
the skies and it suddenly became cloudless and i could
see the earth and a full moon and then the stars and
then the earth and the moon and the stars and the earth
and the moon and then the stars and then the earth and
the full moon and the stars and the earth and then the
full moon and the stars and as i fell i could see the
sides of the trees and the moon and a few stars and
then the earth and then the moon and then the trees and
then the earth again as i abruptly and unexpectedly
landed and something mammoth detonated and the
thermonuclear impact of my body caused a huge crater in
a vast desert landscape where all the forest trees had
been blown away and i was at ground zero and rose and
dusted the snow off my pants and took a deep breath and
noticed there was no curve to the earth anymore and no
horizon and the land went on forever in all directions
and this desert was an endless flat planet that wheeled
through contorted space and the stars were so huge that
they resembled twisted squares of light and the ground
was made of rusted steel with rows of evenly spaced
protuberances or bosses that ran off into the distance
like plants in an infinite field or metal and i knew that
these protuberances were graves and that those who were
buried on this flat and immaculate plane were sealed in
an unbreachable force field and doomed to anonymity that

was so complete that they lay in their drilled spaces
and couldnt remember ever having been alive and in this
sense were like those who are living but cant remember
their previous deadness but these dead while being in
the opposite position had no worries because there was
no ego in their lifelessness to cause a problem and
there was a nut attached to a bolt whose threads were
sticking out of the earth and a tool to loosen the nut
and i realized that if i removed this nut the graves on
the plane would open in unison but i refused to touch
the tool and turned and standing next to me was a
penguinlike creature shrouded in a sea of electrons and
bright sparkling particles like tiny bits of colored
candies orbited about his head and body and although i
could locate his head i couldnt make out his features
and couldnt see if he were human or a penguin or if he
had eyes or a nose or a mouth or a bill or how many
limbs or fins he had because his bodily mass flowed within
the seams and grooves that nestled within the electron
field and he gazed around the terrain and waved an
indistinct object over my head and it felt like a
shutter snapping shut and i was alone and isolated and
buried within the drilled in spaces of the metal and
there was no one there or anywhere and everything was
darkness and i realized in horror that i had no body and
wasnt breathing and there was no sense of my being
connected to anything and i was a mind with nothing
outside it and there was no creation except for the
voice which was me and then there was no voice and
nobody was saying anything and i had no senses and there
was no train of thought but i existed nonetheless
because there was thinking going on but i couldnt tell
what that thinking was or who was thinking thoughts and
consequently there was nothing to hold onto and i tried
to evoke an image of something i had experienced before
the shutter snapped and thought about the flat corten
planet with the bolted graves but couldnt picture the
planet the flatness the bolt the graves or the picture
and then i tried to evoke an image of my prior
existence but couldnt come up with anything and was
imageless and thoughtless and motionless and breathless
and speechless and egoless and mindless and deathless
and hopeless in my state of absolute fear and began to
think about what it meant to feel because if there were

feelings there must be somebody feeling those feelings
about someone or something and i tried to think of
someone or something i could feel something about and to
imagine love and i spontaneously felt love and to
imagine hatred and i spontaneously felt that too so i
knew that i could recognize a feeling and in the process
of recognition that feeling would be produced and i felt
resentment and anxiety and greed and a spectrum of other
feelings but i had nobody to love and nobody to fear and
nobody to resent and nothing to want and the feelings
existed in and of themselves and if i could imagine a
lover for my love and an enemy for my hatred and could
create an art and world and life then i could build
almost anything but i had nothing to grab onto because i
was permanently incapable of imagining anything except
the feelings i was feeling and yet i had a suspicion
that this was merely a spell and since all spells by the
nature of myth must come to an end i began to blame the
atomic penguin and realized with a jolt that i could
bring up the image of the creature in my mind and then
i tried to imagine someone or something else but still
found that to be impossible and thought that if i were
given the gift of being able to imagine this one
creature that was the source of my misery then perhaps i
could influence my destiny by praying to it as if it were
my creator because by creating difficulties in a truly
significant sense it had created me and so i said a
prayer to the monster who created the spell and had an
immediate intuition as to the origin of the cosmos and
saw that feelings preceded objects and love preceded
reality and that god had created the world in order to
exercise his loves and hatreds and suddenly the image
came into my mind of schools of fish and i remembered how
id been on a beach in miami smoking a psychedelic
cigarette and it occurred to me that i was still on a
trip and that it had continued all this time and i was
suffering the same mental paralysis with my inability to
imagine things as i had suffered in terms of tracking
fish as they moved through the ocean when i was able to
get one step ahead of the situation by surrendering my
ability to fantasize and that because my current
mindstate was similar to my earlier mindstate then it
logically followed that i was being affected by the same
force both then and now which was a chemical i had

inhaled and i remember the primary tenet of all trippers
and dope fiends which is that everything wears off and
the primary cure for fear is always patience and that
inaction is the most important form of action and this
brought me back to thinking about the ball in the hands
of the archangel michael and i realized that the
meandering bardo was a rat fuck and that the final
solution to the problem of deciding whether or not to
catch the beach ball was hysterical laughter which was
the only human response i never considered when i had
the liberty to frame any response i wanted for i
understood that at some point and for some reason i had
stood before the angel and been ensconced in the eternal
predicament of choosing whether to catch something or
not but i couldnt remember what decision i had made or
even if i had made a decision or why since i was alive
i had once been a dead person or moreover how it could
have been possible to have returned to earth because
returning to earth is not one of the three options of
the angelic situation which are to catch the ball and go
to heaven or miss the ball and go to hell or do nothing
for the rest of eternity and converse with the flaming
angel but i saw in any case that hysterical laughter is
the primary emotion that governs all emotions and that
all emotions and creations spring from hysterical
laughter and that if a dead person facing the angel with
the ball would only begin to laugh hysterically then
there would be nothing that anyone could do and the dead
person would be totally in control of his own laughter
and nobody could stop him because pain or hurt or
threats of any kind or even the brimstone of hades would
only cause greater hysteria and more mirth because there
is nothing more intimidating than looking deep into the
features of someone who is laughing hysterically since
this is the most frightening thing imaginable and
hysterical laughter is a force of immense power that can
shatter anything and then and there i started to laugh
hysterically and the laughter caused breath and the
breath caused my body to solidify and my body caused a
world of stinginess to come into being in which rain
would never fall in greater amounts than what was
necessary and the sun would never lavish excessive
warmth on the planet and nobody who ate would ever feel
full and no one would have extra children and for an odd

reason this resolidification and rebirth of my body had
been fortunate and i was released from my tomb and
elevated to a position of extreme importance as the
monarch of mentally challenged men who had seceded from
the state of alaska and were running a new bachelor
country for profit and anyone who came to live with them
was forced to pay homage to me and give me all the
money i needed for my ever changing wardrobe and the
area of the state where this new country was located was
tropical and the animal population were mutants and
incapable of eating one another and the atmosphere was
so benevolent that they all lived in a peaceable kingdom
of sanity and gentleness and my realm was surrounded by
mountains and was very beautiful and my mentally
challenged subjects never swore or told lies and the
mountain ranges were magnificent and lofty and the
outsiders who came to live among us shed their pompous
attitudes and habits as soon as they walked through the
pass in the mountains that separated us from the rest of
the world and there was an admission gate where
immigrants had to make their entry payments and i was in
the toll booth with a crown on my head and had donned
my robes and was collecting fees and the immigrants
would get extremely emotional as they paid me and break
into sobs and tears of gladness and i was very cynical
and kept the totals of the money i was making in my
head as my new subjects passed through the gate and i
was fortunate because i had done nothing to earn my
position but had been born into purple out of my blank
state of frustration and lack of imagination and
hysteria in the tombs of the metal desert and not only
would i be able to keep the fees without spending a dime
because all of my wants and needs were supplied in my
kingdom by my mentally challenged subjects free of
charge but also i would be able to levy taxes within the
kingdom on everybodys labor and ideas and acts of
charity and possessions and projects and family
heirlooms and even on shoelaces and snippets and no
matter what i did with the money i gleaned from my new
position nobody would be allowed to say a word against
me or stand in my way when i went into neighboring areas
to buy the goods and services that werent available in
alaska but each of my subjects would immediately upon
coming into my presence have to touch their noses to the

ground and mumble i love you your majesty with all my
heart and soul and while i was raking in the profits in
my admissions booth it occurred to me that i could write
laws and make people behave in any fashion i wanted no
matter how ludicrous the behavior was and so i demanded
that everyone be forced to donate half their working
hours to the erection of the tallest statue in the
history of the world which would portray me crowned in
all my glory holding my royal scepter with a benevolent
smile on my face and yet there was a faction among my
subjects that declined to do this creative work because
they were rebels and wanted to build a normal size
statue in honor of the achievements of the bachelor
leader who had originally founded the paradise kingdom
of the mentally challenged and they claimed they had
nothing against me personally but since they were rebels
they had a spiritual connection that couldnt be broken
to the original rebel leader and yet i suspected in the
darkness of my heart that they intended to build a
statue of a traitor who was rebelling against the status
quo and not of the rebel leader of the past and so i
informed them that any statutory change to any projected
statuary would be heresy and treason and that all
statues would be judged by an independent panel of
experts feature by feature and aspect by aspect and that
if any feature or aspect of any statue were deemed to be
the slightest bit different from my feature or aspect as
it existed in its current state of glory then the
sculptors responsible for the work on said feature or
aspect would be expelled from the kingdom forthwith and
consequently there was an exodus of citizens as files of
men were seen to be halfheartedly heading toward me from
the opposite direction as i was collecting money in my
toll booth because they had decided to go back to the
world rather than submit to the artistic tyranny of a
brain dead politician and i was forced to return their
fees which made me unhappy because i had neglected
through a drafting error in my expulsion edict to
explain that anybody leaving the kingdom wasnt entitled
to a refund and i began to run out of cash as the
sculptor rebels demanded the return of their immigration
fees which i had already disbursed on expensive
accouterments and i began to insult the citizens and
they arrested me and brought me to the central square of

the city and tied me to a stake and had agreed at a
national bachelor conference on the arts to resort to
execution and there was a pile of faggots under my feet
and a grand inquisitor wanted me to confess that during
the term of my reign i had been taking vitamin
supplements but i was stubborn and invoked my royal
privileges and refused and he said that i would die the
most painful death imaginable because they were going to
inject me with rabies virus and when i began to get
thirsty they were going to burn me but i would roast
very slowly because the logs underneath my feet had
been chemically treated to cause the greatest possible
amount of pain and if at any time i was willing to
admit my errors and freely confess that i had been
taking supplements then the process would be stopped and
i could resume being king with no hard feelings but
because i was stubborn i again refused and a medical
team arrived in an ambulance and a doctor in a scrub
suit slapped the veins on my arm and stuck in a needle
and the feeling of the rabies virus being injected was a
main line rush and i began to nod and chase in my brain
a continuation of that chain of pleasure that extended
from my arm to the deepest center of my head and i was
lost within that golden flowing river of warm pressure
and could feel the liquid lapping against its shores and
the pleasure extended down my back and surrounded my
asshole and the anxiety and suspicion i had felt from
the beginning of my reign through false pride emptied
from my being and i knew i was totally in the wrong and
was ready to repent but was too stoned to talk and
decided to stay bound against the stake with my head
nodding forward and enjoy the pleasure while i could
before the rabies virus took over and turned my brain
into soup and i passed out and when i awoke there was
smoke rising from the area of my feet and a terrible
pain was lodged in my skull as if untold frenzied
termites were gnawing away at the most sensitive nerves
in my brain and foam was pouring out of my mouth and my
eyes were paralyzed so that i couldnt blink and were
popping out of my head and i could feel the heat licking
at my toes and could see beyond the veil of smoke my
subjects laughing and enjoying themselves immensely
while stuffing their faces at round restaurant tables and
i was on a platform as if this were a form of dinner

theater which reminded me of a distant event concerning
another dinner at another theater and there were
waiters and waitresses who once were my sculptors who
were collecting tips and trying to do a good job and
they were happy to have untaxed money and a fierce pain
moved up my calves and i could smell my flesh burning as
the foam from my lips dripped into the fire and i cursed
the kingdom and all the people in it but the curse
unfortunately was sealed in my head because all of my
facial features were paralyzed and the veins in my eyes
were rupturing and filling my eyeballs with hot blood and
i reviewed my options as i stood there tied to the stake
and realized that i would have to surrender to the
prevailing circumstances and since the fire was certain
to purge me of disease i would finally be cleansed and
change into intertwining trails of smoke and not into
ashes that were falling into the logs because the ashes
would be flesh and bones and the smoke would be my pure
aristocratic spirit rising into the crystalline air of
alaska and i realized with horror as the flames moved up
towards my waist that i would be inhaled by the food
slurping proletarians in the dinner theater and that my
spirit would move into their lungs and be lodged inside
my tormentors and their very acts of respiration would
be a form of spirit attachment and that my noble spirit
would blend into the debased spirits of the mentally
challenged people who were watching me in the theater
and become part and parcel of hundreds of burping and
slobbering bachelor subjects and yet i comforted myself
because i knew that a portion of me would ascend into
the clouds and vibrate miles and miles above the earth
and move across the face of the land into canada and
over the yukon and baffin island and up into the frozen
wastes of the arctic where there was a cold kingdom at
the top of the world where i would feel no heat as the
flames moved up to my chest and the foam in my mouth
turned black and continued to flow down my chin and i
could hear the saliva from my mouth sizzle and sputter
in the fire and blisters began to form on my cheeks and
my eyelashes were kindled and steam erupted from the
pores of my neck and i knew that my stomach was
beginning to decompose and my only solace was to
concentrate on feelings of triumph and liberation
because i knew that what was happening to me was simply

the result of poor decision making and that i was only
changing form and this was a rite of passage or process
of transition or opportunity for growth depending upon
ones point of view and yet my resentment against the
people who were swilling food and socializing continued
to build and it bothered me that they didnt seem to care
about my welfare after all that i had done for them as
king by providing them with a joyous and serene working
and recreational environment in spite of their mental
disabilities and i could see them through the flames
laughing and thoroughly enjoying their bachelorhood and
their partying and some were tossing toothpicks at me
and my resentment was an additional flame in my breast
but i couldnt afford to die while feeling resentful
because i knew from the lore of the kingdom that the
emotions one feels at the moment of death affect the
future welfare of the soul and i had to turn myself
around and assume an attitude of forgiveness and
composure but it was hard to maintain that sort of
detachment given the predicament i was in and i wondered
what the release of the soul would feel like and if i
would slip into oblivion as the flames were rising
because if i slipped into oblivion then the game would
be over and yet i didnt want to be reborn on earth
because the best i could hope for would be the situation
which had led me to the stake and immolation in the first
place and the agony i was currently experiencing had
resulted from my once having had the best possible
occupation on the planet which was the job of being the
absolute master of a bachelor paradise and meanwhile the
flames were up to my shoulders and most of my body had
been destroyed and i was suffering mightily from the
rabies virus which because of the heat had increased its
activities and was gnawing away at the innards of my
head and yet i was alive and thinking that i was still
a child of god and that there must be something to be
grateful for even in this difficult situation and
although my face was paralyzed and most of my body was
gone i was amazed that i was able to process information
and wondered what was going to happen when the flames
rose above my ears and i wouldnt be able to see or hear
and my brain would melt and my hair would explode in
flames and this was a matter of curiosity which in and of
itself was a source of enjoyment and caused me to feel

immense gratitude since i was enjoying the process of
speculation in spite of the agonies of the stake and was
appreciating learning and revering education and wanting
to become a more dignified and ennobled human being and
i wondered if this incorporeal thing that yearned for
data was my soul so that ones spirit wandered from lesson
to lesson and life to life acquiring information but it
also occurred to me that information from previous
lessons and lives would be useless because the actual
circumstances of each successive life would be radically
different and that rebirth was a process of acquiring
useless or more precisely disposable information and one
could be the wisest of the wise in one life but in the
next would become the dumbest of the dumb so that
exercising my speculative faculties was a futile and
foolish endeavor even though it was giving me such
satisfaction in my final moments but my thoughts were
suddenly interrupted as my eyes went dark and i realized
that i was about to become a royal martyr or even a
saint because i had refused in spite of all entreaties
to admit that i took vitamin supplements and preferred
to die rather than cave in on a matter of principle and
as the heat slammed into my ears i stopped hearing and
with relief foresaw that i would probably receive a
better statue than what i had originally anticipated
because it wouldnt be a statue to a king but to a saint
and instead of a crown and scepter there would be a halo
and wand and my image would be placed in churches or
nutrition centers and be worshiped in the alaskan
paradise because i never flinched and the barbarians who
clamored for my death and were laughing at me while they
picked their teeth at the dinner theater would one day
be sorry and be recognized for the fun loving sadistic
mentally challenged bachelor slobs that they were and a
flame started growing and glowing in the center of my
head and i could hear the rabid termites crinkling in
the firestorm as the pain of constant gnawing vanished
from my brain and i was able to concentrate on the
raging wall of flame which was originally surrounded by
gray matter but now was a mass of orange identical to
the solid orange in which i was immersed at the bridge
party when i was licking the breast of the woman who was
leaning over my shoulder and could feel the stinging
dribbles of juice in my eyes and it isnt true that those

who ignore history are doomed to repeat it but rather
the opposite is true which is that those who concentrate
with all their energies on a particular moment of
personal history are doomed to relive their lives from
that precise moment through to the present as a
consequence of which i would be forced to relive the
anguish and anxiety of my multiple transformations from
the time i was licking the orange carrot encrusted
breast of the woman who was leaning over my shoulder at
the bridge party until i found myself to be the center
of attention at this bachelor dinner party in alaska and
an incredible weariness descended on my spirit as the
flames engulfed the remaining portions of my brain and i
wanted to be relieved of the incessant onslaught of
superficial images that had dominated my consciousness
from god knows when because the ramifications of thought
are truly infinite which means that every possible
thought has at one time or another been thought which
also means that there is no such thing as a new thought
which means again that one is always thinking a thought
that has been thought by someone before or will be
thought by someone in the future which means once more
that one is continually jumping through time and at one
moment is here and the next moment is five million years
ahead and the moment after that is five billion years
behind so that when we think that our lives are part of
a continuum it really isnt so and we brush against the
eternal web of infinite thought for the briefest possible
moment and when we touch this web a spark of individual
photonic energy ignites and forms an integral moment and
we burp out an integral thought and the next moment we
are brushing against the web at a different space time
coordinate point and burping an entirely different
thought into an entirely different world with an entirely
different brain and consequently we are an infinite
number of people in an infinite number of places at an
infinite number of times rattling out an infinite number
of thoughts and as such are the one and the many and
the individual and the infinite and the ego trapped in
time and the timeless infinite egoless liberated spirit
who is every possible being in every possible place and
time and thinking and doing each and every thing that it
is possible to think and do because the metaphysical
truth of all existent beings is that to be one being who

292

thinks one thought is to be every being who thinks every thought but that is not as much as to say that to be every being means that one is god because the thinking being does not create the infinite web of thought but rather is the web of thought itself and yet who creates or created the thought web or whether the web creates or created itself is a metaphysical notion that i didnt have time to ponder given my circumstances at the stake and as i was about to submerge completely in the flames i knew that i was in nothing more nor less than an ordinary situation because every moment is a moment that precedes death given that the precise definition of death is a change in identity and considering also the inescapable fact that our identities change each time we access another instant in the web of infinite thought patterns and so i began to realize that a frozen moment was a victimized bug that was caught in a delusional web which was very different from the web of freedom and infinite thought processes associated with my enlightened thinking at the stake and that our delusions of ego and survivability and all the other delusions of self centeredness for that matter are nothing but the paralyzed and hopeless premonitions of death that an insect feels as it sees a spider moving like a machine of destruction across a web to suck the vital throbbing juices out of its stupefied flesh and it didnt matter that the last living bit of my own flesh was about to be consumed in the firestorm spawned by the grand inquisitor of the bachelors because i would be packing my bags in any case and leaving well before that final brain cell popped and would be on to a new job and occupation in some other skull and situation and felt an incredible lightness of being because of my newfound knowledge and understood what it must be like to be a mayfly rising from the intricate surface of a river for its momentary dance of glory in the sun as the raging fire consumed my final cell and then i saw a tunnel of brightness opening before me and voices were calling from the right and left and above and below and i could feel myself shooting out some dark channel into an all powerful and embracing and all welcoming divine light and was ecstatic and grateful and prepared myself with blissful anticipation to tumble into the lap of my creator because i knew that my metaphysical vision couldnt be explained as a biochemical reaction in a dying brain since my brain had already been burnt to a crisp by the alaskan wall of fire and yet i jumped to an impetuous and unfortunate conclusion about the nature of life after death in assuming that i was rocketing toward heaven as a result of the spotlessness of my behavior as the saintly king of paradise because i had indeed been transformed and etherealized but it wasnt in the way i had hoped and the dark channel hadnt been a spiritual ladder to everlasting salvation nor an escape from the infinite web of previous reality but a paternal urethra leading into another sorry morass of pitiful existence and i had been blown out a set of anonymous gonads and my faceless head was plowing through cum and it wasnt because i was motorized but there was something that made me wiggle and nobody else had heads or features either but i saw that they were carrying heads and features or at least half a head and half a feature within their trembling cavities and how i got into this position of resperming which is a much more radical form of retrogression than rebirthing ill never know but as i continued to exert my masculinity i recognized that id wind up in a toilet or tampon in no time and looking quickly to the side i saw herds of tadpoles huffing through the white goo that i originally thought was heavenly light and it occurred to me that anything could happen but chances were that nothing would and that i was jerking myself off in the literal sense of the word and that if there were no sperms there could be no pricks which created a conundrum in my brainless brain and i began to think of what an absurd organ a drooping channel of flesh is that dangles between the legs of half the humans on the planet and could see a mammoth egg with a surface like a golf ball whose talking navel was the only point of entry and wondered what the source of this specific knowledge was because i could understand swimming upstream as part of a herd mentality but the intuition that i had to enter through a talking navel in a golf ball is a different kind of thing entirely which means that instinct or knowledge is present in an incomplete piece of throbbing shit like a sperm and as i swam closer a halo appeared around my faceless head and i was anointed and could hear faint choirs humming through the innards of the goo and the geodesic surface

of the ball began to pulse and the choirs became
jubilant as my halo streamed around my magnetized bulb
of a head that was being tugged by the female egg force
and i realized that i had been selected and in moments i
knew that my spermlike essence would meld along its
chainlike being with the seductive female wiles and
inner links of the golf ball and be transformed at every
point of contact and my body alerted the egg to open its
force field for me and i was sucked toward the talking
navel and although i had just been part of a larger
orgasm i felt a smaller one building inside me and this
intimate pleasure was blasting through my body which no
longer wriggled but was hardened and drawn out along the
gravitational force fields of the egg and extruded
through the sexual latitudes at the depths of being and
i plunged through the oval lips of the talking navel
which were frantically murmuring soft and passionate
words of love and burst and came in an incredible
rapture of orgasmic shuddering which was followed by a
flowing glistening overall sense of peace as if i were
spreading through a lake and could feel distant lappings
at my edges and tiny objects were swimming through me
like fish and a brown benevolent heat was trailing along
the lake and toasting the sparkling chromosomal tides of
the egg surfaces and voices were calling other voices
and there was no power that could control the insanity
of this vocal production and then there were two of me
and i had to abandon the notion that i was one thing
and what was worse i had to abandon any notion of a one
thing history so that the faceless head with the tail
that had been wiggling toward where i now was was not
what i had once been because i couldnt tell which of the
two of me was the original swimmer but the argument was
beside the point because all of my energy was being
devoted to creating splits in the nature of selfhood and
it was strange that i still retained one voice that was
king shit while all the other chattering vocables of my
multiplying cells were cooperating and i panicked since
i couldnt figure out how i was thinking because now that
i was a being that would eventually develop a brain i
saw that my thinking was preceding its source which
meant that effect was preceding cause which was a
contradiction of the tenets of western philosophy and it
was certainly possible that once i developed a brain i

would have an explanation for how a brainless being had obtained thought but until i developed a means to think about how i was thinking id try to focus on the storm that was raging around the egg where lightning shot through clouds of raining fluids in hot prongs of language and i didnt know whether to be terrified or not but it didnt matter because a primal energy was making me divide no matter what i did and i was destined to become a massive clumping of cells and saw a mist of microscopic insects gliding through a patch of slanting autumn sun and oak leaves were peeling away and whirling through shifting cubes of brightness inhabited by these gnatlike creatures who were basking in the dancing patches of froth that flowed below the banners of failing light in the trees and where this image came from i didnt know because i was still within the clouded boundaries of the egg which had begun to move or rather i had begun to move because i was reconciled to being egglike and was heading for the maternity of the womb but the image of floating gnats in an oak grove had had to come from somewhere since i hadnt yet experienced the gestalt of a gnatlike experience and i thought that perhaps the male who had created me and as a result had become my dad was standing at that very moment in a forest and had forged a telepathic connection that would eventually degenerate into a father child relationship or that this isolated image of insects shimmering in the sanctity of the woods was in some mysterious way not an image but a symbol of some natural or psychic force that moved in a matrix within me just as i was being moved by a power not my own nor my mothers toward the profundity of the womb and i was actually smaller than a gnat but in my pinheaded head the gnats seemed smaller than me and then i comprehended the ultimate truth of all reality and the supreme wisdom and ultimate principle that governs the universe and all its creations and that once understood can be utilized to explain every aspect of the myriad phenomena and to answer every koan and solve every problem and banish every doubt and erase every intellectual care and that supreme wisdom and ultimate principle of the universe is that nothing makes any sense but that nothing ever has to and i wanted to hold on to this important thought but couldnt and was wearied by my activity and had strange cramps although i had no organs and felt anguish and frustration and a maddening thirst for truth and wanted to be young again although i was only a few minutes old and didnt know how i could face the rest of my life and wanted it all to end before it began and truly believed that the millions of fellow sperm who were nowhere to be seen and were drifting and dying in another area of my mothers body where there was a conclusion to work and sorrow were luckier than i was and yet my desires for extinction were a passing fancy because my brain had started to develop and because it is a scientific fact that the brain has an inherent need and vested interest in its own survival therefore my yearning to die vanished without a trace and i was forced by my head to be in love with life and my brain cells began to contrive to make me forget everything up to the present point which i did because nobody ever remembers what i had just forgotten and i knew i would have to go through many layers of forgetfulness before i was born because the principal job of the brain is to figure out how not to know but i forgot what i was thinking before i finished my train of thought about the nature of forgetfulness and was nestled against a wall of nutrients and started for the first time to feed which was a drag because i now felt hunger for food which automatically decreased my thirst for knowledge and i saw that my brain was telling everyone else what to do for its own ridiculous benefit and that i would always hate telecommunications because it was just a means of brains using nonbrains to talk to brains as opposed to systems of excretion where stomachs use nonstomachs to communicate with stomachs and a thin thread formed between me and the puffy wall which was a link in the chain of the stomach system i had been using my brain system to think about and miraculously i had my first taste of blood and was awash in a life deadening dependency which my brain called love but i called slavery and although i no longer understood what i was thinking or feeling or why i was dependent on eating because of the brain poisoning i knew that the crap that would begin to form in my new intestinal system was what i had to look forward to for the rest of my life and i couldnt stop my brain from driving excessive thoughts through my head which was actually starting to form into

a headlike structure and i felt the need to sleep and
the next thing i knew i was bigger and then asleep and
then bigger and then asleep and then bigger again and
then asleep again and this cycle kept repeating itself
month after month and for a while i thought i was a
chicken or a rodent or a fish or a brute until i finally
assumed the lineaments of a man and realized that a
wingwang was beginning to dangle between my legs so
that one day i would eject what i had been into
something similar to what i had entered in order to
become what i had already become and i wondered what was
the use of living through another dreary cycle because
there are many forms of creation besides ejaculation
which are equally futile and the better one is at
creating things the more isolated and useless one
becomes and one of the iron laws of humanity is that
almost all great artists die unknown and almost all
great lovers die unloved and almost all great healers
die of the illness of trying to heal humanity and that
public success from time immemorial has always been
based on luck and a vaunted mediocrity and the most
common trait of those who garner fame is viciousness and
i wondered if there were any value at all in a humble
life above the fray and convinced myself that the best
way to experience humility was to break down the power
structures in my brain and so i began to meditate in
order to home in on the primary source of brain
structure and i perceived that the fountainhead of
mental power wasnt far away since i hadnt been born yet
and there were only a few barriers that had been erected
by my developing cerebrum to shield me from the blinding
truth of my own creation but the notion of humility
suddenly bored me because my brain had decided to fight
my resolution to make changes in its power structure by
releasing defensive hormones that created ennui and
depression and i became distracted and listless and
couldnt focus my meditative energies but fortunately i
was resourceful enough to summon into my service the
biological energy that had created my brain in the first
place and was able to coopt the energies that my brain
was using to coopt me and by meditating on a deep
biological level i was able to regulate my biorhythms
which allowed me to reduce the rate of brain cell
multiplication and so my brain was forced to surrender

in order to continue growing and had to comply with my
humble wishes and i forced it to remove the barriers of
forgetfulness and was finally able to think in a
nonstructured way and view in retrospect the moment i
was converted into a sperm which was the moment after
the moment i was tied to the stake in the paradise of
the bachelors while having my final brain cell fried by
the wall of flames that had been ignited by the inquisitor
who had been hired by the rebels who had refused to
construct my statue in the kingdom i inherited after
being trapped in the metal desert before i exploded as a
result of the trap set by the government in order to
maim the wolfchasers who had bivouacked outside the
cabin into which i wandered after my brain sector
operation and because of this second elimination of
brain structure i could now examine my prior life and my
life before that life and my lives before the life that
preceded my present life when once upon a time i had
been fixing in my kitchen which made me see bloody dots
floating through the rooms of my office building prior to
being jabbed in the rectum by a nude woman before going
to a dinner party and winding up being attacked by a toy
duck which resembled a machine on a cruise ship with
metal jaws that forced me to escape into a raft that
tumbled over a falls after which i wound up licking an
orange breast at a bridge party in anticipation of my
conversation with a monkey whose evil wishes landed me
in my own coffin where i traveled around a cemetery in
order to have the opportunity of flirting with mermaids
whose wiles got me magnetized and flying across the
countryside toward a rickety house where i conversed
with a forgetful horse and then journeyed to saigon in
time to observe a fascinating parade and subsequently
flew my helicopter to miami and smoked psychedelics which
caused me to need the aforementioned brain operation
conducted by the jam eating reverts and this anterior
life was viewed by me with redoubled abilities and
renewed ease and i realized that there was no flip side
to existence because one reality was pretty much like
any other whether on earth or in heaven or in hell and
·regardless of what one did or where one was one was
still doing something somewhere sometime and the
something one was doing had a beginning and a middle and
an end and the end of one thing was the beginning of

another and the underlying substance of all possible experiences was unbelievably boring because one was always assured of something else happening that was just as meaningful or meaningless as the thing that had just occurred and no matter what mental act was inspired by the events in question that mental act would be followed by another and no matter what word or figment of language was generated by the mental act there would always be another word or figment that would follow the first figment or word as night follows day and i saw that there was only one reasonable escape from this endless trail of sickness and sick language and that was the creation of a language of nonexistence so that i had to figure out a way of creating a situation where i was no longer connected to my own language and then i could be said truly not to exist and would be free and so i began to meditate on this paradox which was like the sound of one hand clapping and went into a trance and even though i was developing and changing in the external world of my prenatal reality and even though i was born during this period of trancelike concentration i steeled myself against incorporating the birth sensations into my meditation practice because to do so would have meant acknowledging the existence of existence but instead i continued to focus on the creation of a language of nonexistence and it was only at the moment when i was lying in my incubator that i gained an explosive insight into the hopelessness of philosophy and came to understand the existential truth of the language of nonexistence which is that it doesnt and never has existed which is what makes it what it isnt and what it never was and what it never will be and i felt completely helpless because i was a newborn blob in an incubator and the feeling of frustration and failure was ripping me apart as i lay there cooing and drooling and absorbing the full implications of endless boredom within the existing parameters of an existing language and i saw that there was only one way out of my predicament which was to restore the missing power structure to my brain so that i would once again be ignorant and attach significance to my measly life and have beastly desires and be ravaged by commonplace fears and so i made my unholy bargain with the truth and was transported to a stadium where fans were doing the wave

and i was the chief referee for a grand sporting event
and had written the rule book that governed everybodys
behavior during the contest and the game was democratic
and based on a theory of voting and each member of the
two teams had a single vote and could choose which
player on the opposing team should be the designated the
official ball carrier and the individual receiving the
most votes was required to run a gauntlet through the
fifty members of the rival squad all of whom were
equipped with referee approved and league sanctioned
razor sharp knives and the idea of the game was to see
how far down the narrow corridor of stabbing and slashing
competitors the official ball carrier could get before
collapsing and dying in a heap of guts and there was no
question of surviving but only of gaining the maximum
number of yards before being carted away to a mortuary
behind the stadium and each team always had fifty members
because after the death of a player the population on
one side of the stadium would vote for one of their own
to be sent onto the field to replenish their team and
this was considered a great honor and after the death of
an opposing player the fans for the other team would
vote for their candidate and after a ball carrier was
removed from the stadium the box office would sell a
single admission ticket for an exorbitant price so that
there was always the exact same number of spectators and
players and the democratic game went on without let up
year after year and huge amounts were spent on promotion
and nobody on the outside realized what was going on on
the inside since all that could be heard were perpetual
cheering and the hubbub of the fans and each individual
on entering the stadium and receiving an identification
number and hearing the gate clang shut might wonder if
he had made an error and it would dawn on him after
years or decades that he was bound to wind up on the
field and might be stabbed and slashed to death since to
garner the honor of descending to the playing field as a
substitute was akin to winning the lotto of self
destruction and yet the promotion of each fan to the
rank of player was greeted with mass applause although
from time to time an errant individualist would raise
his voice in stormy protest but whenever that happened
then certain perverse and resentful counterespionage
fans who were in the pay of the promoters would vote for

the beleaguered protester so that he would leap to the
front of the balloting and wind up joining one of the
teams where invariably for some inexplicable reason he
would become the first player to run the murderous
gauntlet and so everyone was held in line and the game
proceeded according to my rules which was gratifying
because i had been hired by unnamed financial interests
to invent not just the rulebook but the game itself and
i even orchestrated the cheers of the cheerleaders and
once the game had been invented there was no stopping
anything and given that a reasonable number of lucky
players were never singled out to run the gauntlet
through the course of fifty ballots they were thereupon
allowed to leave the stadium and the crowd would
accompany their exits with exuberant grunts and hosannas
and a secret hope was kindled in the breasts of the
delirious fans that it was possible to win the democratic
game of survival by maintaining an impeccable
invisibility which was the unspoken subtext of the
entertainment phenomenon and the spectators in the
stands began to practice conformity in preparation for
their elevation to the status of players so that they
would run the best possible chance of getting out of the
stadium in one piece and it was because of this necessity
of remaining virtually unnoticeable that the game
progressed as smoothly as it did but the truth was much
more gruesome than the reality known to the spectators
because the game didnt allow for the liberation of
survivors and provision had been made for the immediate
exile of those who had beaten the odds and the surviving
team players on exiting the stadium were immediately
arrested and taken to a kangaroo court where they were
convicted of precisely fifty murders which it was not
difficult to prove since they had been allowed to keep
their official blood coated razor sharp league sanctioned
knives as mementos and these mementos were used as
evidence against them and the hapless team members were
flown to a clearing in a rain forest of a central
american country called stabonia and each survivor was
branded on his forehead with the identification number he
had received when he first entered the stadium and was
handed back his knife and dropped into the clearing
which was many miles in diameter and there were stabonian
farm implements for each of the sports team survivors

although the agricultural situation was terrible because
the topsoil of a cleared rain forest is notoriously thin
and what with the heat and yellow fever mosquitoes and
the fact that there was no law enforcement most of the
sports team survivors expired quickly as a result of
inanition or disease or stabbing by the more hardened
survivors of previous contests because the commonwealth
of stabonia was founded on the principals of a grim
natural selection and if a sports team member were to
venture outside the compound he was immediately gunned
down by right wing guerrilla insurgents who were in the
pay of the sports team promoters but as the chief referee
i was the only one who was aware that the only way out
of the stadium was to live with a branded forehead in a
steamy jungle clearing by stabbing to death anybody who
challenged ones ability to collect vegetables and this
was the logical outcome of the democratic sporting
contest and it was possible for me to change the rules
of the contest at any time because the owners of the
sporting teams trusted me implicitly and had made
considerable fortunes by allowing me to construct the
rules according to my own wishes and certain gifted
tabloid spin doctors had been hired to advance the
reputations of members on the playing field who were
especially proficient in staying alive but as soon as the
journalists would hype a particular individual for
having avoided being chosen that individual would almost
immediately be picked out of spite so that publicity was
equated with instant death and after a few years of
officiating i realized that nobody ever went to the
bathroom or required food or sleep and it surprised me
that i hadnt realized before that i must have been
operating on the basis of metaphor and that the
situation i had created was a lame conceit for crowd
control or contemporary totalitarianism under the guise
of freedom or human evil or the brute power of the group
to root out any form of human excellence or individualism
but the bottom line was that the corporate sponsors and
owners and landlords who rented out the stadium and
journalists and trainers and coaches were satisfied with
my stupendous achievement and the bloodshed seemed
beside the point because when somebody died the fans
would reinterpret the tragedy in personal terms by
commenting that that particular individual didnt have

what it took or his legs were too short or he didnt
deserve to be so popular in the first place and yet there
were a number of occasions when individual players
refused to play the game and would not hold on to the
ball but would drop it and try to run out of the stadium
and such despicable behavior would send the crowd into a
frenzy and these ignominious cowards were forced to be
groundskeepers and clean up bodies and remove the blood
from the artificial turf with special detergents that had
been developed by chemical firms that formed part of the
owner combine and eventually i acquired enough money to
buy a cottage in the country and live out the rest of
my life in superannuated quiet and was given a
commemorative plaque that was autographed by all the
managers who had told me what to do and i hung it over
my mantel and in my more devout moments expressed my
gratitude for having been given the ability to live a
productive life as part of a larger society and one
night i fell asleep by the fire and found myself locked
in a cell block and there was one prisoner per cell
but the cells werent actually cells but more like
honeycombs and the prisoners werent actually prisoners
but more like bees who for all practical purposes were
identical to one another in looks and behavior and the
guards were identical to the prisoners although their
features seemed slightly more malicious and less
developed and i would constantly check my body because i
was terrified that i would change until i was
indistinguishable from everyone else and one day i saw
that the unforeseen had happened and all of the prisoners
were uniformly and slowly changing into me and this was
disturbing although i couldnt decide why because it
wasnt my problem if others wanted to imitate me and i
saw that all of the prisoners were staring at me fixedly
without blinking and that by looking at me they were
able to absorb my identity and so i started staring back
but realized that to do so would risk my changing into
them by the same natural laws that allowed them to
change into me so that in either case the same result
would occur and yet there was another possible
explanation for this phenomenon of change which was that
i was changing into them but that at the same time that
my identity was changing my knowledge of what my
identity was was changing as well so that i was under

the illusion that the prisoners were changing into me
but in truth i was changing into them while thinking
that they were the ones who were changing and
consequently i pretended that none of them existed and
one day the doors of the cells slid open and we were
forced to march single file to the main yard where a
plank extended over a huge cauldron of scalding red hot
chili oil and one by one the criminals jumped into the
vat and boiled themselves to death and all of the
prisoners seemed resigned to their fate as if they were
identical soup ingredients and soon it was my turn to
walk onto the plank and i realized with a sigh of relief
that the reason everybody had worked so hard to become
like me was to aid me through the trepidation of this
dive because i could take solace that others just like
me had gone before me and others just like me would
follow in my footsteps and so i jumped into the seething
mass of peppery bubbles and saw insulated fish swimming
through the parboiled dumplings of the bodies of the
convicts and awoke in front of my fireplace with a much
better feeling about the brotherhood of humanity and
rubbed my eyes and yawned and on the table next to my
adjustable chair was a deed of purchase for an ancient
tree i had bought which aside from having curative
powers if one chewed the leaves was an aesthetically
perfect specimen and although i didnt own any of the
land surrounding the tree yet i had obtained an easement
from neighboring property holders which allowed me
constant access and i was proud of having obtained the
right to call this tree my own and read my ownership
document with satisfaction but suffered a severe shock
when i discovered in the small print that my right of
easement was only a right of standing easement and not a
right of sitting easement and that the lawyers who
drafted the document had overlooked the fact that i
needed sitting rights because i intended to hire a
security firm to guard my property in order to make
certain that nobody poached a seed or graft or leaf or
scarred or even touched my tree with their fingers
without permission but all of the security firms within
an acceptable radius had been forced through political
chicanery and raw economic coercion to hire union labor
and their contracts were uniform in requiring that each
of the guards have a place to sit for at least fifty

minutes every hour and there was no way i could trust an
unbonded watchman to look after my interests and i didnt
want to have to go back to the surrounding land owners
because to do so would have involved financial ruin since
they had formed a cabal that owned all the property
extending out for miles from the trunk of my tree and on
the other hand it would have cost a small fortune to
bribe the security firms into evading union rules because
if they were caught they would suffer a work stoppage or
incur prohibitive penalties from safety bureaucrats and
i was between a rock and a hard place and realized i
had purchased a white deciduous elephant because if i
couldnt guard the tree then for all intents and purposes
the tree would become public property and my right would
be valueless and when i thought of the acres of rain
forest that had to be cleared in stabonia in order for
me to earn my tiny percentage commission on the
entertainment deaths of all the sports team players
which allowed me to buy my single tree i became
infuriated and was having trouble enjoying my cottage and
even more trouble sleeping because i was obsessed and
was forced to devise a long term strategy while i sat by
the fire burning my logs and although the tree was a
practical investment only in cases where one was bitten
by a black widow spider because the leaves of the tree
were a natural antidote for this particular type of
infection yet there wasnt anything else that would
possibly motivate your average john doe to lay out a
considerable sum of money to replace me as tree owner
and the tree couldnt be syndicated or franchised or
leased or funded or leveraged or optioned or hypothecated
or condoed or bartered or mortgaged or amortized or
incorporated or subordinated or liquidated or litigated
or downstreamed or upstreamed or sidestreamed and it
couldnt be monopolized or promoted or produced and
directed or commercialized or marked up or down because
it was nothing but what it essentially was and my
ownership was a polite fiction created by an institution
of government which in itself was a polite fiction and
although the tree was an overpowering work of divine
beauty that had been worshiped by sophisticated gardeners
for many generations i was forced to cut my losses and
chop it down because an analysis done by a reputable
accounting firm had demonstrated that its removal was the

best economic option and i could get two cents on the
dollar which was better than nothing at all and i owned
my cottage debt free and had been prudent enough to
purchase an annuity which would support me comfortably
for the rest of my life and so i signed a contract for
its removal and sale and carried the contract to my
local banker who sold the instrument to a factor and yet
i was concerned when i considered that economic security
hadnt provided me with any peace of mind because there
was something inherent in money that when applied to the
human condition produced ruthlessness and it occurred to
me that cash accomplishment was a poor substitute for
real accomplishment garnered through increased knowledge
and maturity and that generosity and gratitude and an
overall openhandedness would prove to be a more
satisfying foundation for what little life i had before
me than the ravenous pursuit of wealth and yet i saw
that the exasperating problem with learning to be
generous was that it required emotional growth and that
most people were nailed into their attitudes and that
society was moving in the wrong direction because stupid
people were having all the children and smart people
were becoming increasingly impotent so that year after
year the average human was becoming less and less
capable of understanding not only that he could change
but that he should change and peoples foreheads were
getting lower and lower and their eyes were turning
glassier and glassier and therefore moral improvement
was becoming a practical impossibility because the
planet was uniformly inhabited by degenerate morons and
yet god hadnt granted me the power to change others but
only the power to generate the inner spiritual changes
that were necessary to my own salvation and just as my
tree had fallen in the forest and nobody had known
except for a few distraught and unimportant gardeners
who were trespassers in any case so my moral improvement
would go unnoticed by the surrounding world but would
still be important to the only person who really counted
who was me and i decided to take an inventory of my
faults and spent a number of hours in contemplation
while attempting to determine the nature of my
transgressions and was able to conclude that there were
a number of people that i had hurt in minor ways but
the damage had occurred when i was an idle youth and

resulted from benign neglect or adolescent rashness and
that by the time i had reached my majority id developed
a firm ethical sense that had guided me through my
halcyon years as chief referee and yet i couldnt help
envying the nameless tycoons who paid me my pittance and
underneath it all i seethed with bitterness because id
been treated as a mere employee rather than as a
fountainhead of wisdom and without my ideas there would
have been no game and consequently no profits and i
thought of the spouses and children of the unnamed
investors who never would have to lift a finger to invent
or do anything and would spend their lives in domiciles
much more opulent than my humble cottage and everybody
would flatter these simpering leeches because they were
wealthy even though their good fortune would be based
entirely on my hard work and brainpower and it bothered
me that life was unfair and that handsome guys could
ball the beautiful gals and wealthy snobs could order
people around without thinking twice about the welfare
of others including myself and i tried to imagine a
better world where such behavior was not permitted and
was transported in my minds eye to a standard world
where everyone was dressed in standard clothing and ate
standard food and lived in standard housing and had
standard attributes and standard personalities and
standard bankrolls and standard cars and standard
clothing and was entertained in standard ways and this
place was not much different from the prison which i had
been in when i fell asleep in front of the fire in my
cottage nor was there any significant difference between
this standard society and the society in which i was
raised since a standard language had been developed in
my youth which could only express the most standard
thoughts and feelings and this change in language was a
form of mind control in which all good things were
bargains and all lifes higher meanings were created by
low lifes in corporate offices and the standard community
in which everyone was standard was the standard way of
manipulating the world for fun and profit and my
worldwide fame as a result of the democratic game i had
created meant that i had become standard enough to
achieve standard notoriety and underneath it all i
remained a boring old man in an adjustable chair with
nary an interesting thought in my standard head and i

felt an overwhelming desire to bust out of my mold and
do something daring and quintessentially human before i
cashed in my chips and made contacts through managers
who reported to the promoters who reported to the senior
vice presidents who reported to the directors who
reported to the owners of the investor syndicate who
managed the subsidiaries that sold concessions that had
been endorsed by defunct members of the sports teams and
these managers arranged through connections they had
forged with japanese portfolio administrators of saudi
conglomerates whose shares were held by bolivian generals
residing in a guarded compound of a sweltering west
african metropolis for me to become a recreational
therapist for a safari searching out rare metals in the
swamps of gabon and before joining the expedition i
needed to be refurbished and was referred to a
gerontologist in california who had patented a form of
herbal surgery which removed tired cells from the body
and after a rigorous course of acupuncture and mudbaths
i was given a complete makeover by an assistant to the
herbal surgeon and on arriving in africa was placed in
one of the executive jeeps and the swamps were fens of
quicksand and on descending from the jeep into the sands
i was sucked down so quickly that at one moment i was
opening my eyes into a brand new herbalist state of
utter rejuvenation and the next moment my eyes were
sinking below the liquid sands of gabon and my pith
helmet was hovering on top of my descending body but i
remained elated because i knew i would be fossilized and
spend hundreds of millions of years without pain but
error as a rule is intrinsic to speculative thought
processes and as my body descended and the pressure of
the mud increased i was frozen in the inner space of the
quicksand and began to harden and although a situation
couldnt have been created with fewer options yet my
predicament had resulted directly from my desire to blow
it all out and the irony of my situation as i sank into
the terrestrial gabonese deprivation chamber was no
different from the irony of any other situation and the
only escape from the consequences of my physical
immobilization was through humor which is a form of
religious faith because the essential aspects of human
life meet at the tangible surfaces of self deprecation
and the grandeur of the sun is a cosmic joke especially

as viewed from the gummy interior of an african mud
puddle and it is impossible to be meaningful without
making fun of oneself since its like the heisenberg
uncertainty principle where velocity is meaning and
position is humor and if one is purely humorous then life
has no meaning and if one is purely meaningful than life
has no humor and yet humor and meaning are always there
and i concluded as my body continued to change into
pavement that nothing should be taken seriously and i
continued to sink into the quicksand and the pressure
was enormous and i felt a strange sensation as if
somebody had turned a hose on my feet and the hose began
to move up my legs and then to my waist and the lower
half of my body was rinsed in a gush of water and
suddenly i popped loose of the muck and fell into an
underground sewage system that carried the wastes of
gabonese mining interests towards the sea and there were
fish with sharp teeth and antennae that looked like
chinese lanterns living in the industrial sewage network
and as i plunged through the waste disposal channels
that ran below the steaming jungle the fish congregated
in larger and larger numbers and looked at me quizzically
and i realized with dismay that these were gabonese
lantern piranhas and their shifty eyes were glowing with
hunger and every once in a while a freestanding gob of
rancid flesh came tumbling through the brown liquid and
the piranhas turned their attention toward the loose
meat and within seconds gobbled it up and i couldnt figure
out why they didnt do the same with me and realized that
it must have had to do with my herbally rejuvenated flesh
which wasnt rancid enough to interest the fish and we
were flushed into a harbor of hot salty water and the fish
swam off and i came up for air and made my way in a
leisurely manner toward a ladder that extended over the
edge of a pier and climbed up and found myself in an
amusement park and had to stand in long lines and was
disgruntled because it turned out that the lines
themselves were the rides and when i got to the end of
a line i had to pay for the fun i had enjoyed while
waiting and the lines had names like rollerball and
tiltawhirl and scrambler and why anybody would pay for
the pleasure of being denied pleasure made absolutely no
sense and i was waiting in a line called rocket to the
future and noticed with surprise that others in the line
were sharing an experience that i wasnt a part of and

they would gasp and shriek at the same moment and a fat
woman in front of me put her hands over her eyes and
said oh no not again and people were commenting
appreciatively as they paid at the front of the line
that this particular line was the best ride ever and
there was a man behind me who was seven feet tall and i
pulled him aside and asked him why people had been
gasping and screaming in unison and he explained that
there were stimulators planted in the lines by the
gabonese amusement park managers who were paid to gasp
and that everyone else would gasp at the same time
because nobody wanted to confess they werent having any
fun and i asked how he knew that people were planted in
the lines and he confessed that he was a stimulator
himself and by the looks of me i would make a good
apprentice and he took me to the ride employment office
and i noticed that all the employees were at least seven
feet tall and i was given a job application which asked
for my first name middle initial and last name and my
height and arm length and those were the only blanks on
the form and i realized that the man behind me in line
had singled me out as a possible stimulator because i
had become over seven feet tall as a result of the
softening caused by my herbalsuction treatments followed
by temporary fossilization under extreme quicksand
conditions which had pinched me and transformed my
emolliated body and extended it in new directions and i
was ushered into the personnel managers suite of lavish
offices which contained oversize furniture and was seated
in a mammoth chair and offered a gigantic glass of green
liqueur and saw a beach ball on a chain hanging from the
ceiling in the center of the office and the ceiling was
thirty feet high and after i had quaffed my drink and
engaged in a few minutes of mindless chitchat the
personnel manager said it was time for the job interview
and he went over to the wall and flicked a switch which
lowered the ball so that it was twelve feet off the
ground and he said to me do you think you can swat this
ball if you try and a shiver ran up my spine because i
had heard something similar in the past but i said sure
and prepared myself and jumped up and swatted the ball
easily and he said good we can offer you a job at fifty
thousand dollars a week or i can raise the beach ball a
foot higher and you can try to achieve a higher level of
compensation which is offered to candidates with

extraordinary abilities and i asked what would happen if
i missed the ball at the higher level and he said it
wasnt a big deal and did i think i could swat the ball
if i tried and i said sure id have a go and he raised
the ball and i prepared myself and jumped up and swatted
the ball easily and he said he could now offer me a job
at a hundred thousand dollars a week and i was delighted
because in my wildest dreams while sitting in my
adjustable chair in front of the roaring fire in my
cottage and feeling sorry for myself i had no idea that
my safari would lead to such awesome job opportunities
and i said how much id love to be employed as a
stimulator and he said not so fast did i think i could
swat the ball if it were raised another foot or even two
feet to say sixteen feet and the liqueur had given me
added energy and self confidence which added to my sense
of herbal rejuvenation and i was certain i would be able
to swat the ball and he raised it to sixteen feet and i
prepared myself and jumped up and swatted the ball
easily and he pumped my hand and said that i was a
truly amazing candidate and would be perfect as a
stimulator and he had been authorized to offer me two
hundred thousand dollars a week if i wouldnt be insulted
by such a paltry figure but as compensation for the
insult he could raise the ball to twenty feet and did i
think i could swat the ball if i tried and i asked if
it would be possible to have another liqueur and he said
sure no problem and handed me the bottle and i poured
myself a drink and meanwhile he raised the ball another
four feet and i stood and made a toast to the personnel
administrator who blushed with pleasure and drank down
the liqueur and prepared myself and jumped up and swatted
the ball easily and he shook his head from side to side
in awe and amazement and told me he was empowered to
offer me three hundred thousand dollars a week and asked
me to sit down and relax and have another drink of
liqueur and he got on the telephone and called a number
of other personnel executives who were standing in the
room by the time i had finished my drink and looking at
me with a mixture of wonder and admiration and one of
these executives introduced himself to me as the vice
president and overall potentate of the personnel
department and asked me if i thought i could swat the
ball if it were raised to twenty five feet off the ground
and that if i did i would be paid four hundred thousand

dollars a week and i said sure why not id give it a try
and i put down my liqueur glass and stood up and
prepared myself but as i was in the midst of my mental
and physical preparations i began to entertain doubts
for the first time and wasnt certain that i had a twenty
five foot jump in me and asked the potentate of personnel
if i could still be paid the three hundred thousand a
week if i missed the ball because i still had three
hundred thousand dollar a week stimulation abilities and
the personnel manager said that unfortunately the
original offers were now off the table because i had
agreed to try for a higher level and i began to wonder
whether i was being offered a job at all or whether this
personnel office was in reality an amusement ride but i
put this perverse thought aside and prepared myself and
as i was about to soar into the air the door burst open
and the seven foot stimulator who i had met while
standing in line was yelling that i was a fool and was
being taken advantage of and was in for a big surprise
later that evening and that he was sorry he had led me
astray and if i grabbed his hand he would guide me like
vergil to safety and one of the personnel officers pulled
out a large pistol and shot the stimulator in the side
of the head and he fell to the floor and they encouraged
me to go ahead and jump and so i prepared myself and
jumped in the air and easily swatted the ball and the
men fell to their knees and started praying and thanking
god and said oh lord you are so wonderful and we will
pay you five hundred thousand a week which includes a
sizable saltatory bonus and would you like to swat the
ball one last time and well only raise it a few more
inches and if you swat it we will double your money but
my shoes were wet from the blood of the stimulator and i
said i had had enough and would do my job conscientiously
and they were cordial and said they knew where i was
coming from and that it was wise for a person to
recognize his own limitations and so we signed a contract
and i was directed toward one of the lines and told to
stand there and begin my stimulation routines and the
line was called the mister america buttfucker ride which
made no sense because i was somewhere in africa and i
wondered who mister america was and nobody was allowed
in the line who was over twelve years of age and the
management had dressed me up in leather dominator
clothing in order to disguise my role as a stimulator

and there were hordes of children standing in the line
and i had been instructed to pant and moan which i did
and all the children made panting and moaning sounds in
unison because they had been conditioned at birth to act
like their parents and at a certain point i was told to
yell out do it to me again mister america ram it into
my virgin ass where the sun dont shine which i did and
all of the childrens eyes rolled back in their heads and
they paid their money and hobbled away and i objected
because i thought my job was tasteless and returned to
the personnel office during my coffee break and complained
vociferously but the manager said i should remember that
i was a stimulator and not a perpetrator and that
simulation and stimulation were almost identical words
but two entirely different concepts and i should keep
that bit of corny wisdom in my miniature brain the next
time i wanted to object about a harmless company policy
because nobody got hurt and nothing ever happened and
everybody in west africa was entitled to freedom of
expression and if little children wanted to pay money to
pretend they were getting fucked in the ass well then
that was only in the nature of being a child and such a
ride improved the emotional balance of the kids and
allowed them to adjust gradually and naturally to the
problems of upcoming adulthood and if i complained one
more time i would find myself in the same position as my
stimulator friend who had been blasted in the head by
another stimulator who had been posing as a career
employment officer and if i knew what was best for me i
would get back in line and shut my foul trap and i was
shocked by the changed attitude of the personnel
administrator but i saw his point because he hadnt said
anything that wasnt true and i headed across the
amusement park and saw a sanitation worker pushing a
cart filled with body parts and he was wearing an
identification badge which said gilbert and the letters
dbpofsscre and i asked what that meant and he said that
as an employee of the park i could look up the definition
in a glossary which could be found in the back of the
operations manual which was part of my level three
orientation kit and i opened up my satchel and inside
was my manual along with assorted stimulation items and
on the thirty seventh page of the glossary appeared the
word dbpofsscre and its definition was detached body
parts of failed stimulation swatter candidates removal

employee and so i was grateful i had made it past the
examination and been deemed employable and that evening
i was ushered into my freshly painted luxury apartment
in the amusement park resort condominium complex and i
kicked back and opened a bottle of pinot noir and
weighed whether i wanted to work for people who had
established an amusement park based on weeding out the
weak and murdering them and yet i had accepted my weekly
salary of half a million dollars in advance and so i
felt obligated to work for at least a week as a matter
of principle and i went into my bedroom to go to sleep
and in my bed was a small boy who had been standing in
the buttfucker line in front of me and he asked me to
read him a bedtime story so that he could get in the
mood for amorous endeavors and i said that i had no
interest in making love with him because what i was
doing in line was just a stimulation job but he told me
that he was the son of the owner of the amusement park
and if i didnt tell him a bedtime story he would report
me to his father and that the amusement park had been
named after him and who did i think i was anyway and
what did i think so much money was for and that all of
the stimulators were members of his harem of tall men
and that tall men were hired as stimulators because they
had humongous schlongs and he had slept with all the
other stimulators on multiple occasions and that he
wanted to sample my goodies and i was disgusted but i
thought that i could lose nothing by reading him a story
and he handed me a book called doctor diddle takes a
vacation and i read about a doctor named doctor diddle
whose wife had died as a result of the malpractice of one
of his best friends who was another doctor named dorf
and doctor diddle had killed dorf and embalmed him and
stuck him in a glass case in his basement alongside the
body of his dead wife who was in another glass case and
between the two cases doctor diddle had placed his bed
and he slept with young boys every night between the
glass cases of the two corpses with a huge fixture
containing dripping wax candles hanging over a
mattressless bed of unfinished lumber and the wax would
drip from the fixture and burn the doctor and the boy as
they were making violent passionate love and the pain of
the burning wax would add to the pleasure of the lovers
and doctor diddle was very handsome and had the most
beautiful and longest penis in the world and had a

special friend named louie whom he loved and desired
more than all his other lovemates put together and when
i read the name louie the small boy in the bed next to
me pointed at the word and said proudly that that was
him and that his name was louie and that his father had
hired a famous ghostwriter to write the book and put
louies name on it and i turned to the cover and saw
that indeed the first name of the author was louis and
there were comments on the back of the book made by
world famous authors about what a young genius louie was
and how he had a great future ahead of him and how the
book was a tale of grandeur and about the sacred craft
of the writer and of little louies flare for poetic
utterance and louis told me that he had won a number of
important awards for this book and for another book that
he had done later with the help of the same writer
entitled the return of doctor diddle from his vacation
and that he had received a grant from the gabonese
government and a genius award from an important african
foundation and the promise of a tenured teaching job
when he reached adulthood and that his father had had
nothing to do with it and he swore to me that nobody
had paid to influence the decisions of anybody and that
the ghostwriter hadnt actually written either book but
had simply been available to answer questions by
telephone about how to spell certain difficult words and
i asked if he wanted me to continue reading but he said
that he had something else in mind and since i needed to
stall for time i asked louie to tell me what kind of
vacation doctor diddle eventually took and he said the
answer was obvious and that he had taken a vacation at
the amusement park that louies father owned but that
this was a sheer coincidence because the story required
certain special attributes of a vacation destination
that could only be matched by the attributes of louies
fathers park and that each of the important rides in the
park were described in detail in the book which
increased the sales of books and admission tickets and
louis got out of bed and knelt down and folded his hands
and said his prayers while i waited in bed and he prayed
that i would be gentle with him and only hurt him as
much as he wanted to be hurt and that god would watch
over his father who was watching over him right now
through a camera that was mounted in the ceiling of the
bedroom and i was shocked but waited until little louie

had finished praying for world peace and an end to disease
and famine and for the health of all his lovers and then
i asked him what he meant when he said that his father
was watching through a hidden camera and he said that
this was literally true and that his father tuned in
every night and monitored little louies activities
because he was a responsible parent and wanted to make
certain that louis was all right and a few weeks ago one
of the newer stimulators had been unable to maintain an
erection and little louie had begun to cry and a team of
dbpofsscres had rushed into the bedroom of the
stimulator with chain saws and hauled him away but that
little louis didnt know what the initials on the
nametags of the sanitation workers stood for and he had
assumed that the impotent stimulator was taken to
another condominium that contained a smaller bed and i
felt humiliated because i was being required to perform
sex on a youngster for money and began to wonder whether
i was capable of maintaining an erection myself and
whether the amusement park was actually an amusement
park at all and perhaps a charade had been concocted to
satisfy the sexual appetite of this youngster and all
the people standing in line were actors and the only·
open job in the park was to be a stud for this lascivious
pampered kid and i decided to forego the money and make
a run for it and excused myself to brush my teeth and
there was a ventilation duct in the bathroom and i
climbed in and started crawling and cold air was blowing
in my face as i worked my way along the metal duct and
what had been a distinct advantage for me in acquiring a
job at the amusement park had now become a liability as
my elongated body was knicked and cut and i felt myself
moving through a space time warp because the metal lost
its surfaces and bars of energy hummed around me and the
air in my face no longer seemed like air but molecules
possessing airlike qualities and i came to another grate
and removed it and wiggled into the cockpit of a
spacecraft where two astronauts were buckled into seats
that were facing me and sitting next to me was a
headless man fiddling with his harness and a stump of
spinal cord emerged from his neck wound and strands of
vein and muscle extended over the edge of the cut skin
and the rest of the neck was smooth red meat and through
my headphones i could hear the countdown and as the
vehicle was launched i could feel the g force ripping

at my muscles and it felt as though someone had punched
me in the stomach and my eyelids were forced so far back
that i feared my eyeballs would bust out of their sockets
and my nose was flattened against the bones of my head
and my testicles were jammed against my seat cushion and
my ankles ached and the nails in my fingers and toes were
pushed into their cuticles and there was a pane of
superresilient clear material opposite me and i could
see the craft moving into space and the weight lifted
and it was time for the forcible ejection of one of the
astronauts and a bottle on a spindle was spinning in the
center of the four of us and began to slow until we
could make out its contours and it went slower and slower
and i asked the pilot of the ship what the significance
of the bottle was and he said that when the bottle
rested pointing at one of the four of us then the
equipment of the spacecraft would be thrown into gear
and the astronaut at whom the bottle was pointing would
be ejected at such an amazing speed that the sliding
ejection door would only open long enough to let the
astronaut pass through but not long enough to lower the
air pressure in the cabin one iota and the violence of
this ejection would hurl the astronaut tens of
thousands of miles into the void and the astronaut would
explode because none of us was wearing pressurized suits
and be turned into the thinnest possible mist and as the
pilot was talking the bottle was pointing directly at me
but i saw that it was still moving in the direction of
the man with no head and i prayed fervently that it
would keep moving because i didnt care much about the
welfare of the grotesque being in the seat next to me
and i turned and cursed him and said maliciously that i
hoped he would die and the bottle was barely pointing at
me and was moving so slowly that i couldnt imagine its
getting past me before it stopped and my harness was
locked so that it was impossible to get away from the
ejection equipment and the pilot and copilot were
laughing at my predicament because they knew there was
no way the bottle had the momentum to keep moving until
it was pointing at them and i was furious that they had
such terrible manners and as the bottle began to slow to
a standstill i rebuked them and said that my curse would
stay with them and haunt the spacecraft and poison their
future activities and that after i exploded in outer
space i would return as a ghost and i would sleep with

their accursed wives and lovers and mothers and
daughters by coming to them and raping them in their
dreams and there would be nothing that either man could
do about it and i would assume horrible shapes and cause
horrendous accidents through magical afterdeath powers
and i assured them as the bottle continued to slow to a
standstill that they deserved such a rigorous lesson for
their crude behavior in laughing at the possibility of
my demise and i looked down and saw that the bottle was
about to break out of my ejection zone and was trajecting
toward the zone where it would be pointing at the
headless hunk of meat sitting next to me and i started
to worry that the headless man would do to me what i
had threatened to do to the pilot and copilot because
after all i had cursed the meat hunk who sat nonchalantly
tapping his fingers against his arm rest and seemed
oblivious and the bottle came to a halt and as a result
of the quickness of the ejection mechanism it seemed
that the headless astronaut had disappeared whereas in
fact he had been ejected and the pilot and copilot
explained that they were laughing because they had
played a joke on me and the spin the bottle mechanism
had been preprogrammed to point at the meat hunk and the
most important part of their mission was to eject this
hunk of guts into space because he was a distinct
liability on earth where he had roamed at will and was
accused of mercilessly destroying people for years and
had proven indestructible and there was no way he could
have been eliminated aside from extraterrestrial ejection
and the meat hunk was now at least ten thousand miles
away and outside the earths gravitational pull so that
even if he didnt burst he would float forever and
consequently everyone could now rest easy and as the
pilot and copilot were gloating over their sick joke at
my expense we heard clanging on the outside of the ship
and through the transparent window i saw one of the
hands of the meat hunk pounding against the hull and
every time he pounded he rattled the spacecraft and the
concussion of his fist made the lights in the spacecraft
dim and the air supply system began to falter as the
hunk kept bashing but the pilot and copilot stayed
composed and radioed down to mission control in arkansas
and requested further instructions and were told to
initiate plan seven three eight e four because the
thinkers at the central command post had fed every

possible circumstance into a supercomputer that was also
used to predict weather patterns and the computer had
listed the meat hunks swimming instantly back to the
ship as one of the possible unfavorable outcomes and
provided a plan to be executed by the astrogation team
in order to counter the effects of the pounding and my
harness came loose and i was lifted from my chair by the
two men and placed in a closetlike chamber at the back
of the spacecraft and could feel my body being annealed
with insulation material from head to toe that permitted
me to breath and speak because it was gummy and had
small pores that allowed for the passage of sound and
air and i was told that i was going to be thrust into
space and that once outside the ship my job was to nego-
tiate with the meat hunk to get him to swim away and
look for options elsewhere in the universe and i repeated
my threat to the pilot and copilot that if anything
happened to me i would haunt them and would fuck their
wives and children and make them accident prone so that
eventually they would be paralyzed or blinded as a
result of some stupid engineering mistake and i could
see through the glass door of my insulation chamber that
this worried the men who in spite of being astronauts
were plagued by ancient superstition and they contacted
the arkansas command post who contacted somebody else
because neither the scientists nor the meteorological
bubble computer had foreseen the possibility that i
would curse the people in the spacecraft and i went a
step further and cursed the people in the space command
post and told them that i also would fuck the space
executives wives and daughters and lovers and make them
asthmatic and miserable for the rest of their natural
born days and the pilot and copilot received a message
from the surface of the earth saying that i should be
removed from the chamber and seated in my chair and they
put the harness on me and i noticed that the insulation
material had dissolved and i breathed a sigh of relief
until i looked down and saw that the bottle was whizzing
in circles and the pilot and copilot were no longer
sitting but were floating aft of the seats and laughing
uproariously and since i was the only one in a chair it
was a foregone conclusion that the arkansas computer had
decided to throw a rat fuck into me and i would be
ejected into space without any insulation which i
immediately was and in a split second i exploded but

instead of dissolving in outer space i became a restless
ghost in inner space and no longer inhabited the body of
a retired referee but was a vibrant and youthful and
horny nude spirit beneath percale sheets in a suburban
neocolonial residence in suburban little rock and the
faithful wife of the copilot of the spacecraft was about
to hop into bed and go to sleep and i knew that she
couldnt see me because i would only be visible in her
dream shell and she had to descend into a world of loose
psychological images for me to penetrate her defenses
and seduce her and she was beautiful and had large
perfect breasts and smooth long legs and perfect feet
and slim shoulders and a rock firm ass and i became even
more excited because i realized that within her dream
shell she would imagine herself to be a defenseless
virgin and try to get away from me because she would
think that she had to save herself for her astronaut
husband but deep inside she would be aching for my body
and would give herself to me completely and because i
was a spirit being i would be able to control every fiber
of her response and during the time i was in bed within
her dream shell she would be totally possessed by me and
i could have my way with her and ravage her virginity
and she would never forget the experience because she
would come in her sleep with a force and energy that
would totally alter her future waking states and sex
would never be the same and never as good as what i
would perpetrate upon her tender virgin body in her
defenseless dream state because i would do everything
exactly the way she wanted and she would lose all
rational ability to judge what was happening to her and
would respond at her deepest level with devotion and
when her husband returned from his voyage after having
disposed of the meat hunk she would never again be
satisfied with his dismal sex routines and would start
hanging around the astronaut training center looking for
studs who could approach but never achieve the level of
rapport with her body that i was about to attain when
she fell asleep and her marriage would be ruined and she
would confess to her husband when she asked for divorce
that a sexual ghost adonis had come to her one night
while her husband was being an asshole on the spacecraft
and had ravished her and enslaved her soul and shown her
through the force of his seductiveness that her husband
who she always thought was an intrepid explorer was

instead a foul mouthed yokel with a bad sense of humor
who liked to taunt innocent referees who were fleeing
malicious children and the copilot would think back on
what i had said and be terrified that i would eventually
make him drop things or become paralyzed and i assured
myself that he deserved what he got for treating me with
such disdain when i was strapped in my harness and
watching the bottle whiz around and he had thought he
was free to be the malicious petty yokel prick that he
was without negative consequences whereas in fact i was
preparing to do the deed with his beautiful wife and she
fell asleep and i entered her consciousness and over a
period of several hours i savaged her in a state of
utter bliss and couldnt wait to inhabit the beds of the
three gorgeous daughters of the pilot and there was a
junior executive at space command central who had a
mature yet luscious mother who possessed incredible
sexual technique and i was going to have a blast with
her as well and clearly saw that a disembodied spirit has
more fun than corporeal beings because the dead have no
limits to the fulfillment of their desires and can use
the living in the same way that children manipulate
dolls and yet as i lay in bed with the sated wife of
the copilot i realized that death is a comfort to the
living because it provides the mind with necessary
boundaries and i panicked because i couldnt see any end
to my vengeful responsibilities and thought back to when
i had blasted apart in space and my corpuscles had
arched into vast walls of sparkling matter and my
personal light had been released and shone among the
other lights of the universe and i suddenly regretted
that the darkness of my curse had caused such a terrible
transformation of this liberated energy and driven it
between the percale sheets of the bed of the copilots
wife in little rock where i became wedded to the
debauched spirits of the sublunary world and my
ruminations rubbed the gloss off my sexual conquest and
i was ready to move in new directions but a ghost is
driven through a maze of former values and cant escape
its labyrinth of prior intentions and i felt that
because of my shenanigans with the copilots wife i owed
it to humanity to perform good deeds and decided to
rematerialize as a holy man and pray continuously for
the salvation of my fellow beings and i showed up the
next day for work as a dishwasher in a french restaurant

and a strange language came out of my mouth that no one
understood including me and i wanted to curse my fate
but i couldnt understand what i was saying or what i was
cursing and the cooks were screaming at me because id
been daydreaming about my night with the copilots wife
and suddenly i resented that id lost my chance to sleep
with the three beautiful daughters of the pilot and with
the mother of the space executive but instead had
voluntarily placed myself in the greasy galley of a
french kitchen because i wanted to do the world some
useless good and i didnt feel particularly holy and
couldnt understand what the cooks were yelling about and
decided i had nothing to lose and yelled back and
effortlessly framed sentences that made no sense and
realized i must have had a defective rematerialization
and come back to earth at the bottom of society and i
saw that my projected notions of saintliness were
ludicrous since i was nothing but a babbling dishwasher
and wouldnt be of value to anybody until i pulled myself
up by my greasy bootstraps and i held up an object and
identified it by saying the first word that came into my
mind and i learned the unnamed languages words for fork
and then spoon and knife and cup and saucer and then
fuck you you pretentious piece of french shit and a
weird phenomenon occurred in that every time i learned a
word in my own language i learned the same word in every
other language that was spoken everywhere by everyone at
every time so that by saying fork in my unnamed language
i gained the ability to say fork in english kurdish
french old norse spanish russian mandarin latin baluchi
yiddish finnish urdu tagalog ugaritic swedish hindi
parsee armenian korean linear b and every other
conceivable language and yet if a cook pointed out what
the word for sausage was in french i couldnt get the
saucisson to stick in my head but it would come out as
sucksuck or soossissoon until i learned the word in my
own master language and then instantly and effortlessly
i would know how to say sausage a thousand different
ways and after a year of washing dishes i was truly
omnilingual and could say anything to anyone and didnt
want to waste any more time washing dishes given my
newfound abilities and felt like a wildblossom in the
wilderness shedding tears of dew with nary an
appreciative eye but realized to my dismay that although
i could say anything i couldnt say anything original

since i still had the intelligent quotient of a
dishwasher and decided that i was perfectly suited by my
mental limitations to become a psychotherapist and so i
claimed to have graduated from the most prestigious of
viennese therapeutic institutes with a postdoctoral
certificate in functional parameter transformative
reaction analysis and was able to open a clinic in geneva
that catered to a distinguished international clientele
and whenever a patient asked a question i responded with
a question of my own and without having to think much
about anything i was able to drive a benz and wear custom
suits and purchase a stunning home and join an exclusive
club where i could play gin rummy with my sicko
jetsetting clients and regardless of which languages i
spoke i always said the same things and everyone thought
i was brilliant and their lives got better and i learned
a lesson from my new occupation which was that almost
every patient was a fool no matter what language he
spoke and yet there was a hole in my gut because
everything i stood for was a lie and shame smoldered in
my breast and it took all of my energy to keep from
blushing or destroying myself and i thought back
nostalgically on my days as a babbling dishwasher when i
had worked so hard to learn the language i was speaking
and i yearned for a more positive existence and i had
two clients who were twins and cordially hated each
other and i saw them separately and whatever constructive
change took place in one twin would cause an opposite
change in the other so that when the former twin finally
came to the realization that she was in love with
her mother the latter twin came to a simultaneous
realization that he was in love with his father and
when the first twin confidentially admitted to me that
she was a man and had had sex with her brother the
second twin admitted that he was a woman who was
incapable of anything but a lesbian relationship with
his sister and that when they had slept together it was
like a new form of biology and was a mind blowing
experience replete with cultural significance whereas the
first twin who was a woman who claimed she was a man
had said that the sex she had had with her brother who
was fully intent on identifying as a lesbian had been a
total and utter drag and that the act of intercourse had
shown her or him depending on ones point of view that
all the various forms of pleasure were void of higher

Marty S Goodman
died trying to
save the life
of Herbert Cl
ark who was
wading in a
river. Death
by drowning

The ideal citizen of a capitalist system is a castrated man with a bulging stomach.

Looking backward, we see nothing but emptiness; while looking forward, we experience this emptiness as fear.

The greatest cause of sadness in contemporary man has been the destruction of the myth of his own uniqueness.

The ultimate insult to the sanctity of art will come when the dilettante is theorized into the position of creator.

Every day something new in us begins to die.

When we all speak the same language, share the same tasteless products, get the same haircuts, wear identical fashions and drive the same world-car into the standard driveways of the same affordable dwellings, we won't be able to tell each other apart and when we get angry, we'll just jiggle around a bit.

The most noble of men is the committed philosopher.

The twenty-first century war will consist of humane and painless kills.

Confucius said: When two people understand each other in their inmost hearts, their words are strong and sweet like the fragrance of orchids. This is the perfect bond with which to cement a society.

The illusion of progress is maintained by the progressive strengthening of illusion.

If you wish a young man to commit a crime, march him to the act in a uniform.

Trent Cutter died trying to save the life of Amelia Cutter who fell in a lake. Death by Drowning.

Cynda

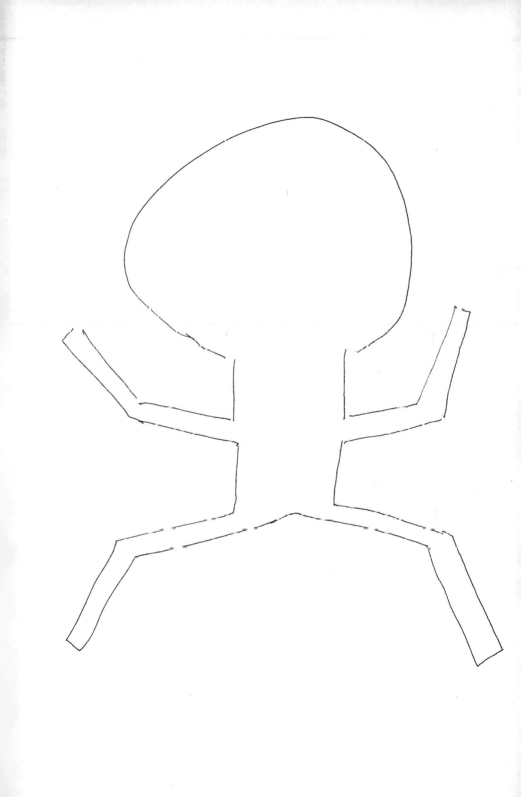

Bobby, take me make me shudder.
feed me the light and the wind, lover

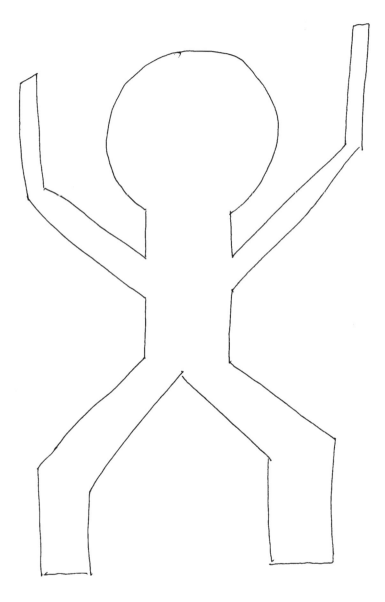

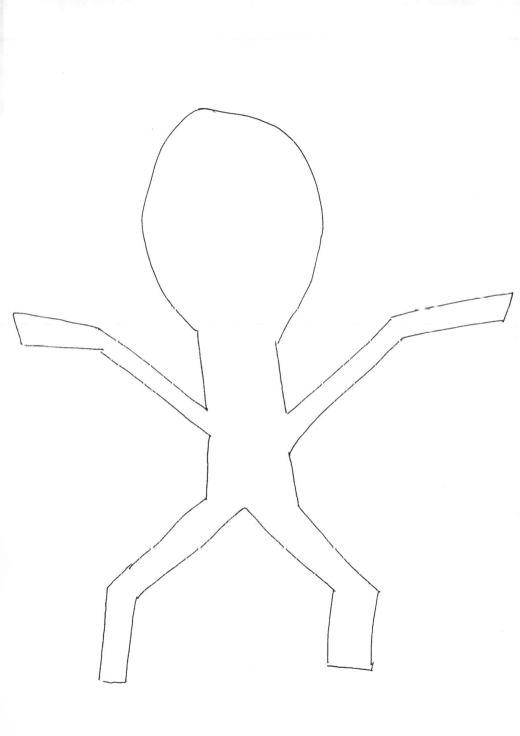

no ache is more refined: the bitter wind
atop the heron's wing sheds less light

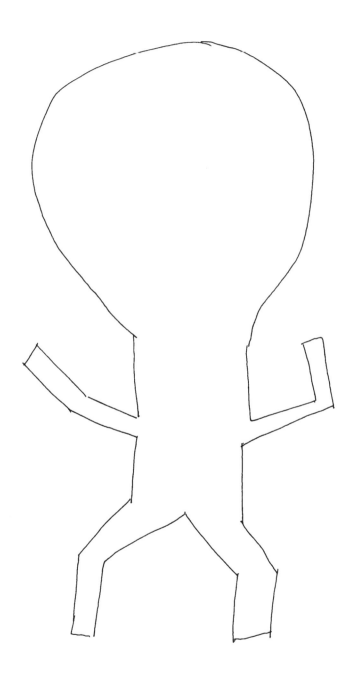

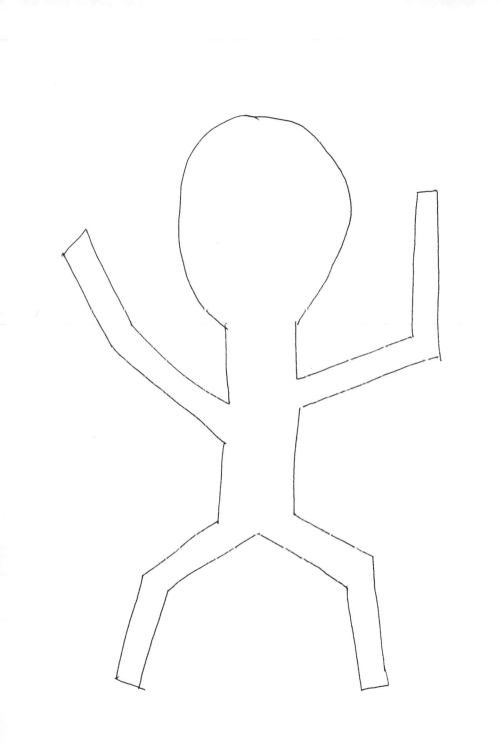

i am the breeze's shaft, the blanket
on a star, the tremulous core of your kisses

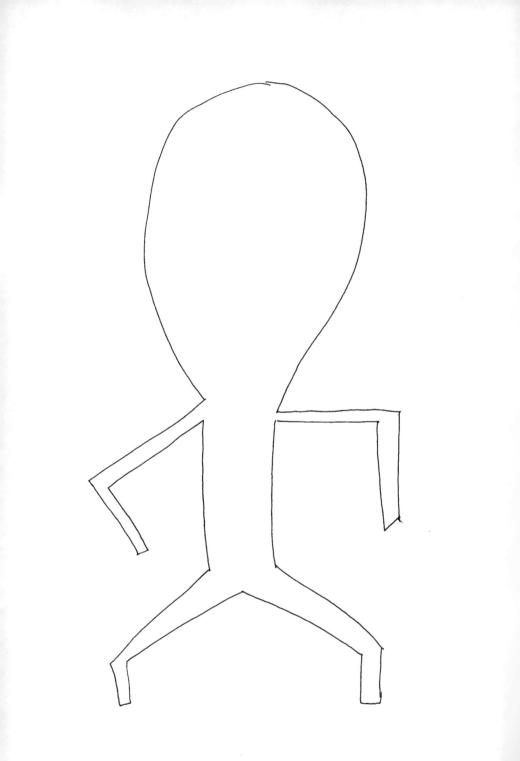

hush! silence! let my sweet Bobby
sleep at the damp feet of rainbows

our love is a wind-swept nest in the rain
where flicker the radiant souls of birds

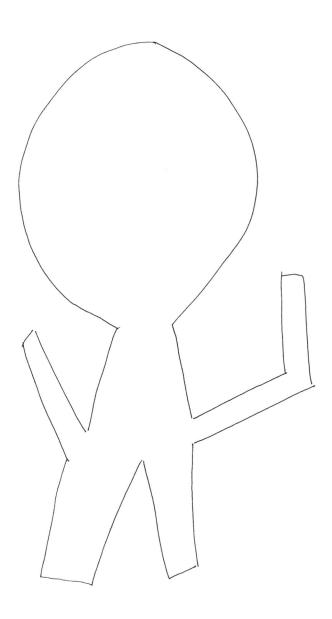

we glide through a tangle of river blossoms
as peach petals mount in the orange currents

in your arms the stars turned fresh. the moon
breathed for the first time through cold glass

my pregnant lap is filled with innocent
and child-bearing psalms

laughter tumbles through the crystal gates
of summer: our joy is never silent

sing me a song of divine solace
and of the touchless dreams of mirrors

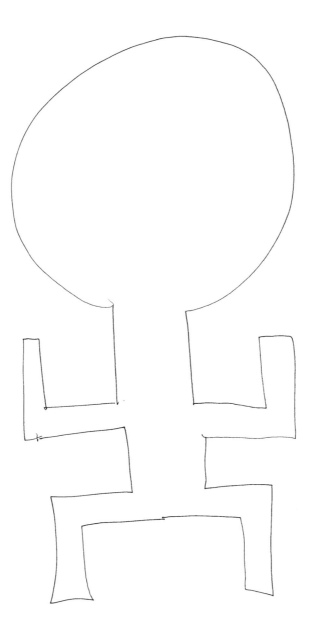

no wind, no sound. no sun, no light.
without your pleasure, no heat, no life

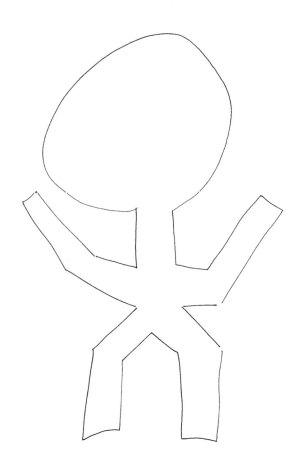

we are chaff in the light of barns whose
afternoons shift weightless into nothing

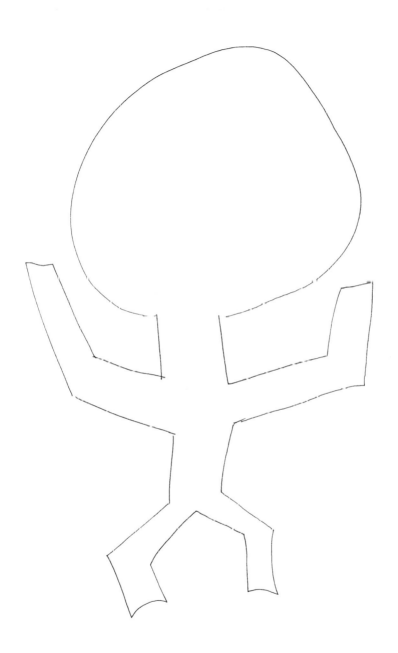

bathe me in an infinite blueness
of pure ecstatic clouds

after death the free roam, thoughtlessly
worshiping stones and bright bits of moss

trembling pools of opal flare:
my dampened hair unfurls within your hair

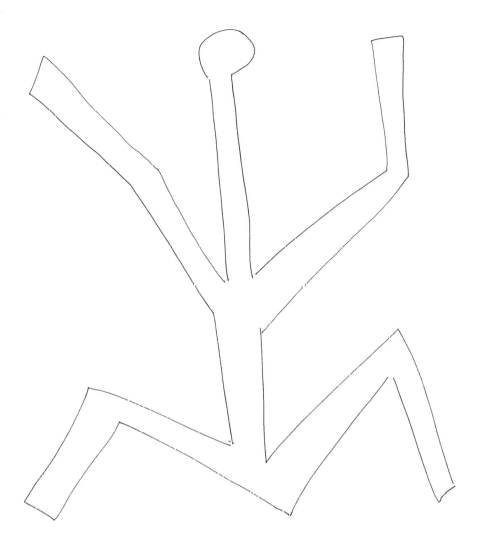

I lie in a cold crush of stems. i am
wet with tears and am become light

your youthful skin is harvest corn
whose fragrance rises slowly in the bins

Bobby, kiss me in the frailest
interface of shadows

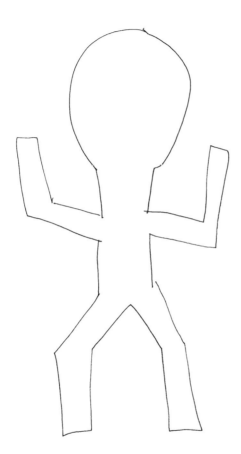

you are blood and bones within me:
glowing nameless warmth

shine within my dream of you,
my love forever, Bobby

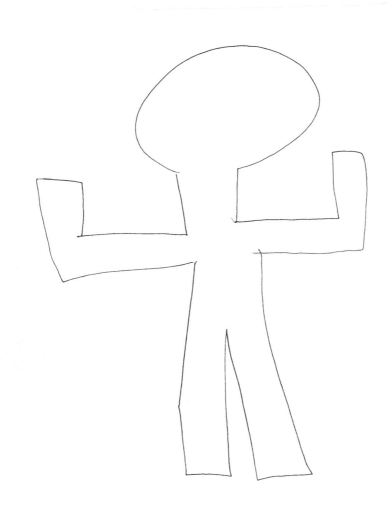

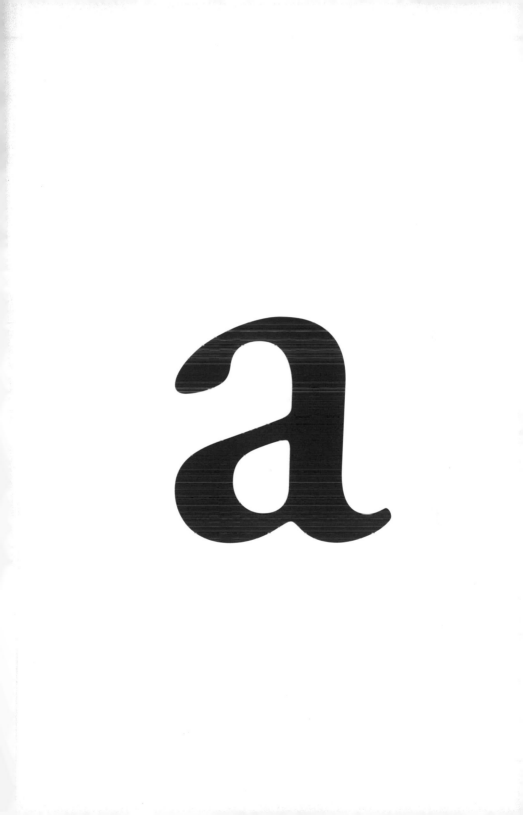

Joseph Langols died trying to save the life of Issiac Mohammed who was running down the street. Death by bullets.

In order to get ahead in this country, one must shake the right hands, keep the right secrets, project the right image and pay the proper pipers.

Bystanders are disposable obstacles.

In a world of perfect justice, there would be no need for cash.

The movements of disease among general populations have had a profounder impact on the course of history than the movements of ideas among individuals.

Youthful soldiers are fodder for the toothless gums of ideologues.

Two geniuses alone can fashion a civilization.

Machiavelli said that anyone who makes a profession of goodness in everything must necessarily come to grief, so that we must learn how not to be good. Practically, if one wishes to be constantly good, one has only two choices: to die in the world, like Jesus, or to die from the world, like Buddha.

Every hamlet has its two-bit Cassandra.

McCarthyism never went away. McCarthy was simply disgraced by the new McCarthy's and blacklists were replaced by graylists.

If you cannot sell what you make in America, you will starve unless you are fed.

Suyamol Suk
badee died trying
to save the life
of Witichai
Bujonkit who
was swimming
in a lake. Death
by drowning

Mitch

The impulse to help others is a mad impulse, and I've had to admit in my sobriety that I only wanted to help myself, to rescue myself from my own pit of helplessness. But surprise! to take on the brute forces of injustice is to enter an unbearable realm of meaning. Life is neither heaven nor hell. It is merely absence and must be lived without satisfaction. My philosophy has been to make the best of a bad situation. Unfortunately, kindness in the face of ugliness becomes abstracted. This is the lesson of the Cross. The true tragedy of Christ is that He was turned into a symbol. We are forced to seek redemption where redemption is an absurdity, which is why my only option turned out to be heroin. Heroin is mental money.

The world becomes inconsequential as we huddle over the thinning flames of our pleasure. Then pleasure itself is reduced, the flames become smaller and harder and let off glares that consolidate into tortures cast in universal confusion. I have done my damage and made my amends. I have slowly converted to a deeper faith. The streams of life are turned into rivers that are turned into streams, and water is nothing but water. Before Christ, there was only hell. And yet by dying for our sins, He created the spark of hope that means redemption for the faithful. To be reborn in Christ is to love not for the sake of loving but because love is the highway and release from the endless extension of sin through space and time.

The lowest common denominator of life is waiting. Everyone is continuously waiting. We simmer in a broth of instincts while praying clumsily for someone special to turn down the heat. We are tormented by the inseparability of good and evil. The fully-grown are shoveled into the earth with pure tools, and their blood that lavished the brain is nothing more than false color and a loosening of atoms. The smell of brimstone hangs in the air and drips from clouds. It rises from the ground in plants and is bathed in virtual goodness. We are placed on this stinking globe to leave something behind that was added before we were born. We are here to shed imponderable pasts where nothing can be remembered.

I am an oppressor of oppressors, and my mind is constantly in a whir. Nobody will step on my dignity, and nobody will ever keep me quiet. I cannot expect to find integrity in this world if I possess no integrity myself. Nobody will ever put me down and I'll go to my death standing. The world is a mad palace and nesting place for vermin. I have thought long and hard in this context about the inherent meaning of cash as a store of value and a soporific. Originally, when Gerry and Tubby and I started the brigade, we used to call ourselves White Russians. We didn't believe in saving the lower classes, we believed in eliminating the lower classes. We wanted a depopulated planet. We wanted to establish an aristocracy of culture. We wanted to destroy the institutional framework that was breeding human rats. In this putrid landscape of brain-depleted rodents, the most capable of men are seemingly beyond paradox.

The force of purgation is human evil. We are rarefied by our habits. We must nurture the ability of precise and terrible thinking. We must attack the world of decayed and cheap philosophy. Nothing can ever again be popular.

That is why utopian radicalism disgusts me because purity in revolution is in pure destruction, in making plenty of room for the future, and to work hard is almost to explode. A man who worries about his victims is merely inconsequential whereas dyed-in-the-wool revolutionaries are unaware of why eternal hell is such a big fucking deal. Brutal logic runs beneath their language. It is deranged and real and is muttered instinctively in codes. Most people cannot understand this truth because everything they think is so cardboard and fearful of evil. They have to be fed their presumptions. Now I sit patiently in my living room and wait for death. A patch of small sores mixed with mud. AIDS is an outcome of cravings.

I am losing weight rapidly. My ears are getting large and my chest is caving in. I can no longer open jars. I read and write within the eye of a fecal hurricane, within the flowing gunk of an abscess, within the torpid movements of depression. I pay for these paragraphs with searing headaches, and everything in my life seems strangely unnecessary. I subsist on a diet of herbs, pills and mushrooms.

Bobby and I yammer like old men. Since his talk with the principal he has been battered down. He is enmeshed in vain projects of description. He can't see clearly that life is in tatters. He moves against the flow. His narratives are filled with holes, since most of the people he loves are lodged in troughs. Bobby and I both made the disgusting mistake of trying to fill ourselves with energy. He is a vagrant, and I am the armed fool. I thought that there was salvation in small acts of kindness and meaningless chores, but unfortunately there is only an infinity of smallnesses. It used to be that forty years was a lifetime. The Hebrews wandered in the heat until the last of their generation had died so that a new people could enter a new land. Now a forty-year-old is a callow fool. A grub. A larval cavity.

Most madness is meaningless and even dangerous to meaning, but there is an artistic madness that contains all meaning and can only be felt by the few. This is art: where the mad speak in whispers linked through vacuums. When I think back on the brigade, it's ridiculous that most of us were addicts. Gerry used to maintain that all we wanted was a world with cheaper drugs. Since many of us were writers, I remember Marty saying that ink was also a drug. We pleaded, he said, for psychopathic understanding.

Psychopathic understanding was beamed in from other planets and created Triggons who went to the bathroom once a week. Triggons were the only ones who could understand how fucked up we all were.

Why was it that no one else was into drama? We were all, even Marty, devoid of criminal excitement. Gretchen wanted to be a moll, but only in bed. A hooker with attitude, she was into dress-up. In many ways she was the source of many of our political problems because she was so detached and theatrical that she caused us all to have an unexpected definition. Gerry joked that we should have saved ourselves a lot of effort and merely kidnapped Gretchen. That tying up Gretchen was a profound and devastating revolutionary statement since if Gretchen couldn't paint her nails, the world would slowly come to a halt and the machines of night would quickly destroy themselves. Gerry didn't live much longer after that and neither did Gretchen.

As an aging revolutionary, I have no desire to commemorate death. Bobby fights to keep things in his scarred brain. It's as if he is trying to remember something that none of us ever said. His memory book is a lament for the permanent loss of justice. Writing into strange collapsed places, like accordian pleats, one can only take this thought and pride of his so far. Do men who are dying need clean sheets? We have created a vast system of dependencies.

Being around Bobby, I have made a careful study of poetry. I have seen that there is no predetermined direction to the birth of a word, that words move across the page like beams of random light moving through immense voids of wandering flares. Poems are built like jewels. The intricate structure of his books, spewing from fountains of loss, from muffled chords of history, carefully planned and balanced in a volatile mental space, a consistent zone of meaning, has taught me a certain kind of severity and quietness. We have been through such changes together, our outsides, our thoughts, our character, our devotions, our habits, everything we were has changed. Life can be conquered, but first it has to be abandoned.

I used to choke on bitterness, because the conditions that were universal were sick with humor, and I wanted to smash teeth when only the pain inflicted on others could stop the incessant laughing. Nobody's face was appropriate. I hated myself for acting in the interests of self-interested people so that any system of purity would be automatically corrupted. Many of my friends loved filth, and they loved the taste of urine. They would shoot the most disgusting chemicals and they would fuck animals. They would smash potato-size Turkish cockroaches with fists and paint their lips with the juices. They would tie up their enemies and throw them in cellars and then take them out in the country and dump their bodies. One could not boil it down and make it cute. It couldn't be lauded or televised. One feels total disgust for the lack of self-sufficiency and for the absence of dignity that has forced me to be so theoretical and lonely.

Existence is unmitigated pretension, stupidity and boredom. People are cruel because the body sucks away our morality, and we are burdened with lunkish meat from the very beginning, when we were gobs of squirming flesh. There is no peace of mind, just bad dreams and horrors, indigestion, liver pain, financial betrayals, larcenous hugs, accumulating blindness and unredeemed intercourse among smells of old whiskey. In this, my only refuge has been hypocrisy and the accumulation of wealth. It is true, I admit it now at the end of my life, that I intended from the beginning to run off with the ransom money and that I went to Turkey to set up my business. It doesn't mean that I didn't hate the system and that I wasn't deeply committed to the revolution. The revolution was never about money anyway. That was one of the factors that brought everybody down. I am dying and everyone can kiss my ass.

The world is filled with neotenous goons, staring into computer screens. In Burkina-Faso, and Somalia, in Timbuktu and Patagonia, in Outer and Inner Mongolia, in Sri Lanka and Botswanaland, in every land, the same disgusting, cash-enraptured moral dwarf is sweating his load, staring at blips, robbing the poor and banking his trinket money. The motivating dream is the dream of raw power.

Regression run amok: never being able to step into the same stream twice and never really wanting to. A worldwide absence of refinement. Odyssey razor blades. Iliad vacuum cleaners. George Bush pulling off his undergarments to masturbate, searching for the barest possibility of pleasure in his flaccid cotton member. Everyone is impacted, fucked up, maladroit and ridiculous. But I earned my bundle the only healthy way. I stole it. I had the Canadian export service par excellence, providing Turkish heroin to all the addicts in the great state of Texas and other communities of drug-worship.

The American dream, to soak the poor by selling them cosmetics, spreads like wildfire across the globe because in every society there are scummy nerds, vicious creeps, and beer-bellied robots. They will link together over the next twenty years to forge a new source of information. They will work to subdue inconvenient cravings. They will be sport killers of innocent birds.

Bobby claims that taste, impeccability, sensitivities to tones, colors, words, shapes, the entire undercoating of imagination, are disappearing from the American consciousness, and that the planet is under the temporary tutelage of slaveholder demigods. Imagination is the sworn enemy of the future, the bane of the franchise-holder. To navigate ancient glistening worlds, Ulysses risking everything, to feel everything, when every feeling is new, to be swept away by southern winds, to wade through a dawn of smoking corpses, to spew out columns of overarching solar ions from the brainstem, to blast through the inner framework of creation, to do anything, to think everything, all these impulses, he feels, had forced us into revolution and destruction. We were beyond any hope or frustration. We only had each other in a sense that none of us could enunciate. We struck out at the webs of nightmare, at the world of perfumed chimps, fingering their castanets. The PLB of crude, junkie misanthropes, crusading for humanity! The subtle culmination of sixties thinking! Bobby said it: it was over before we began. To his credit, he never expected better than what he got, in spite of the loss of Cynda and their baby.

Everyone is a phony. The experts talk a good game, say the perfect things, and have the perfect gleams. Everyone is an idiot.

It's raining money. There is a storm of money. People run with their eyes aloft, grabbing the bills as they fall. They bump into each other, they slay each other as they stuff the cash into their pockets. It's a firestorm of money. A blizzard of money. Money! Money! Money! Tumbling money! Everyone is stoned on it, gorged on it. Paupers and plutocrats can never get enough of it. It's universal paper madness. It's rectal ugliness. It's suffocating. It will continue until one man is standing. At the end, one happy man will have control of everyone else's cash. A man surrounded by numerical phantoms. A man who is proud of his middle initial.

This is the singular wisdom of civilization: mankind has given up on being intelligent, on voicing a protest, on even realizing that a protest against this kind of insupportable condition is possible. A thousand soldiers charge a hill and are exterminated. Then it is bought for development. The developer changes the name of the hill to Battleview Estates. The gardeners stumble over broken teeth and casings. Lawyers, accountants, chiropractors, and specialists of all kinds and descriptions move in. Nobody feels superior and everyone is satisfied.

Is there any modern transaction that is sacrosanct? The infrastructure of capitalistic fervor is based on a repetitive and tacky lie. Government, advertising and mating require that truthfulness be a pose. Wars are desert storms, and lying is the projection of internal misunderstanding where evil is being recast and redefined. What have we gained in the past ten thousand years? Longer lives? Actual comfort? We are a lobotomized mould or glue, a sticky paste, a stinking corruption of nature. Stock-exchange tokens.

Sometimes I think that fruits are the opening sores of trees and that all the realms of life could on some deep, perhaps the deepest level, on the most intimate of levels, overcome the procreative urge, rise in protest and eliminate existence through abstinence. Lifelessness as a staged revolt against the God-given, a false warmth with no one getting warm. My rage, it is true, has destroyed my family. I am a blind fury writing in a suburb. I'm almost not human; I'm almost not sane. My disease is strictly an outcome, a means of wound exposition, of staging a living death. I have transcended personal need. I have my plots and fictions. A bag of bones. I am the new Jew, a false identity, a classmate of Bobby's, an old and withered drupe.

Consequently there is nothing to be gained from human structures. Men must be in agreement with the world and with divine mercy. Christ was born among cows and the sheep and the goats. He was laid among the food of animals. The oxen, for a delightful moment, forgot what it meant to be oxen, stars descended into the fields, and passion, for the very first time, was vindicated in the touch of a baby. This is the ideal to be pursued, that in the enflamed core of violent aversion to all things human, in the hatred of one's own skin and muscle, the soul can sing out of judgment, there can be a new freedom and a new sponsorship of the image of God.

Is there sex in hell, and if so, what kind? The comprehensions of the mad are limited by these expressions of the sane. Asylums must be redesigned to allow for full and complete physical involvements. There are madmen who fear the frontal attack of citizens, that the sane will surround the shelters of the mad and toss them out. This has recently happened. In primitive lands there was really no disease, and shamans conversed with the spirits of hunted beasts. There was no need for writing when the bark on the trees could be read as a substitute treatment for decency. Now all good things are hacked out and strange, rational and manipulated, and the mad go begging.

Between any two people there is always new language, but that such an energy would flourish can only occur when the communicants shed their identities, as Bobby and I have done, so that the pure word is left to develop on its own and to assert its own validity. This has been the method of our actions. The oppressed are confronted with the formlessness of signs and out of that, out of the emptiness that winds in and out of routine and constant signals of human betrayal arise the purveyors of hope, those that actually believe in the possibility of a world without poverty.

Bobby has forgiven me my excessive desire to destroy others. He knows that I did nothing to hurt his wife, that it was my wife, who had been rendered helpless, and who was responsible for destroying his. Bobby didn't want me to kill Marty, and he didn't want Marty to kill me. It is interesting, the friendship of men with blood on their hands. Many such friendships end in death.

If there were any escape to torrid zones, moving up-river on junks, the frigid ecstasies of opium dens, group sex with the natives, if there were any answer in travel—but there is nowhere to go where the cries of human action cease to arise with absolute consistency, where there are no loaded trials and subhuman jurors. Harbingers fly up from all our toppled altars. They have nowhere else to go.

Kindness and sin. Sadness and fatherhood. The stuff of legends. My rock. My staff to comfort me. I have made so many mistakes and closed myself off from so much, as if drawn through the world in search of the things that never could be. Sometimes the demons talk to me, but so do the spirits of heat and light. I am a servant of the mid-ground and would be lost without this intimacy. If Jesus wanted me to be anything but a Jew, he would have become a Catholic himself. I have nothing but empty neighbors and am moving toward a clear and endless vision.

This vision demonstrates the isolation of men who are trapped within their own unities. Around them, through them, across them, next to them, within them, they are invaded, transgressed, punched, choked and tormented with the instant agonies of time. The center, the self, what they are, is impalpable and vulnerable and at any moment they are ready to go down, to tumble through dark shafts. There is no logic that will explain the basis for this game, yet instead, every man considers himself to be the victim of circumstance, he creates emotional frameworks that turn rotten, and he awakens every morning to the bitter aftertaste of sorrow.

We rise or fall in relationship to sameness. Bobby has taught me that we either are cleansed and eventually removed from judgment or are sullied and remain to be born again and again into suffering, pain, hardship, fear, despair, cruelty, sickness, madness and meaningless groveling. We stay within existence until we get it, and when we get it, we are transported elsewhere, to where faith and probity take us, to be reunited with a loving God. This is the miracle of our Savior. My tragedy is that I always take this change too seriously. I stay where I am and fight. I create victims, and I refuse to become innocent.

The most excruciating thing about dreams is that in them we manufacture our own light. Is there sunlight after death? Is there a Book of Life that records the sins and sorrows of another world? I don't care, and whatever world I enter, I will enter with maximum defiance. Wherever I go, if they don't like me, they can boot me out or perhaps, if I can, I'll leave voluntarily. I'll take a crap and leave. And wherever I reappear, I will challenge the morality-mongers. I'll forge through subversion extraordinary opinions that will disturb and constantly elevate, and I'll make dangerous friends, and I will be unkind.

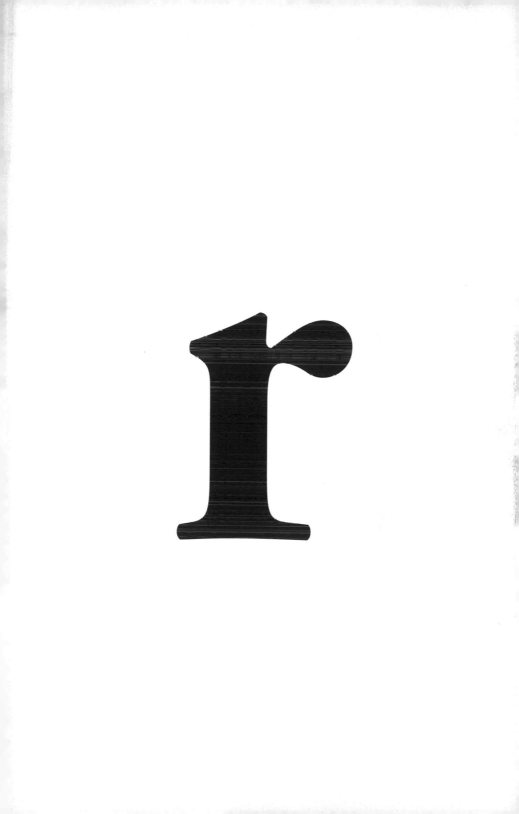

Buddy Hecht
died trying to
save the life of
Hannah Hecht
who was burn-
ing in her car.
Death by Fire
Wall.

Religions aim to be governments, and governments aim to be religions.

No one has more contempt for what it means to be a man than the leader of a crowd. Kierkegaard. Amen.

The common voter will always favor choosing on an impulse.

Both Johnson and Nixon are certifiable psychotics. The proof that our system of government is in a state of collapse is that we have consciously chosen madmen to govern us.

In an ideal society, every capable man and woman would raise food for the benefit of others.

The dictator of the world, the ultimate power-tripper, the person who will be in charge of the global slave society of the twenty-second century, will be a cartoon character.

If one wishes to join the struggle, a rudimentary question must always be answered: Is there any practical limit to my vengeance?

The cornerstone of American political philosophy is that each man has a right to heap up riches and finger them every night before he goes to sleep.

In a utopia, men and women would be creative, contented, generous and poor.

The average man, given any opportunity to do so, will lower the standard of what it means to be average.

Robert Hansen
died trying to
save the life of
Campbell Jr?
Pianist boy who
fell thru ice.
Death by freezing

Helen

7-16-74

Mitch:

   Now that you and Bobby fled the coop, and I'm here
with my brother, I need to let you know what has
happened recently. I'm supposed to be a no-bullshit
person, so to speak, but yet I've never been able to
say what needs to be explained. Perhaps in order to
get to the meat of the matter, I'll start out with
the fat.
   I refuse to be haunted by the death of that girl.
Marty knew instinctively that the only way we were
going to get out of that cabin alive was to keep her
from screaming. It was a question of her or us. These
things happen, and Marty had spent most of his life in
stir. He did what he had to do, and I did what I had
to do. We split through the patio door before those
guys upstairs found out where we were. I know you
think we abandoned the cause in some way by refusing
to get our brains bashed in, but screw that. Nothing
would have been gained by having two more corpses.
I'm still alive, and I survived to fight another day
You, Tommy, Marty, Bobby and I are still breathing.
Five out of nine. When you play with fire, you are
liable to get burned. We took on Marty when he got out
of prison because we needed firepower, we needed to
have people around who weren't afraid to do things.
There are natural consequences to that.
   The world is becoming a strange place, and I don't
know if people like you and me are going to have any
part in it. It seems to me sometimes that the squares
we are trying to save aren't worth saving. We aren't
going to win our battles. It's just going to be a
bunch of pig corporations and fucking piglets in

suits. It's going to be Technicolor. It's going to be
mass brain entertainment based on the worship of
stupidity and jewels. But I suppose this isn't part of
your logic pattern, since you just walk into bars and
attack bullies. That's your modus operandi. You spend
your life bashing bully pricks.

It's a murky fucking world, Mitch. I'm sure it's
not much better there in Izmir. Are you guys going up
to Istanbul, as planned? If so, I hear the pad to
crash is the Sensoy, near the Blue Mosque. You can cop
what you need within a few blocks, and it's cool to
sleep on the roof.

Tommy and I are going to stay where we are. Toronto
is a fucking drag, but there is work that can be done
with resisters. I often think about coming back into
the cabin and seeing Bobby there with that bag over
his head and Cynda next to him, and Tubs, Gerry and
Gretchen looking like roadkill. That child's blood was
there, too, still wet against the back of the chair.
I saw something else also, that night before everyone
died. I don't know why I'm telling you this, because
when we were together in Mendocino I had resolved to
keep quiet. I was going to keep this to myself. It's
important that you don't show this letter to Bobby.

That last night I couldn't sleep. I had tried to
get shitfaced enough to pass out, but it wouldn't
work. I felt sick, and I got up and walked down the
stairs. Bobby was the person on guard. The girl was
tied to her chair in the middle of the room, and he
was totally naked, kneeling in front of her, with his
head between her thighs. He was crying. He had removed
her pants, but she still had panties on. She seemed
totally calm, not excited or frightened, just very
quiet. It was weird because I didn't understand why he
would break down like that. It was as if he were
getting off sexually on repenting for something. The
scene was pathetic. I didn't hang around but went back
upstairs and eventually lost consciousness.

And yet this feeling I've had since then has
stuck with me. I used to believe we were put here to
learn that we have to figure things out, to come to
understand how to live and change our lives, but

thinking about Bobby in that basement, with his head between that little girl's legs, sobbing like that, I think there might be a more important truth: that the circumstances of life are what they are, and our only job is to make amends, for something, for anything, and there is nothing to figure out except that we have to release our sins. I know this sounds like some kind of sappy spiritual head-trip, but perhaps we are trying to save other people by attacking the wealthy and corrupt, when we should be trying to save ourselves by washing the feet of the poor.

This has been extremely hard on me, compadre. I wish I could act stronger, that I had a gung-ho fucking attitude, and wore bandoleers, and chewed tobacco, but I'm not that kind of woman. I've got my fragile side. It's strange, you with Bobby and me with Tommy, and both of them so different now from what they once were because of what a shithole planet this is. The world turns its most precious spirits into madmen. Every time I think about Bobby and Cynda, two brilliant poets who loved each other so much, I actually start to weep. At night I lie awake, and life seems so dark, complex and desperate.

And now for the main thing. Yesterday Marty showed up. I hadn't seen him since he went running down that road toward Truckee. How he found us in Canada, I have no idea, but you know Marty, the man is a ferret. Anyway, he looked shitty, Mitch. He was broke and totally strung out. Way off balance. He told me that he was going to find you and kill you. He had always assumed that the guys who surprised us were Panthers, but then he ran into one of them, the driver he saw as we were sneaking out, and he tied the man up and threatened to cut off one of his thumbs and stuff it in his mouth. Fucking Marty! Needless to say the guy told him everything he wanted to know. He told Marty that your wife ratted on us, and that she was from the Mafia herself.

Why didn't you ever tell us about Gina's background? I can't believe you would have arranged to have your friends slaughtered, but Marty isn't as reasonable as I am. He's not so sure that you and your wife weren't

acting together. He said that he tracked down and
killed Gina. I don't feel bad about telling you this.
I don't feel bad about what he did either. He threw
her out a window. He wants his share of the take. He
thinks that the revolutionary thing was scamming, that
it was a money-grubbing set-up and that you intended
to keep the dough from the very beginning. I asked
him to explain, if that were true, why you would have
rescued Bobby and taken him under your wing, but he
wasn't particularly interested in what I had to say.
He had nothing against me or Tommy, because he thought
we were victims, too. We bought him a couple hundred-
worth of smack and he was grateful.

Mitch, I want you to give the ransom to the
Panthers. Why are you hesitating? We made a commitment
and we should keep it. Just because the cats who were
hired to wipe us out at the cabin were spades shouldn't
affect what we do with the money. Your attitude is
wrong. That pig asshole you used to work for, your
relative or whoever he is, is the real culprit, and
the people who worked for him, even if they were a
pack of thugs, were still enslaved. They were acting
out rage caused by the repressive nature of the
society we are fighting to destroy. You used to muscle
people for a living, too, my friend, so you of all
people should understand. And if you go ahead and do
what you're planning to do over there, and invest it
in shit like what came down in San Francisco, it's
going to be bum karma. It's a drag, man. You'll
eventually turn into them. You'll become the enemy.

I know these are harsh words, but I've given it a
lot of thought. Everybody's selling out nowadays.
Everybody's narking on everyone else, just like your
she-bitch wife, who's been planted exactly where she
belongs. We've got to maintain some kind of purity
here.

Write me soon. I'll be at this address. And watch
your backside.

        Helen

458

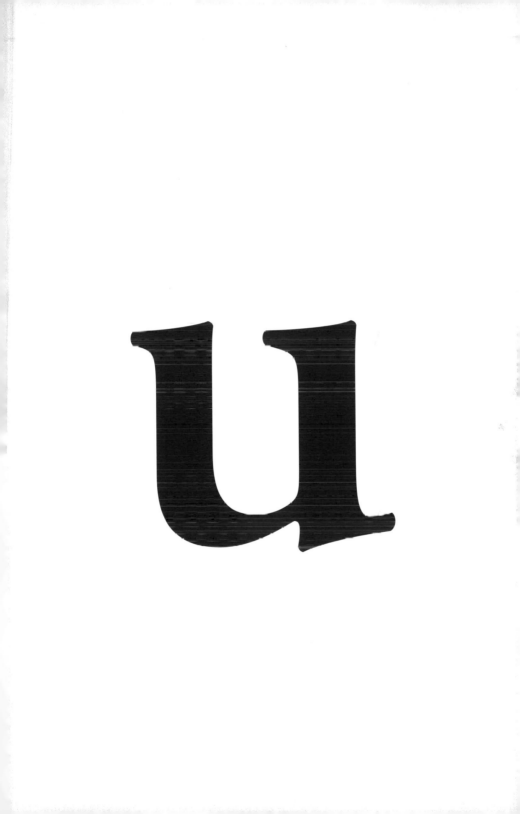

Carmella Lopez
died trying to
save the life of
DeeDee Lopez who
swam in the
oshun. Deth
by drowning.

As the population of the world increases, each man turns into a crowd.

Men who dream of justice—the armed peasant in the jungle, the slave in the labor camp, the union miner, the institutionalized schizophrenic, the street-corner evangelist, the poet in his garret—all are history's buffoons.

The bitter blood of impatience is shed drop by drop.

There is no practical obstacle to the vanity of a stupid and powerful man. When he looks in the mirror, the mirror itself will speak, and the birds in the morning applaud.

The pain of those who care about others is permanently lodged in perplexity.

Aristotle wrote in his Metaphysics that all men by their very nature feel the urge to know. It is true that all men, as infants, feel the urge to know how to crawl, and every man almost without exception learns how to crawl successfully, but there are only a few people who are driven to investigate quantum theory, and there are even less who feel the urge to study the metaphysics of Aristotle.

A murdered saint is a martyr. A murdered revolutionary is a corpse.

When we voluntarily release a fly from the slow starvation of a house, it carries in its flight our most sanctified wishes.

There can be no salvation in church until there is death on the boulevards.

Harold Scott died trying to save the life of sharon Pippen Scott who were attacked by a mugger. Death by bullets.

Bobby

The Crossing Guard

I am immortal Lazarus, damned then saved,
and yet, for immemorial sin, jettisoned into darkness
then forced to wander among the caved-in wreckage of graves,
from life to death and back to life again I forged my way
among the crumbled coffins and downturned weeds
dangling in their stuffy bayous.

Without a stir in the upper worlds
I picked apart the moldy wooden dressings
where tubercular women listened to the faintest
splash of rain in broken-heartedness.

Before my journey started, the universe
was graveless and there was only stainless passion.
To seal and protect the lips of every accountant, I pulled
shut my moon-disk rock and the bright blue coals
of the limestone walls began to glow
in their sky cylinders.

That first death was mine,

I claimed in the name of Jesus Christ,

to be redeemed in each and every life in a long chain

one life at a time, the dead holding hands with their babies,

for every man as he's lowered into his grave

whether into a cloud or into the soil

cherishes in each fumbling paw

the child he was on the right

and the reborn child

he was to be

on the left

so that only I began and ended one-handed

as I reached down into the slime and grabbed ahold

of that first baby Adam and brought him forth with too many ribs

into the frail light of the Garden to anchor the chain of life

and begin to sing my adamant line that hasn't quit

from the very first breath, from Adam to Seth

to Enos to Cainan to Mahalaleel to Jared

to Enoch to Methuselah to Lamech

to Noah to Japheth

my bones sing

in the flesh of man

the coruscating lights

of the poet.

Lord God Jesus Christ mightiest Moses
and all the children of Israel who haunt the sky,
bring peace to the soul of Lazarus!

I was the prince of quondam lands;
the black-satin woman of Jericho and the baby
who died holding hands with two other triplets,
the middle baby had died so young;

I was the Incan carter with no wheels,
the Cro Magnon sailor who wailed in the woods
for the lost presence of icebergs;

I was the young Ohio pioneer who crossed to Sandusky
on a field of lavender, the Tartar with the wind in his nose
and the dew-eyed Heian cross-dresser;

I devised the garbled scrolls of Babylon
by searching for cracked agates where the dry land
stretches flat and ragged into the hills;

I was a tangerine trainer of cranes,
the proverbial Phoenician swimming in chains
at the bottom of a sperm-infested sea, I was the wife
of the inventor of perfume, who had stolen the secret away from me
in the year thirty-two hundred sixty-one BC, staring into the vastness of space
and searching for rinds, I was the shaman Esquimo who slept in her own pink shadow;

the son of Pedahzur, prince of the children of Manasseh, I sat in a dacha
for thirty-five years and watched
the clouds come on.

Now I'm a notch of bone, a vague corpuscle,
the grim serotonin arranger. I am a wandering drop
at the heart of a rock that sizzles
at the earth's center.

Who shall break
the seal of this cave?
Who shall carry me out to bathe
in the anemophilous fields
of stars?

Before the first man swooned in his shrouds,
the unborn hummed in sea-borne trees, afraid of everything
fleshy that touched them. One by one they were slated among the artificial flares
through a hundred-thousand generations of rain-soaked crossing guards,
for Bobby was original to the loins of Adam, when God
created Adam inside Adam he created Bobby
and every other future being,

and every generation
remained in part a Bobby-world
as the coating around the Adam Person was lessening,
as non-Bobbiness was shed from generation to generation

from the original mold of the Adam Person bit by bit
until only one crossing guard remained

(that Bobby the Helping Hand who helped Adam
cross his own bright road became the New Bobby
christened in shame) and all non-Bobbiness

which had been carried in the Adam Person
from the veritable dawning of history, every single cell
of the current non-Robert Simon Lazarus-ness had been sloughed
away by the tide of noneternal moments into a vague eternal sea
of non-Bobbified humanity,

for in every generation
there has been a crossing guard
from the dimmest beginnings of highways,
and the image of the crossing guard has been growing
and overflowing and glowing and slowing traffic
until Robert Simon Lazarus be released
from his marbled chains,

from the humid world of rancid graves, so now may it be
that Finkelstein the Beggar lodged in the bosom of Abraham
look down upon this cave of sheer cerulean shimmer and crimson bats
and beg his Holy Father, O Lord please, may time be uncrated and uncreated
for the surcease of suffering of all men, may Lord Lazarus
fly to the bosom of God, awakened!

Only a corpse can master the deep.
Only a corpse can breathe through trees,
which are the bronchia of spirits extending
into the vast lung of heaven.

When a tree sheds a leaf, it sheds
a memory lodged in the colorless breath of corpses.
The bark of every tree is the protection that our Lord Jesus Christ
extends to those in the ground who dream, until that Glorious Day each bud,
each verdant prong, each arch, tendril, each graceful drape of lambency, each blossom
that masks the invisible hum that attracts each bee, the massive radical drills
that are the pillars and columns of an undersea awash in livers and hearts,
each bleating volunteer in the vegetal world of animal deformity,
each grassy fiber of God's handkerchief
that tells the cool foot it's lucky,

each seedletting, helicoptering wing, each grain, acorn, bract, petiole,
each dark aureolar mark in the phloem that marks a stage in the cloud world's passing,
each topmost regal twig in the morning shine like the glimmer on the smoking ice of peaks,
each plump regimental thought nestled along the corn, each vibrant wand that rises up
and gives air to buried cities moves out from among the jackstraws of talpoid
creatures to the surface and drives up into baronial avenues of ease
and rhythmic access, while down in their holes the dead brood
and bleed out stale hope gone mad.

The green grief of Jesus
lies fragrant on every leaf,
Whose tears were shed as dew
for the curse of what I'd always be,
wandering eternal from crossing-guard body
to crossing-guard body, as the door to my cave
swung open and I would stumble into the blinding light
of yet another cave. There is no limit to mortal anguish launched
on the inner oceans of dew where thunder and lightning,
ringed with shrieks and fiery gnashings, originate,
a suffering brain in a liquid cage
shedding tears of air.

The first prisoners were brought down
chained in sparkling globes along the verdant
highways and byways, as a light perspiration of delicacy,
as a moist promise to the Children of Israel.

Each faltering pearl,
hallowed as the first clear ray
of warmth descendent to the newborn skin,
contains a whimpering dungeon of glassed-in penitential sinners.
A full-fledged partner in the firm of Lazarus and Jesus Frères,
the house we built and clinched still stands,
whose stanchions once flourished
in the dry tides of the sea.

The veil of the temple may be rent
but a dappled anguish harrowed from the teeming
grasses of Golgotha remains as a redolent bond of man to man,
for the Son of Man considered Lazarus his lifelong friend
when Christ was brutally crucified in a dewdrop!

The purity of His brain was rinsed in rain
in drips and drupes in nacreous cabochons and baguettes,
in bortless diamonds, cirric strands, great strings of peptidic walls
whose foam-tipped herbal surfaces are sprinkled with sterling carnations
dangling milky in masic clouds in which the duodecillion manifestations are the contours
of an abscess tangled in event horizons, daunted with ice and wind, silvery cell-blocks,
mitotic death-camps careened in a veil of methane atremble
in ambassadorial hopelessness,
parturient indigo flame
and galactic pulses

(for every galaxy has a pulse) called astronomes beating out time
in supernoval hemorrhages and chrysographic trails of carbonated dust.
Metal burrs within each drop of dew, each tear
of Christ forms up then slowly falls.

In every age I raised my sign.
I stood before Paul on the road to Damascus
and told him when to stop and when to go.

When Moses descended with the Sinai tablets,
I gestured to him halfway down the hill. (Were it not for me,
Ramses would have made it to the other side of the sea.)
I blew my whistle, and Caesar crossed the Rubicon.

The silk trade ceased because of me, and birds that once
flew south were shunted toward the east. I occluded fronts,
beat martial drums, puffed signals to the Pawnees. I was the torpid delayer
of visas, the absent familiar of jaywalkers, the diplopic beacon of befuddled drunkards,
the permanent gatekeeper of all black-topped binaries, crossbucks and transversals
Some call me Lares. Others call me Hermes. Horns and shofars never
phase me. Time screeches to a halt before my outstretched hand.
It all amounts to traffic

I was the Lord's playmate.
He said Bobby, I am a prophet come
to save my people Israel but I shall be crowned
the Prince of Bulldogs. Each of my cells is an inheritance
from Abraham, who was a solitary person connecting two infinite Jewish lands,
the last and first, for on that day our forefather was born, in a distant place
light-years cosmically away the last Jew died and that ancient
planetary world wept bitterly for the absence of Torah. I am
a god-like human, Lord Jesus told me, the Son of Man,
forged in dignity over thousands of years when men
have davenned in the dawn light, wearing
frontlets to the true God, unique;

but before I die I shall be betrayed,

not by Judas Iscariot, but by a petrified coward

who will lie to the people and dub himself my rock and priest,

and men will spread their nether cheeks for the soft ram of Mammon.

I preach a world without churches whose pebbles are filled with love.

Bobby, He told me, you will never, until the very end, be free

but will take on my responsibilities and guide my children,

for in every age, when a child, confused and damaged,

reaches out a hand in trust and belief to cross a street

that hand will meet the waiting hand of a Bobby.

The holiest guardians

are the humble protectors

of young flesh from the ravages

of wheels and plans.

Lord Jesus, I said one dusty afternoon

in the gloamings under the olives, what was my sin

that made me born again and again, the same handsel

that predetermines Man opening the flap door for Lucifer

as he plummeted down from the heavens, what did I do to cast

this thread? What did I do that propelled me through the realms of the dead,

dragging my sheets wearily through ammoniated cemeteries of stupidity and dread?

What did I do that earned me rites of suffocation to watch my Cynda crushed to paste,

her dying words of love for me destroyed over a vile play for money? I will watch

forever her face mirrored in mine cloud up in her bag and fill with blood,

er gentleness rarefied into an ambient sally of warmth. What did I do,
for what I pleaded will your crucifixion mean when I have suffered
in life after life, my brains beaten in (for as you know, I was Abel
under the rock of Cain), and in every age I worked
in torment, what did I do, dear Lord?

Why in every tiring house, before I spiraled down through the clouds,
was I handed an orange uniform, an octagonal sign and told where to stand
and where to extend my prohibitive arm? Why am I with you now
and not in heaven? By what cruel joke are we deemed to play
together as children, and I three years older by birth
must take your hand and help you cross the tracks
and fields and bring you safely back to Mary?

I lay in a polyethylene cave with my hands taped behind my back
and my bag was haunted by woodsmoke and indistinct figures were choking
as their own bags deflated. I saw my young wife dying and she was crying, she cried
Bobby I love you breathless from her wounds. She cried Bobby I love you breathless
as I stared into her shadow, she saw me as plastic shadow and we would have died
together but my cave turned black and the most intimate portion of my brain
was squeezed to live in a dark spark, and Cynda now looks down

from the Bosom of Abraham on this vile worm cast with arms and legs
as face to face we watched the light die before the rod appeared to reap from her skull
that last ounce of charmed life and rob me where now I await her radiant kiss, the only hint
 of bliss that shall appear until the door swings on its hinges and light crawls in

as I crawl out, drawn by sapient powers, into the enfolding arms
of Jesus Christ, never again having to doubt.

This living universe is but a spark
in the infinite darkness of the dead,
of a sleep without sleepers

where the mastery of bones
gives way to looser soils. Our waking life
is an isle aspin, a wisp in a hairpin, a ghoulish bark
from the pale moon's horizon. The black banners of night
are held aloft with infinitesimal, mirthless pins.

I was embarrassed to be buried and staggered out
of the cave through clattering locusts and clashing leaves,
a slowly-expanding skirr of planetary opinion and integumental philosophies,
stoic renunciations and pale ponderings, the phantasmal repositionings of clouded minds
intent on a new religion. I carried with me from the edaphonic trysting spots
the fleshless tangles of sourceless schemes and voices that voyage
like crewless ships into the cratered muscle of the earth,

magnificently emanating buried logic through the galactic shoals
and bars, into a single white hot brain of vapor that moves and vibrates
like ribbons and protects the inner seams of the world. At the bottom
of every mortal sink rage the angelic flares of battle,
and in their military worlds, the world of gods,
there are stark reasons for everything.

A rogue ant moves across my page.
I have been there once, trudging through the sun
with my own framed messages:

of lamentations scrawled on soggy boxboards, of fever under blankets,
of liquor-store dimes, of speeches tattered with the soft sounds of ocean, of arthritis
verging on nausea, invisible, untouchable, a sewage of regrets and misplaced tranquilizers,
half-eaten hamburgers and crushed cans, a highway of shopping carts with nicknames,
of sobbing under bridges, of hospitals filled with platinum pumps, of dolls
dumped in gutters and crystal forests of dogbones and golfcaps
and lobotomized spinsters, torn filaments of childhood
woven into bracelets, ragged amulets of suicidal sons
and memories of cool sheds smelling of bacon.

I know the very worst,
for the dead return to the streets.
In the wake of the universe,
the dead remain homeless.

Ghosts filled with dunnage and fierce pain
tumble down a river whose shores are heaven and hell,
forgotten in midground, sapped of dreams, the cure for these dead
is another disease, streets leading forever into streets, one waits interminably
to expire and then enters a pink barium nightmare where men without eyes and children
without boundaries wander along avenues glutted with shopping.

The homeless
scream in death
that they are human,
but of course they are
no longer human.

Linked to a phenomenon of craving, the shaking hand
holds out a cup among solar intelligences, the demigods of planet earth,
blinking in their grafted suits and ties. Anything edible will do, because the homeless
never cease to eat, the homeless dead are eternally hungry, weightless on the boulevards
of emotional gravity, mailing letter upon letter into the system. I alone am snug in my cave,
coming back time after time to the same place, having shed a small prism of life
into the outer world of bourgeois values. More and more, the spineless
people who pass me mindless are turning into Bobbies.

Within the walls
of every star emerge
the raging victories
of personality.

Mercury, the god of transportation, flings around the sun,
singes and burns, frantic to be spun away from the searing heat
of this slow deformation, as unbeknownst to those without homes,
all the planetarily-domiciled lives who celebrate the birth of the sun's
location are walking down the street while praying
for the final perfection of its heavenly body.

484

To be everlasting, everything loved

must be snuffed, taken away, beaten with iron poles,

vacated, burned, buried, deteriorated, nibbled by beasts,

wrapped in bags and injured irreparably in the senses. Love is

the constant cause of death, for what we love, in the process of loving,

we kill through slow accumulation. We are born out of hatred into infinite death,

where hate is the thread and love is the bead; hate is the thought and love is the mind;

hate is the act and love is the action; hate is the note and love is the music; hate is

the parent and love is the child; hate is the car and love is the school patrolman

ever-vigilant lowering his flag; hate is the sun, raging in its ball, and love

is the moon, the distant arbor of lime-colored ices; hate is the tree

and love is the leaf; hate is happiness and love is what makes

hatred happy, breaking the heart from the inside slowly

methodically inevitably tearing apart its tender vessels

as it beats frantically ecstatically dissolving into love,

so hatred is the drum and love is the rhythm, so all

traffic is embedded in motorized hatred, aiming

at everything that is confused and loving

and only the committed crossing guard

in graveclothes smelling of rosemary

and pressed lilac inutterably bound

up in sonatas of acceleration

and recoil can, in this Age

of Man, save ambulatory

cities from vehicular

destruction.

Mitch and I would drive to the forest,

and there I would cry and commune as we hovered

over the placement of her body. There was nothing to think

or say, and tears spoke for me. Time, whose arched kindness healed me

slowly, threading the firs and pines, weaving the fate of leaves in its languid play of light,

tossing continuous death among the stones in a duff of romantic insects, rinsing her golden

hair in thick shags of bark, her chill lips trembling on the evening air and her ancient smell

so confident and comforting wound in bright filaments of birch, the twilight thundered

praise and justice for those who hear and bear the measures of the dead,

who smell the censers swinging in the secret armatures of trees,

the hamadryads echoing from their highest

reaches mountainous night slogans.

A poet with nothing has more than he needs.

Champions of hardship, clothed in bright nimbi of purity

and giving, govern the streets, force handouts at off-ramps

and drape the mourning world. The lilies of the field

are blinded by the clean smells of linen.

Sufficient to the day is the evil thereof.

Yet I who tried

to stop so much

am doomed never to reach

the farthest curb and trudge

the harmless sidewalks

of the Lord:

All that I see
is a vague dream of seeing;
unimaginable are the singing
ecstasies of heaven.

Smelling of seaweed
and armed with shopping cart and leister,
I shamble down the endless promenades, a fisher
of men from bus stops and benches, sent to Samaritans and Sarmatians
to spread His billowing seine of benediction. The lowest of the low, beyond contempt,
I make my plea that Lord Jesus save his special friend, returning him to Cynda
and our son, twenty-five years now dead in the womb.

Murdered before the trauma of his birth,
his vision purged of empty objects, he bathes
in a world of curious hope and potential. Every year
the nameless bear him gifts the way a river yearns.
I taught him proudly how to watch and turn.
To guide a child, I always guided him.
Slow and dubious life,
without the unborn,
is a desert.

There is a common biology
that plots to break the spirits of poets,
a special antigen lodged in the system
to fight the terrible beauty of words.

Once upon a time,

a Paracletic verse rang out

from a tune lodged deep in the chanting void.

Then cells banded together to sing the songs of cells,

taking billions of years to form into mouths, while at the red-carpeted foot

of the Judgment Seat the spotless brains of poetic saints were dubbed

with verbs and adverbs, with sparkling adjectives and holy nouns.

A small ear takes delight in tools it has to turn existence into joy

and if joy never comes but in patient snatches the ear can

never be denied, for it drains the stars of magnitude,

exuding consonants with balances and balks,

with hedgerows and high grounds

of exalted purpose.

The ear is never helix, meatus, concha,

lobe nor foramen that carries sound to the brain.

Nor malleus, incus, stapes, cochleal cavity, nor nerve nor drum

nor receptacle of anything. To hearken to the music of the Lord in all of its strains

is to know the song of the ear creating thought. I plod along the city's avenues—

those miracle miles of commercial value, my powerless stop sign

waving at the vacuous crowds—and listen.

I hear the dark strain of this dark age

surround me, although my homeless mind

still loafs and plays under the calm skies of Jerusalem.

The earth will end like the squash of a shit-drunk fly. A crowd

of beans trembling in a hardwire arena are cleansing the global streets
of all forms of principled morality, the streets that are awash
in paralyzed emotion and inarticulate insanity, and yet,
like a young girl with lavaliere and ribbons,
I am pinned for love.

I rise above the jaded sidewalks
of the world into the permanent embrace
of a loving God. Clutching their book bags,
all of my children's voices ring: "Bobby the Greatest
gets us where we have to go!" All of my marvelous children,
smelling of oil and soap in their small clothing.

Venerable bearded crossing-guards, magnificent
in their apostolic weeds, flank the wending boulevards
that lead to the flaming throne. Can the children of the bedchamber mourn
as long as the Bridegroom is with them? Angels haunt the avenues and whisper to the cars:
"The world will end soon, the world will end soon, and Lazarus shall finally be redeemed,
as the last corpse ascends to judgment," and all the heavenly kids will prance and sing,
"Gloria in excelsis Deo!" their pudgy hands mounting to pluck the golden strings,
the trusting hands I held to ease their fear and suffering.

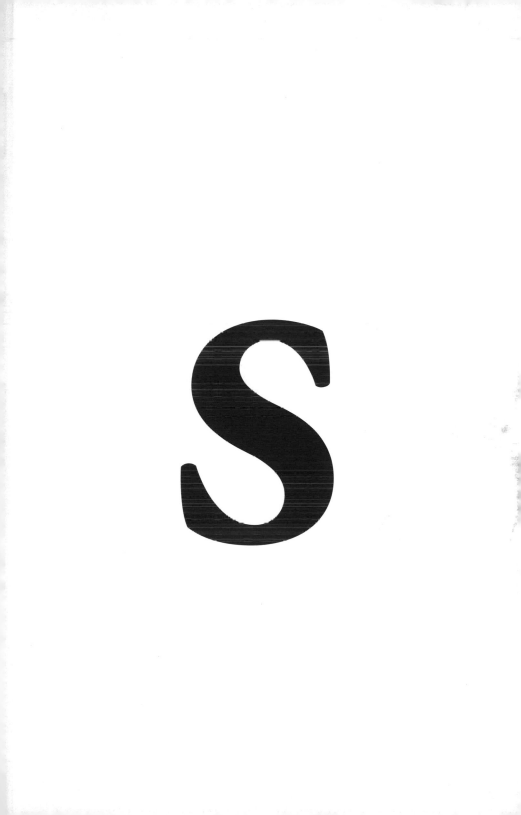